i |

LATER DAYS & NIGHTS

A NOVEL BY

LAWRENCE CHRISTOPHER

Ebony +
I hope that you enjoy
this read and find
it uplifting !
From yo' mama &
Christopher
'09

MF Unlimited
Atlanta

Later Days & Nights

Copyright © 2008 by Lawrence Christopher
ISBN 0-9712278-6-1 ISBN (13) 978-0-9712278-6-6
Library of Congress Control Number: 2007940160

This novel is a work of fiction. Any references to real people, events, establishments, organizations or locales are intended to give this work of fiction a sense of reality and authenticity. Other names, characters, places, and incidents are either the product of the author's imagination or are used fictitiously, as are those fictionalized events and incidents that involve real persons and did not occur or are set in the future.

"Fool Fool Heart" (In Prose) © 2008 Ronika Jones
"Are You Really Ready for a Relationship?" © 2007 Dr. William July, II

Cover model: Dani
Cover photo: © 2006 Jim Demmers
Cover design: Tri-Union Entertainment and Tolbert Graphics

Printed in the United States of America

MF Unlimited
Civic Center Station, P.O. Box 55346, Atlanta, GA 30308
Publisher@MFUnews.com www.MFUnews.com

Books by or including Lawrence Christopher

- All About Mary: A Mick Hart Mystery (out-of-print)
- Dog 'Em: A Mick Hart Mystery
- Ghettoway Weekend
- Journey to TimBookTu: An African American Poetic Odyssey, edited by Memphis Vaughn, Jr. (Sadorian Publications)
- Later Days & Nights
- Mary's Little Lamb: A Mick Hart Mystery
- Tickle Fingers: Where Is Pinky
- Tickle Fingers: Five Finger Prayer Book

Visit www.TimBookTu.com and www.LiterateNubian.org for short story fiction by Lawrence Christopher

For more information about Lawrence Christopher's writings, visit www.MFUnews.com

Acknowledgements

Giving honor to God-

I thank GOD for blessing me with cognitive thinking and an active imagination. (Deuteronomy 8:18)

GOD loves me so much that He will accept me just as I am… but He loves me too much to leave me that way!

"I can do all things through CHRIST who strengthens me." Philippians 4:13

Dedications

This book is dedicated to S. Danielle

To the unbreakable couples:
Antae and *Felecia*
Anthony and Tiffany
Barack and Michelle
Clarence and *Shantae*
Dennis and Melissa
Donald (*Mr. Arrogressive*) and Anita
Dustin and *Beth*
Michael and Teri
Ontorio and *Sherhonda*
Rodriquez and *Annie Belle*
Rudy and *Bobbi*
Anthone' (Tone') and Schveka
Willie and Sandea

In memory of:
Bernard Jeffery McCullough – "Bernie Mac"

Even after all this time
the sun never says to the earth,
you owe me.

Poem by Hafiz the Great Sufi Master

<u>Introduction</u>

The road to joy and happiness is not straight. There is a curve called Failure, a loop called Confusion, speed bumps called Friends, red lights called Enemies, caution lights called Family. You will have flats called Jobs. But, if you have a spare called Determination, an engine called Perseverance, insurance called Faith, a driver called God, you will make it to a place called victory.

Prologue

TAG YOU'RE IT

IT'S AUGUST 2005, A YEAR AND A HALF LATER AFTER MEETING AND MARRYING MINA AND ADOPTING MERCEDES. My twin cousin Emily and I are sitting on the deck, looking out on the bright sunshiny beach of Oak Bluff, Massachusetts. Our legs are dangling over the deck's edge and we're kicking around the sand and memories. The Frankie Beverly and MAZE *Anthology* CD is playing; the song *Happy Feelings* is coming from speakers which has practically everybody singing along. Wherever Mina is, I'm sure she's singing what is one of her favorite songs as well.

Our parents and other older relatives are sitting behind us, performing their roles as griots passing on the rich and varied history of the town that sits on the northeast shore of Martha's Vineyard. Their storytelling not only includes our personal family history, but also that of the Native American fishing villagers, West African slaves, and the current upper middle-class property owners of the New England beach town. They also reminisce of their own childhood of Blackjack gum, wax Coke-Cola shaped bottles filled with colored sugar water, the collecting of Green Stamps, and roller skates tightened by a key.

The conversation changed its focus when our grandmother wanted someone to recite the ingredients of her favorite fast food sandwich.

"Come on Emily; say it for your Nana" requested the respected matriarch.

"Aww grandma, can't Matthew do it this time," pleaded Emily.

"Girl, what I say?" Nana said with an authoritative voice.

"Yes ma'am. *Two all beef patties, special sauce, lettuce, cheese, pickles, onions on a sesame seed bun.*"

Nana provided applause in show of her appreciation.

Emily and I turned our attention to the children playing a game of tag on the beach. Running behind them is five-year-old Mercedes who is kicking up her heals, along with sand, as she runs. She repeats an acronymic chant "sugar honey ice tea - sugar honey ice tea" of the zebra character from the *Madagascar* movie. There is such a beautiful innocence of a child. She calls me "two daddy" as in her second daddy.

She rarely asks about her parents who abandoned her. Their never returning from New Orleans made the adoption process easier for Mina and I. Once Mina told her family the truth about her aunt, they then supported her actions. Most of the family had not ever met the little girl until we traveled to Louisiana and Mississippi or when they came to our wedding held in the backyard of our Ellenwood home.

My former girlfriend, Natalie Pennington-Peel and her husband walk by. She's still wearing her white Keds® sneakers and walks in them like she was of great physical beauty and appeal. Her husband Vernon Peel is a real-estate broker. The upwardly-mobile couple is destined for greatness if you believe the press written about them in *Jet* magazine where they announced their wedding. They are expecting the birth of their first child in a few months.

Natalie speaks and waves to my parents and family, but she doesn't acknowledge or say a word to me. When we've run into one another and we have a private moment, it's quite a different greeting and story. Then I'm "honey and sweetie" with a great deal of flirting. I don't understand it. Emily says she still loves me and all I need do is ask and I could *have the panties.*

It doesn't matter the least bit. I've never been happier than I am with my wife Mina. After she accepted my second proposal to marry at Disney World, we were technically engaged. Yet, we still had to complete our last date, which lasted just a little over the nine hours it took for us to drive back from Orlando, Florida to Decatur and Ellenwood, Georgia. During the ride we talked about everything and nothing, but all of it was enjoyable and sometimes laughable.

Once we reached home, our lives returned to our daily routine. The only difference was that we both had new goals in mind. We were working toward our future and having a life together. The one thing we agreed upon was to not to lose our individuality. I would maintain my life and friends. Mina would do the same. Well, almost. We compromised when it came to our friends Marcus being mine and Tyriq as one of hers.

Mina and I would bring our two lives together where and when it made sense. She doesn't hang out with me at Starbucks and I don't watch *Girlfriends* with her. Then there would be the life we shared together with Mercedes.

When I met Mina, she was a college dropout, one year short of graduating. She was working full-time as an office mail clerk in the Bank of America building where I work. She worked to support herself, her live in aunt and niece.

It was *like at first sight* between us. I'm a contract management lawyer, who met my wife-to-be delivering mail to the law offices where I work. The funny thing about our meeting was that my best friend Marcus who chased down the hall after Mina. She shot down his advances. Later, she and I went to lunch and the rest as they say is our history.

Mina completed the professional development program through the ASK ME Foundation. Being community conscience, she heads her own social service program called FREE (Financial Reward Empowerment and Enlightenment). The program is geared towards those at low to medium income level. Many of the people who attend her workshops are from her old Easywick Village community. She focuses on getting them off rent-to-own purchasing, pay-day loans, using the corner convenience stores to cash their checks to instead establishing a relationship with traditional financial institutions. She's now re-enrolled at Clark Atlanta University to complete her studies to earn a dual bachelor's degree in Business Administration and Social Work.

As far as how my life has changed; first and foremost I have a wife and adopted daughter. While I don't take Mina for granted, I do take her as she is and I love her. The true strength of the relationship between Mina and I is that we are aware of one another's weakness, yet we still respect and compliment one another's strengths. Getting to know Mercedes is day-to-day. We spend Saturday mornings together eating breakfast and watching cartoons. We mostly watch the lineup on the Qubo Channel, which offers *Jacob Two-Two*, the *Veggie Tales*, and *Jane and the Dragon*. I think our favorite Saturday morning show is *Beakman's World*. Somehow, in getting to know a child is getting to know one's self.

~ ~ ~ ~ ~ ~ ~

Mina has come out of the house, bringing me a tall glass of ice cold lemonade. She kisses me on the cheek before going to help my uncle barbeque turkey legs. I catch my father giving an approving smile as he watches Mina walk by. His smile might have been brought on by the undeniably nice way she fills out her shorts.

My family loves her and Mercedes just as much as I do. As I watch Mina laughing and carrying on with my relatives, my heart does swell with pride.

"I'm so happy for you Matthew," claims my cousin.

"Why?"

"Look at you. You have a lovely family. I am just so proud of you. What was it that made you ultimately choose Mina?"

"There were two things. One, you're going to think is stupid."

"Try me."

"It was such a little thing; I never mentioned this to anyone."

"Go ahead."

"Well, it was early in our relationship. Like the first week. We had gone to lunch, where we had wings at JR Crickets. On our way back to the office Mina noticed something on my face, probably sauce from the hot wings. She reaches over and picks it off."

"Yeah . . . so?"

"It was something about that moment that did something to me and stuck in my head. Had that been Natalie, she would have told me that I had something on my face or handed me a napkin. But she would have never used her own hand to get it off."

"Oh I see. Mina pulled the nurturing move, which made you see her as a mother figure."

"Get out of here."

"Yeah, I was just kidding. I think it was the intimacy of the act is what it was."

"I guess. To be honest though, it was also her caring, compassionate and giving nature that persuaded me. When we met, she was always giving of herself to others. She would do it so genuinely, without looking for anything in return. I realized that it would be good for me to have a woman like her in my life as a reflection of me and a reflection to me to make me a better person. I guess I know why she's in to my life."

"They say 'when God wants to bless you He will bring a person into your life.' But have you ever thought that He brought you into her life to be her blessing?"

"You know, I never even thought of it that way."

"God is blessing you so that you can be a blessing to her and Mercedes as well."

There was a time when happiness wasn't what I was after, because I thought I could make myself happy. In life, there are the experiences and happenstances of happy feelings, joy and pain. As Mina told me early in our relationship; "joy comes from what you know and not your external circumstances. The joy of knowing life will get better, the joy of knowing when you have no one, you have yourself, the joy of knowing love is but a word but responsibility is not. I am (we are) responsible for maintaining joy in our own lives. Look to have joy rather than to merely be happy."

With Mina and Mercedes, I know my life is better. With them in my life, I have accepted responsibility. Now it is up to me to keep that joy I now know.

~ ~ ~ ~ ~ ~ ~

Late in the night, under the starry lit sky, Mina and I are standing out on the deck holding one another. She is clutching my t-shirt, with her head leaning against my chest. When I asked her once why she held on to my shirts like that, she said "so I won't lose hold of you." She went on to tell me that when she was about three or four years young, her father was carrying her and a bag of groceries. When he stumbled, she and the bags fell to the ground. He told her from then on to always grab his shirt so she wouldn't lose hold and she would never fall.

In return, I have both of my hands tucked firmly in the back pockets of her khaki shorts.

"*Bookie*, I never thought it would ever be like this." Mina whispers.

"Like what *babe*?"

"Like this. This is the closest to my dream that I have ever felt."

"And what exactly is this dream?"

"I don't want to say just yet." She says as if speaking it out loud would jinx it, like the telling of the birthday wish after blowing out the candles. "But I will say that I love you for bringing me this close, closer to my dream."

"You're welcome, but our journey together isn't over."

"I know. Your being in my life has made me feel more empowered to go and do and not dwell on the things in my life that I want to change but haven't yet. You have also helped me realize that life is not instant and things take time . . . even dreams."

"I do know. Dreams do come true."

"How do you know?"

"Because I'm holding mine," I clinched a handful of her backside. Mina turned her head and lightly bit my chest. "Hey . . . hey!" I protested.

"You silly," she followed those words with a light giggle. "When you say things like that, it just does things to me."

"I'm glad that I still have that affect on you."

"You do in so many ways. Besides being good looking and fun to be around, you help me get to my full potential in life by being there for me when I need you. That is far beyond anyone's anything."

"I don't know exactly what that means."

"It means, I truly appreciate your love and support *Bookie*; that you didn't even know you were giving. I love you and I like you."

"I love you and I like you too."

The Beginning.

Fall

OCTOBER

"GETTING TO KNOW YOU."

THEY SAY IT TAKES A MINUTE TO FIND A SPECIAL PERSON, an hour to appreciate them, a day to love them but then an entire life to forget them. This could not be any truer for the way that I feel about my wife, Mina.

It was a whirlwind romance from the start. For those in favor of Mina's and my union, it was a love affair of the heart that worked out for the good. Those who were oppose, saw it simply as an affair. Truth be told, both views were correct. Mina and I were caught up in the romantic moment; raised in each other's lives due to our circumstances. I fell *in like* with Mina in less than a week. I grew to love her in a very short month to follow. It wasn't a case where I wanted to tell my mind not to listen to my heart. My mind was made up and it knew that it liked Mina. My heart was easily persuaded.

Two years ago; there wasn't a hint of marriage in my thoughts. At that time, I was in a long-term relationship with my girlfriend Natalie. It was a relationship of convenience, where it turned out that both of us took the other for granted. We treated each other decently, but we were just going through the motions, headed for nowhere in particular. It wasn't until the later days and nights, right before our breakup did Natalie mention marriage; when she actually proposed to me. Being the high-powered mergers and acquisitions lawyer that she was and still is; Natalie had a marriage proposal drawn up in the form of a contract and had it delivered to my business office. That act alone showed me that marriage to Natalie would be nothing more than an arrangement.

Now, here I am and I can't imagine myself not being married to Quijelmina, pronounced *Kee-hel-meena*, with our adopted six-year old daughter Mercedes, nicknamed Sadie. Many people said that it wouldn't last. I will have to admit, at times I had my doubts as well . . . before and after we were married. When I confided in my mother and my twin cousin Emily, they said that "some doubt was only natural."

"If you are waiting for the perfect person and time to get married; it will never come." My mother voiced.

"Yours and Mina's is a fairytale romance. Even fairytales have their dark moments." Emily offered.

They were both right; and I won't say that Mina and I have been happily married ever since. As a matter of fact of life, we have had our challenges. Those challenges presented themselves at the very beginning of our journey together.

A big part of our struggle was that we had been successful as independent, strong willed, single or head-of-household people. Instead of working together, for about four months in to our marriage we were still living as singles only in the same household. We didn't see it because we thought that as long as we were handling our individual responsibilities, it meant we were taking care of home. In most respects we were. The bottom line was we needed to bond as one, come together without losing our identity.

There needed to be an adjustment and some compromises made on both our parts in order for us to get along.

We did not begin to live together until after we were married. For less than a year we were engaged, still living apart. So it wasn't until we moved in together did we learn of our personal habits and little idiosyncrasies that required a change on both our parts. Those required changes were needed in the way we lived and related to one another.

"CLEANING DOWN THE HOUSE"

When I wash dishes, it is usually at the end of the day or when it is convenient. Mina on the other hand likes to clean as she cooks. Our compromise, as we share the responsibility of kitchen cleanup; whoever's day it is to cook or clean, that person can clean as they see fit.

As for the cleaning of the rest of the house, we split those chores. I'm used to waiting until Saturdays to do household chores. That's how it was when I was growing up. Mom would get me up early to sort the clothes in the laundry room. Then I would go through the house and *clean down*. Moms says that you don't *clean up*; meaning starting from the floor. You start by dusting and wiping down the furniture and then you sweep and vacuum last.

I turn on the radio and tune in the 102.5-*The Grown Folks Station*. The play list is soul music from the 70s, 80s and 90s. Usually, I open the windows throughout the house. Between the Lemon Pledge, the Original Scent Lysol Concentrate cleaner and Murphy Oil Soap, it can become a little toxic in a closed area.

Mina likes to clean and keep up the house throughout the week. An example of our differences in style; there were some crumbs on the coffee table which I proceeded to brush off on to the floor. In my mind, I was going to vacuum on the weekend, which happened to be the next day.

Mina looked at me and questioned; "you couldn't have put that in your hand and placed it in the trash?" To be only twenty-five and to have an old mother's wit, she amazes and shames me.

We share in the clothes cleaning. Mina drops off and picks up the dry cleaning. I handle the machine washing and drying of laundry, except that I'm not allowed to wash her personals. That I don't get. Any given day or night, I could have my hands inside those same personals, while she's wearing them. Yet, when it comes to retrieving those panties out of the hamper, I'm not allowed to touch them. Not that I really want to, but women are funny.

"LIKE YOU FOUND IT."

When it comes to the care and handling of one another's belongings we needed to learn to respect one another's personal property and space. At least, that's how I saw it. My CDs and DVDs are kept either in their respective players or in their cases. Mina and Mercedes had a habit of leaving them lying about, prone to breaks and scratches. Mina and I exchanged a few choice words about it.

"Ain't nobody trying to tear up your stuff," Mina defended.

"All I'm saying is that you can do what you want with your own things. But when it comes to mine, I wish you would take better care." I replied.

To avoid further incidents, Mina burns her own copy of any CD of mine that she may like listening to. I'm teaching Mercedes my father's golden rules. *If you open it, close it. If you move it, put it back where you found it when you're finish with it. If you break it, tell someone. If you make a mess, your mother will clean it up.* That last one remained under dispute.

The first time that I had to speak sternly to Mercedes about writing on the liner note insert to one of my CDs, I made her cry. When that happened, Mina and I had to have a heart-to-heart conversation about my being able to discipline the child. I explained to Mina that proper disciplining of a child was just as much a show of love as a kiss on their knee when they scraped it from a fall. She knows that I love Mercedes and that I wouldn't intentionally do anything to hurt her emotionally or physically. Still, what was necessary was our first family meeting. Mina called it a *come to Jesus meeting*.

"OVER OR UNDER"

In matters of the bathroom, Mina and I are alike and opposites. When it comes to placing the toilet paper on the roller, I like for the paper to pull from the bottom. Mina on the other hand likes for the paper to unroll from over the top. The obvious compromise was whoever gets the last swipe or wipe, whichever the case may be, chooses the direction of the roll. Sometimes for *giggles and kicks*, I will reverse the roll even if Mina changed it. It keeps us talking.

Even with the things we had in common, Mina and I had to make adjustments as a couple. Both of us use separate washcloths for washing our face and our bodies. That means where there were two washcloths in our bathrooms before we began living together, now there are four. Mina bought little hangers with clips, to hang the washcloths on. This keeps the washcloths separate and able to dry properly.

Oh, and it took only one time for me to accidentally use Mina's body washcloth on my face, to learn not to make that mistake again. Let me just leave it at that – except that she thought it was funny.

"WAS THAT YOU?"

While Mina thought that washing my face with her body washcloth was funny; she didn't think it was humorous at all the one morning I forgot she was in the bed with me and I *passed gas.* Yes, it was unfortunate, but it was also tear jerking, side splitting funny. Why don't women get that? Mina hasn't let me forget that indiscretion to this day.

Before marriage; when it came to sleeping I never had to choose what side of the bed I liked. I had the entire bed to myself. Mina likes sleeping on the convenient sides of the bed. Like closest to the door, to allow for easy and quick access for Mercedes. When she rearranges the bedroom furniture, Mina may want to sleep next to the open window, especially if it's raining.

Other than that, everything else between Mina and me in the bedroom is just fine and that's all anyone needs to know about that.

"HER KNIGHT IN SHINING ARMOR"

Being old school and traditional, I believe that a man's role in marriage and in the home is to provide for and to protect his family. As a provider, I feel that I do pretty well. We have a roof over our heads and plenty of food on our pantry shelves. Our needs are being met and occasionally, a surprise want is shared.

As a protector, I felt that I could handle or at least I was prepared to step to anything or anyone who would threaten the safety and welfare of my family. If there would come that call in the night when Mercedes would have a bad dream, I would rush to her side and assure her that everything would be alright. When Mina would need me to dispatch with a hairy spider or its bug relative, I would be there with broom or shoe in hand at the ready. So I thought I was prepared for anything . . .

"MATTHEW! MATTHEW," Mina's cry came from our bedroom.

As I raced to the room, I saw Mercedes dart in ahead of me. When I entered, I found Mercedes outside our bathroom door jumping around mimicking Mina who was in the bathroom naked from the waist down. The bizarre scene struck me as comical at first, and then I noted the look of panic on Mina's face and in her voice.

"GO TO YOUR ROOM SADIE" she instructed.

"Why? I *wanna* play."

"I said go to YOUR ROOM."

The little girl reluctantly did as she was told. I grab the toilet brush out of its holder and looked around the bathroom in search of the eight legged invader of our home. But I'm unable to follow Mina's line of sight to guide me.

"GET IT OUT. Get IT out." Mina commanded.

"Where is it Mina?"

"In THERE."   She pointed toward her bare legs and the patchwork of curly Qs.

Then I felt a sense of panic, "What!?"

"Matthew, get it out. I can't reach it."

"GET . . . reach . . . what?"

Mina's jumping settled to an antsy two-step; though her hands continued to wildly shake about. "The damn tampon, get it out."

"WHOA. Hold up. Uh . . . a tampon?"

"YES, it's up in me and I can't get it out."

"How did that happen?"

"How do you think? I need for you to get it out."

"Wait; maybe I should get Sadie back in here."

"NO. Don't *chu* call that child. That's why I called you."

"You aren't serious?"

"The hell I ain't. Matthew, I need for you to get it out." She said quite seriously and still panic stricken. "You don't have a problem putting your hands down there any other time."

"Yeah, but . . ."

"Matthew!"

After the emergency extraction, I was sent on my first errand to purchase some Always™ sanitary pads.

"Be sure to get the ones with the hand wipes," Mina reminded as I headed out the door.

As it turned out, this was Mina's first encounter with using Tampax Pearl® tampons. They were suggested to her by a girlfriend, in place of her usual pads or napkins.   For the rest of that day, I showed how truly brave I was by giving her a teasing grin whenever our eyes met; which was often followed by something being thrown at my head.

Needless to say on that occasion; I became more intimate with Mina than I ever would have thought imaginable.

"WHAT'S MINE IS MINE. WHAT'S YOURS IS OURS"

The handling of our household and personal finances is one major area that we had to address. Initially, we continued to pay our individual bills as we always had been.   Mina felt it was her responsibility to pay off her Sallie Mae student loans and her own car note. I continued paying the mortgage and what bills were in place and in my name before we were married. While I went along with this approach for about five months out of respect for Mina's wishes, it didn't sit well with me.

Now, I'm not as old school as my father who believes that the man of the house totally provides for his family. Whereas, I do feel as the man of the house, that it is my ultimate responsibility to ensure things are handled. That could mean through collaboration and coordination of Mina's and my income.

There wasn't much convincing needed to persuade her to combine our resources, especially with Mina's financial management background. We sat and listed all of our expenses, discretionary or otherwise. We then separated our total monthly expenses into *need to pay* bills (car notes, school loans and tithes) and *want to have* expenses (credit cards to clothing stores, dry cleaning and Starbucks coffee). We agreed to both pay on the *need to pay* bills.

To determine how much we would contribute to the joint expense checking account, we based it on our income percent comparison and not on whose bill was being paid. So my salary being seventy percent of our combined income, I deposit that much of my check into the expense account. In the joint savings account, we both deposit ten percent. The rest was ours to spend on discretionary purchases or in our personal checking accounts.

Because Mina has the bachelor's degree in financial management, I assumed that she wouldn't mind handling the household bill paying. That was a poor assumption on my part. To her credit and wisdom, Mina convinced me that we should alternate every other month paying the expenses. That way, both of us knew what was going on financially in the household. Being born digital, she set most of them up to be paid online via the internet.

I don't think I could have found a better *help mate*.

"*IT'S THE THOUGHT THAT COUNTS*"

The reason that I know that I'm *in love* with Mina is that I'm often thinking of her when we're apart. Though she may be out of sight, she is never out of mind. To make sure she is in my line of sight as much as possible, I have a photo of Mina and Mercedes set as the wallpaper on my computers, both at home and at work. Because of the blood relationship between the two ladies in my life, it's quite natural for people to mistake them for natural mother and daughter. The truth is they are cousins. We adopted Mercedes after her mother, Mina's aunt Brianna, and father abandoned her.

One afternoon I was called into the office of one of the law partners. Sitting across the desk from him, he slid a sheet of paper over to me. On the single page was a memo outlining my annual bonus and salary increase. I received a six percent bonus and a four percent salary increase. Based on the bonus alone, I was looking at fifty-five hundred dollars before taxes. I thanked the partner and headed straight to my office to call Mina.

Mina was back in school during that time, earning her degree. Realizing that she might be in class; I texted her cell phone about the bonus.

Me: Hey, guess who just got a $5K bonus?

Mina: Would that be my *Babe*?

Me: Yup, that would be. How about we go out for dinner to celebrate?

Mina: Great! Don't forget your tithes.

Me: Right. ILY

Mina: ILY2

The tithes reminder is the kind of the thing that I love about Mina. She's always being supportive of me and making sure that I'm doing the right thing. She makes me a better man to provide the security, strength and stability to our relationship.

When the bonus was deposited in my checking account, I transferred a tenth into our joint account. I figured that I wanted to show Mina my appreciation for her being in my life. Knowing how much women like shoes, my very next act was to go on the internet and order Mina a pair of designer Jimmy Choo, *Adina* Suede/water snake dress shoes. The price of the shoes was $560. I had the shoes shipped overnight to my office.

As soon as I walked in the house, I found Mina in the bedroom sitting on the bed, heads down studying. I laid the shoe box beside her and waited for the anticipated excitement. There's nothing like a *just because* gift.

"What's this?" She asked with a smiling face.

"Go ahead, open it and find out."

"What is it for?"

"For you being you."

The minute she laid her eyes on the shoes, her face lit up.

"Wow *Babe*, these are beautiful."

Mina literally bounced off the bed in order to put the shoes on and walk in them. My knowing a little something about women's tastes came as a transition benefit from a previous relationship. My ex-girlfriend loved shoes and they had to be designers if they were to make it on to her feet. I sat through enough Saturday afternoons at Bloomingdales watching her try on pair after pair of shoes to learn what works. Well almost.

"Matthew, who helped you pick these out?"

"Nobody . . . can't a man know a little something?"

"I guess." Mina was strutting around the room wearing her baby doll lingerie and those high heel shoes. She was looking damn sexy and I was sure glad she was my wife. Just when I was about to put in to action what my mind was salaciously thinking and what my body was erotically reacting to - - - everything changed. "*Babe*, these are really nice. Do they come in other colors?" She asked the first of a flurry of questions which caught me off guard.

"I suppose. I think gray."

"Where did you get them?"

"I ordered them online."

"How much did they cost?"

"I don't think you're supposed to ask how much a gift cost."

"Oh, I asked because I'm thinking of getting another pair in another color. I really like them *hun*."

"I see. Well if you must know; they were five and some change." See, that was a mistake. I felt it as soon as the words left my mouth. The stopped in her tracks look on her face confirmed it for me.

"Five . . . five what and some change?" She posed with an astonished look on her face.

"Five-hundred."

"*Babe*, you know I believe that you feel good if you look good, but five-hundred dollars for one pair of shoes. Un - un. Do you know what we could do with this money? You're sending these back."

"No I'm not. I bought them for you and I want you to keep them."

"Matthew . . ."

Mina went through a list of reasons why she didn't need to keep the shoes; obviously, cost being first. It came to a point where I was getting upset because she seemingly didn't appreciate my gesture. In my mind, the price I paid for the shoes wasn't an issue. It should have been the THOUGHT that counted. So what if I wanted Mina to have the best money could buy . . . but nooooooo. Then I made matters worse.

"You know what Mina; Natalie would be undressing right about now getting ready to show me just how much she appreciated me buying her those shoes." I blurted, in a poor attempt to justify my action.

"Excuse me. I know you didn't say what I thought you just said."

"I'm saying she would have appreciated the gesture."

"What you're saying is your girl would prostitute herself for a pair of shoes; and you know what that makes you."

"WHAT!"

That's how our first fight began. And no, the shoes did not go back; though she did exchange them for a different color.

"TWO FOR YOU. TWO FOR ME."

We agreed on a "two for two" year agreement of support of one another. The "2-4-2" idea came from my friend Tone'. The base of our agreement was that for two years, one of us receives the full support of the other while pursuing a personal or professional goal. Since I was in a permanent job and had the most tenure, then the first two years of support would come from me.

Mina would have twenty-four months to secure whatever accreditation and certification needed to increase her overall occupational knowledge and competency in the field of financial management.   As a financial and life coach to the underserved community, Mina would save them from making financial missteps. It was suggested that she would need more than her Bachelor's Degree from CAU. Mina met Synea Jackson, her mentor by joining The Financial Management Association.

My support would allow her to focus her attention and time on obtaining her goals. If that meant for me to take the lead in caring for our daughter Mercedes, or meaning that I would chauffeur her to the extracurricular activities, to drop her off and pick her up from school – so be it.

"OUT OF SIGHT, OUT OF MIND"

How ironic was it that the very thing that drew me to love Mina was the same thing that often took her away from me. It was this caring nature of hers that made such a distinction between her and my former girlfriend, that it made all the difference for me to ask Mina to marry me. It was her compassionate and giving personality to a fault that had Mina spending a lot of her effort and time helping others. So much so, that sometimes I feel slighted in the lack of attention given me. I know that it sounds selfish on my part.

I was left wondering how different our lives would be if she were to focus on our household, knowing how attentive she is toward her family, friends and clients. As a life coach to many who call upon her, Mina felt obligated to be at their beck and call - by phone, text or instant messaging. Everybody wanted Mina. That included me and Mercedes.

With the heavy burden of being a lifesaver, Mina was sometimes absentmindedly away even though we're sitting right next to one another. When she was physically away, she would easily forget about home while being so wrapped up in helping others.

The only time that I truly believed that I had her undivided attention was when we made love. Otherwise, sometimes with Mina it was a case of *out of sight, out of mind.*

NOVEMBER

"WHY I GOT MARRIED?"

HERE WE ARE, THE TWO OF US TOGETHER; married for a little over two years and we couldn't be any happier. We've become the classic suburban family, with a four bedroom house in the suburbs, a two car garage and a white picket fence. Mina planted perennials in the front of the house. We sit on the back deck at dusk and, on occasion, make love under the stars. We laugh together, love one another and care for Mercedes to make her life well. If it got any better than this, it would be a sin.

Committing a sin is exactly what I would be doing if I weren't married to Mina, as I lust for her while she walks around the bedroom, naked as the day she was born. She doesn't do it for the sexy effect, or to get me to look at her. She just likes "being natural," she once told me, "Lingerie is fine and everything, but it's just the wrapping on the gift." She's intelligent with a bodacious body. What makes her sexy is that she is modest. Modest yet confident, even with the stretch marks where her mother's genes blessed her with plenty of bounty. Especially her bouncy dark roasted cinnamon crumb cake of a behind.

It's a Saturday afternoon and Thanksgiving is two weeks away. I'm folding clothes from a recently washed load of laundry while Mina goes from dresser to closet putting them away. My eyes aren't missing a jiggle or a wiggle of hers as she flits about the room.

She's talking about our trip for the holiday to visit her family in Louisiana. We flipped a coin to decide whose family we visit for Thanksgiving, while the other gets Christmas. It's the first time we're visiting family for the holidays as husband and wife with child.

I'm listening to Mina, sort of, but I'm looking even harder. Yeah, right then; I had a one track mind. My mind and eyes are tracking Mina's every move.

"... and *Bookie*, will you watch Mercedes while I go to the mall?" Mina asked, giving me something else to mentally process.

"Sure."

"Good, she's asleep and I didn't want to have to wake her."

"Asleep, huh?"

"Yes. Do you want me to pick you up anything while I'm out?"

"No. I don't need to buy clothes every time I go out of town."

"Of course you don't. All you need is your driving gloves and driving shoes."

"And?"

"Whatever. May I take your car?"

"Yeah, I'm not going anywhere. I'm going to watch the game with Marcus."

"Marcus," she says his name with disdain, "Don't he have a home?"

"Yes."

"Maybe I *should* take Sadie with me."

"She'll be okay. Plus she likes her uncle Marcus."

"He ain't none of her damn uncle."

"Why don't you like Marcus?"

"I just don't. By the way, my uncle got you a ticket to the Bayou Classic."

"Who's playing?

"Who's playing? Grambling and Southern and my family is all about Southern."

"Really. Are you going?"

"No, just the guys are going."

"I don't have to go you know."

"Yes you do. He bought you a ticket. Besides, Sadie and I will be visiting *fam*."

"I don't think we're going to be spending much time together while we're visiting your folk." I express with some trepidation. Walking to where Mina was putting socks in the top chest of drawers, I put my arms around her. My hands come to rest on the slight pooch of her belly. "Hmm, is there a brownie in the oven?"

"That's not funny." Mina pushes out to break free of my hug. "It means I'm coming on my period. I told you that there won't be any baby coming out of me."

"I was just kidding," I grabbed hold of her again. This time we're face to face and my hands set comfortably in the deeply indented small of her back. It's a perfect fit.

"Like I said, it's not funny. Besides, you said you didn't want any kids."

"And I still don't. I mean, we have Sadie."

"Okay then. Leave it alone." I sensed an unusually edgy tone in her voice.

"*Alrighty*. Can we still do that thing people do to make babies?"

"If I feel like it when I get back," she breaks free from me again and gets dressed.

As Mina walked out the door of our house, Marcus was pulling up in the drive. He and I both watch her walk to my car. She's wearing three inch high heels, skinny jeans and a short leather jacket. She makes it difficult to take our eyes from her. Marcus calls her a ghetto beauty. There's no mistaking the allure of her curvaceous body from lips to her hips. While she might not ever make it as a runway model, I think she would easily win "Video Vixen of the Year" if she would choose to compete.

"Hey Mina," Marcus yelled to the back of her. She throws him a wave and nothing more. He reached the front door. "Man, your girl is mean as a snake."

"Only to some people, and know this, her hiss and her bite both can be deadly."

"So why'd you marry her?"

It took close to the entire first quarter of the rivalry that is Ohio State and Michigan football before I attempted to explain to Marcus how much Mina and Mercedes mean to me and how they've changed my life. Without spouting poetry or breaking into song, it was difficult to explain to another man how being in love made me feel.

Aside from seeing Mina as cute, smart, courageous, principled while being streetwise tough, I see her as a compliment to who I am and who I want to be. She is an extension of me to lean on, when and where I'm weak. She doesn't try to control me; she ignores one of my friends that she doesn't care for as opposed to trying to keeping me from him. Instead of allowing me to spoil her, she makes me comfortable enough about my manhood to want to give to her just because. She makes me want to come home.

"I married Mina, because she makes me a better man," is what I tell him.

"I ain't goin' to *front* Matt man. I'm happy for you. I mean your girl ain't *chittlin'* ugly that's for damn sure. She's got that Nia Long, Sanaa Lathan cute *thang* going on and she can handle her business. It funny how I used to watch them *pork chops* walk around the building delivering mail, and you done married her."

Mercedes comes in to the family room, wiping her sleepy eyes. The six years old walks to where I'm sitting on the couch and stands next to me. I kiss her on the cheek.

"Good afternoon." Mercedes greeted.

"Good afternoon sleepy head," I addressed the child. "Do you see Marcus, tell him good afternoon?" I tell her, reinforcing the social rule my mother instilled in me - it is the person who enters the room, who should speak first.

"Good afternoon," she offered, while still wiping sleep from her eyes.

In a falsetto voice, Marcus responds, "Hey Sadie Mae."

"Where's Mommy," the tike asked.

"She went to the mall."

"I want to go to the mall. Why didn't she take me?"

"You were sleep."

"Why didn't she wake me up?"

"Because you were asleep."

"She should have waked me up."

"But you were asleep."

"That's why she should have waked me up."

"Right, but I told her it was okay to leave you here with me. Is that okay?"

"Yeah," she answered with little assurance. With that, she turned to leave the room. Just as she reached the door, I heard her say, "She should have waked me up."

"GOING HOME"

Early start road travel is another characteristic that I've picked up from my father. Whenever our family went on a road trip, we would always leave before dawn. Before we would pull out of the driveway, my mother would have us recite *Psalms 23*. To this day I carry that practice forward. With Mina and Mercedes, I recited the Psalms.

Wednesday, Thanksgiving Eve, the normal 7 ½ hours drive to Franklinton, Louisiana took close to ten hours due to the holiday traffic and occasional fender benders.

"Welcome to Franklinton – Courtesy of MaGee Financial" reads the sign that greets us. Franklinton is about 90 miles or so east of Baton Rouge. Mina said that Franklinton is this rural small town, in the Washington Parrish of about 3,700 people. She explained that Louisiana is the only state in the union that recognizes Parishes; which corresponds to counties in other states. Other than my *baby love*, the main thing Franklinton is known for is its Annual Fair. Otherwise, there was where I learned of Mina's country living roots.

We arrived at Mina's mother's house around six o'clock in the evening, central time. From the moment we arrived, phone calls were made to the family and friends in the neighboring communities, parishes and towns announcing that Quijelmina, better known in these parts as "Tweety" was home. The people traffic in and out of her mother's small two-bedroom flat was like that of the Parade of Homes. Aunts and uncles, cousins, nephews and nieces - by blood, by marriage and by baby making, all came over. Family members called on the phone from as far as Hattiesburg, Mississippi wanting us to drive up to visit.

Throughout the evening, I received and gave hugs and kisses to the visiting women. Poor little Mercedes was picked up, hugged and passed around like a little rag doll. Almost the same type of handling happened to Mina by the men in her family. Her brothers are all bigger in stature than she, in either height or girth or both. Mina is the youngest of five children and the only girl her parents had together. From the overflow and gathering of folks, I gained a newfound meaning for extended family. There was plenty of beer, bourbon and whiskey to keep the merry mood of the evening.

Being back at home where Mina was born and raised was like traveling back to another place and time. Everyone called her by her childhood nickname of Tweety, as if she'd never grown older.

I had not seen Mina for about thirty minutes. My guess was that she was in the kitchen or outside visiting. Mercedes was with her, while I'm being entertained by Uncle Raymond. Forty-seven year old Uncle Raymond is Mina's mother's brother. He shared a bedroom with Mina's youngest brother Jarvis, who was twenty-eight.

"Yeah Matt, you did good marryin' our little Tweety," Uncle Raymond assured.

"I think so too."

"The family is proud of her – both of you, the way you stepped in and takin' care of Brianna's child and all."

"Well, we love Mercedes."

"Yeah, that's real nice. Did you ever see ya'll picture in the newspaper?"

"I don't think so."

"WHAT! Jarvis, where the photo album? – IT AIN'T UNDER THE COFFEE TABLE. LOOK IN THE CHINA CABINET AND BRING IT HERE?" The burly, slow to move about man ordered. Jarvis arrived with the photo album, handing it to his uncle.

"Thanks, you lazy bum. Here you go Matt, you and Tweety made the *Daily World* and the *Bogalusa Daily News*. That's big time you know."

Raymond handed me a laminated newspaper clipping of the wedding announcement.

"Yeah, this guy name Randy cuts out these pictures and stories, have them done up like that and mails it to the people. He's been doin' it fo' years."

"That's nice. So he just does this for anybody?"

"Yep. But you know Tweety's a celebrity around here."

"Really?"

"Oh yeah. She graduated top of her class – went to big city Atlanta and graduated from Clark Atlanta College."

"Clark's a university."

"Say what?"

"It's Clark Atlanta University."

"Shoot, that's even better ain't it. Ain't any of her brothers done nothin' like that. They mother is smart and all. Tweety is the only one who takes after her. That's why she's the first one of 'em to move up. Take a look through the book."

The proud uncle gave me a guided tour through the photo album which seemed to focus on the life and times of Quijelmina Parker. The thick album was mixed with Polaroid photos of Mina at various ages and venues. Some of the photos were at obvious personal settings, while others are at school or church functions. I smiled at photos where the flash from the camera are reflected off Mina's heavily Vaseline covered legs and patent leather shoes.

Mina was a highly decorated and recognized academic achiever. She was the valedictorian of Franklinton High School - the winner of a number of highest grade awards and a United Negro College Fund recipient. Seeing the number of accolades and touted accomplishments of young Mina had my chest swelling with pride. Her mother walked up, catching me with a broad smile on my face.

"Look at him smiling from ear to ear. He knows he got him a good girl. That's my little Tweety Bird," said the woman who looked as if she could be Mina's older sister instead of her mother.

At fifty, Rosemary Anne Parker was still an attractive woman; dressed in a gold and blue velour sweat suit that might have been a little too clingy. If by looking at her, I saw Mina in the future, then I was pleased. So would be Marcus, who'd often warn me to check out the mother of any woman that I was considering dating, to know what I could be in for if I decided to make it long term.

Other of Mina's family members entered the room, volunteering personal stories of her when she was a child. The memorable tales spanned from humorous to most certainly embarrassing.

According to Uncle Raymond, Mina was branded with the name *Tweety Bird* because when she was younger her speech was impeded by what he called a "thick tongue, which made her sound like the cute chick Looney Tunes character." She grew out of the impediment to where she now speaks with only a slight lisp.

Also, when she was about three, Mina was helping her grandmother in the garden and she found a baby chick that had fallen out of its nest. She picked it up and brought it to her grandma. They brought the bird inside the house to take care of it.

"Tweety's brothers would dig up earthworms to feed the little bird. One day Tweety decided that she wanted to be like the baby bird, so she thought she'd eat a worm . . . and she did." The laughter filled the room. "Where is that girl anyway . . . TWEETY?"

"She's gone," offered a relative whose name I couldn't put with the face.

"Gone where?"

Almost in unisons the answer came from multiple members in the room, "Hackley."

"OH LAWD! You can take the girl out of the country, but you can't take the country out of the girl."

"Where's Hackley," I asked.

"Not where sweetie, what's Hackley. It's a little country community just across the tracks. Tweety loves to hang out over there. Especially with that girlfriend of hers who can't seem to keep her legs closed. What did the reverend say last Sunday, 'when you lay and play, you pay.'" That comment was followed by a few "um hmm."

From the gist of the conversation from that point on, I learned that Hackley was not a city or town as I assumed, but merely a community not worthy of its own zip code according to the storytellers. From their derogatory description of the group of people who lived there, it was considered as some sort of a country ghetto. I was surprised to learn that class-ism existed in the rural country of America.

Because the hour had gotten late I heard that we are to spend the night at Mina's mother's house. In my mind, I remembered a hotel that we passed while driving in. It's after 11:00 p.m. While people have slowed coming over, they were also slow to leave.

Mina had left in a car with someone to go visit. I'm not happy to learn this second hand and at the late hour. When I called her cell phone which she is never without or far away from, there was no answer. I'm tired and I couldn't get comfortable, neither do I want to in this house.

At one thirty in the morning, Mina comes in the door carrying a sleeping Mercedes. Mina avoids looking at me as she lays the little girl on a love seat. She grabbed a laid out blanket and pillow and begins preparing a makeshift bed for the child. As feared, we're asked to sleep over. Reluctantly, I agreed. The sofa that I had been sitting on all evening opened up in to a bed.

Not more than a dozen words are exchanged between Mina and me while others are around. We can sense how one another are feeling and I'm sure Mina knows that I'm upset. After everyone was behind closed doors and in bed, Mina and I have a moment to talk.

"I know you're mad," she opened with.

"You were gone most of the night and you had Sadie out with you. And why didn't you answer your phone?"

"I left it in the car."

"So where were you?"

"I went to see my friend from high school."

"In Hackley?" I ask, judgmentally. "That couldn't have waited until tomorrow or Friday?"

"No. She's going through some things. You wouldn't understand."

"Help me understand then."

"She's pregnant, with her fourth child."

"So she's having a baby. Women do that all the time you know."

"She's a year younger than me."

"What, she's never heard of birth control?" As soon as the words leave my mouth, I knew that meant trouble. The confirmation of that was the flinch, then stiffening of Mina's body lying next to me. "I know how that may have sounded, but you know what I mean. Doesn't she know how to show some responsibility for her actions?"

Mina doesn't answer right away, then "She's had two abortions. It's too late to kill this one. She's talking about giving the baby away as soon as it's born."

"What about the father of the baby?"

"I don't know."

"This sounds like something straight off of Jerry Springer or what's his name, uh Maury."

"What it is, is a hard life for some people Matthew. Not everyone can live a perfect life like you."

"What is that supposed to mean?"

"Never mind, I'm tired. Good night." She turned her back to me.

There was nothing I could have done to make the situation better, so I let it go for the moment. Time passed and I'm in and out of a shallow sleep. A bedroom door opens and Uncle Raymond goes into the bathroom. The next sound heard throughout the small house was a loud and ripping fart.

"Un unn," commented Mina. I chuckled. Her mother yells from her room, "RAYMOND."

Behind the closed bathroom door he responded with, "THERE'S MORE ROOM OUT THAN THERE IS IN."

"BUT WE GOT COMPANY."

"IT'S BETTER TO PASS GAS AND BE ASHAMED, THAN TO BUST A GUT AND GO LAME."

"RAYMOND."

I chuckled.

Mina says, "Un umm."

"SLEEPLESS IN FRANKLINTON"

At five o'clock in the morning I'm wide awake. Needless to say, I didn't get a good night's sleep. As to why, I had my pick of reasons. There was the bar from the sofa bed that wanted to remind me that I wasn't at home in our California King Size bed, on a firm mattress and Egyptian Cotton Blend 400 thread count sheets. Or, it could have been the cricket somewhere in the house that chirped well into the morning, before I could tune it out. The obvious reason why I didn't sleep well was the way the day concluded between me and Mina.

Mina's mother was the second one in the house, aside from me, to stir. I got up and joined her in the kitchen.

"Morning Ms. Parker."

"Hey Matthew, what you doin' up so early?"

"I'm usually up at this time."

"I know that Tweety is working on her second dream about now."

"Yeah, she's a late sleeper, if not for Sadie and me."

"The two of you are a blessing to Tweety."

"She's a blessing to us."

"Well, I think y'all are a beautiful family."

"Thank you. You did a great job in raising her."

"You just take care of her. She's always taking care of others."

"Yes ma'am. Uh, is there a Starbucks around here?"

"The closest one is in Covington."

"Where's that?"

"Oh, just about an hour's drive."

"What?"

"Oh yeah. I've been making that drive for twenty years, working at Lakeview Regional Medical Hospital. Every morning I stop in Starbucks and get me a hot cup of coffee before clocking in."

For breakfast we had eggs and Canadian bacon, cheese grits and shrimp with biscuits. That was the beginning to a daylong of Thanksgiving eating. In between, I managed to watch a game and a half of professional football.

Because of the influence of her brothers, Mina has a fondness for some sports. She was by my side watching along during the game, when her cell phone rang. It was LaDessa, her friend from high school. She moves off the couch to take the call in the kitchen. I turned my attention back to the game, allowing Mina her space. After about forty minutes she comes back in the room and takes her seat next to me and Mercedes. She holds my hand and leans in to me.

"Is everything okay?" I asked.

"Yeah, she'll be okay."

Thanksgiving dinner Louisiana southern style was deep fried turkey, with oyster stuffing. Jambalaya Gumbo with crawfish, shrimp and okra was also on the table. Mashed potatoes, turnip greens and *Ho cake* bread rounded out the meal. For after dinner, we had yellow pound cake for dessert. After everyone had their fill, Mina begins preparing plates of food. I'm in the kitchen with her.

"*Babe*, I'm going to take this to LaDessa and her kids and I'll be right back."

"Alright. Do you want me to come with you?"

"No, that's okay. Why don't you get us a hotel room for tonight?

"Are you sure? I was sort of looking forward to your Uncle Raymond's midnight serenade."

"You silly."

"THAT'S WHAT FRIENDS ARE FOR."

Mina's mother was thrilled when we asked if Mercedes could stay the night, while we made the long drive to Baton Rouge to check in a LaQuinta Hotel.

"Of course I'll watch my grand-niece." Technically, Mina's mom was Mercedes' aunt.

In Baton Rouge and vicinity, Mina had more family. It was where her estranged father lived and more relatives on her father's side. During the drive there, Mina tells me the depths of her friendship with LaDessa Trufant.

"We met during my senior year at Franklinton High School" Mina began. "There were but a handful of us black kids in the whole school. The local black community complained that the school system was being prejudice. To deal with the complaints, the school board came up with the ARK Bussing Program, where they bussed in two students from Pine High of each grade level. Pine High was an all black school in Hackley. Eight students were bussed in.

"LaDessa was one of the eight and she was in the eleventh grade at the time. There was this math teacher, Miss Anne who liked me. She gave me private tutoring in Advance Math so that I could get preparation for college. No one else in the school wanted it *'cept* me. Miss Anne said she liked my ambition.

"So sometimes I would be in her classroom during other hours, like when LaDessa's junior class was there. At Pine, LaDessa was a top student. That wasn't the case when she came to Franklinton. It wasn't necessarily that the class work was harder, but she did not have the help from the teachers that she got at Pine. LaDessa is dyslexic."

"That means she reads backwards, or something, right?"

"I just know she had trouble with word problems in math, and Miss Anne asked me to tutor her."

"You . . . why you?"

"Miss Anne was tutoring me, so she said this was a way I could payback a good deed. I didn't mind. So me and LaDessa became best friends during that time. The only problem was my own grades for the first time in four years started slipping." Mina chuckles aloud, but more to herself.

"What?" I asked.

"LaDessa *is some kind of special*. When I told her that my grades had dropped off, she said 'Oh no. Is it my fault? Did you catch my dyslexia?'" Mina and I both laughed. "I told her no and that I wasn't worried because my grade point average would still average out to be an A over the four years. Well, there became a problem."

"What?"

"Laura Howard."

"Who's Laura Howard?"

"Check this out, she was this white *chick* who was a junior and decided that she wanted to graduate early and get married."

"Wait a minute. She wanted to graduate early just so she could get married, at what sixteen, seventeen."

"Sixteen and a half, but they do that a lot down here."

"Was she pregnant?"

"No, that's what everybody thought at first. But get this. Her boyfriend was the star quarterback of the football team right. So he was about to graduate and go away on a full ride scholarship to college. So her family wanted them to marry before he left, so she wouldn't lose him. At least that was what people were saying."

"So how was that trouble for you?"

"Ole girl was the top of her junior class, right. By her wanting to graduate early, her mother wanted her also to be named valedictorian of the graduating class – when everyone knew I was the valedictorian. See, Laura had a four point GPA too."

"Okay, so you two tied for valedictorian."

"NO!" Mina vehemently defended as if she was reliving the moment. "See, mine was a four year four point O, where hers was just a three year. IT WASN'T FAIR!"

"Alright. Alright, no need to get excited. So what happened?" I glanced over to Mina who appeared to be at a quiet boil. "Mina."

"They made us co-valedictorians."

"And you didn't think that was a good compromise I suppose."

"Oh, I was cooler about it than my mother was. Mama went off, but not because of the co-thing. No, Laura's mother had the damn nerve to claim that they were being discriminated against because at the Mayor's Scholarship Ball, I got a UNCF Scholarship. Oh, my mother was ready to *snatch that woman a new one*." Mina's demeanor returns to a simmer as we approached Hammond, the halfway point to Baton Rouge.

"*Bookie*, are you okay?" I asked

"You know I said LaDessa was *some kind of special,* right."

"Right."

"Don't get me wrong, country and all, LaDessa is my girl. When she found out what Laura and her family did, the day of graduation, LaDessa waited until after the ceremony and jumped on Laura. I mean and she beat her bad."

"No."

"Yup. They had to take Laura to the hospital."

"Aw man. What happened to LaDessa?"

"She got arrested for assault and battery and she was kicked out of Franklinton. The ARK program was canceled and everything."

"Dang."

"Oh it got ugly. Some of the blacks who lived in Franklinton was on the side of the white people, like they was different from the blacks living in Hackley."

"Are you serious?"

"Me and my mama even got in to it about the whole thing. I told her she was wrong for thinking she was better than anybody."

"You said that to your mother."

"I sure did."

"Okay. What about LaDessa and her family."

"Her family *caught it*, but LaDessa was fine. When I went to see her, she was all happy and braggin' about what she did. She told me that she told Laura *'I'm goin' to beat yo' ass so bad, yo' unborn baby is goin' to think it did somethin' wrong.'*"

"But I thought you said that she was pregnant?"

"She wasn't. She was just saying that's how badly she was going to whoop her butt."

Once again, the two of us shared a hearty laugh. Now I had a better understanding of the bond between Mina and LaDessa and an idea of Mina's sense of responsibility to LaDessa's current personal situation. Mina tells me how the two of them promised to stay in touch. But once Mina left to attend Clark Atlanta University, she had a new focus.

Mina confessed that she discovered that she was one of those "out of sight, out of mind" types of people. One has to reach out to her if they want to stay in touch. She said that she doesn't mean to be that way, but that she focuses on "where she is and where she intends to go, not where she's been."

"LOVING YOU"

That night at the hotel Mina and I made intensely passionate love well into the early morning. We took a shower and go for round two under the hot steamy water. We dried each other before climbing in bed only to get all sweaty again. My internal clock woke me at the usual 6:00 EST time. I turned to Mina to arouse her with a head to toe sensual massage.

"You do know that I was asleep," she stated.

"Oh, my bad . . . I'll let you go back to sleep."

"No, no, I'm just sayin'."

"So how were you sleeping?"

"Good."

"Have I told you lately that I love you?"

"You know what, you haven't."

"Well, I do." I admitted.

I left Mina at the hotel, returned to a sound sleep after another sexual romp. I followed the road directions given to me by the hotel desk clerk to the Starbucks in downtown Baton Rouge. My mind was revisiting thoughts and visions of Mina. My mind's eye could see every inch of her body and every strand of her hair, from the wispy sideburns to the pubic coiled Qs. I find myself becoming aroused again.

Once inside the College & Bennington Starbuck's store, I sat with my comforting thoughts of Mina, and a steaming Grande Chai Tea Latte. Mina requested that I stop drinking so much coffee, so I alternated to an occasional Chai Tea Latte. Her genuine concern for my health and well being was but one more reason why I love her so much.

The baritone vocalizing of Teddy Pendergrass' *This Gift of Life* was being played throughout the store.

♫ *This Gift of Life / Oh I treasure it above everything / This Gift of Life / I'm so thankful / Lord knows I'm thankful to be living / It's the only thing you can't buy with money / It's the only thing that you can't buy . . . it's such a blessing,* ♫

The old school, rhythm and blues balladeer crooned aloud my thoughts, so that the others in the coffee shop could know this joy that I had. Together, Mina and I had Mercedes as our common goal to make sure she had the best life we could afford to give her and to prepare her as best we could for her life ahead.

If life could be any better then . . . I'm suddenly struck with an overwhelming sense of despair. Outside of the large storefront window was a woman approaching a man with her hand out, appearing as if she's begging for money. Intently, I watched with a personal interest though I wanted not to recognize the familiar face of the woman. *No, it can't be. There's no way.* I looked away as she glanced in to the store. *If I don't see you, you don't see me.* That was my illogical thinking.

As the door to our hotel room swung open, I found Mina sitting on the side of the bed slipping on a pair of Steve Madden ballet flats. I'm hoping that my uneasy demeanor was unnoticeable to the normally keen sensory perceptive woman. Chicly dressed for our day of visiting more of her family, my unassuming sweetheart looked at me with wide-eye innocence.

"Let me guess, you went to Starbucks," she correctly figures.

"Yep."

"Did you drink coffee?"

"No. I had tea."

"Good. That's my *Bookie*. Is anything the matter?"

"Nothing at all, why?"

"I don't know . . . you seem different."

"Everything is fine." I lied, but I'm not sure about what.

We headed north from Baton Rouge to begin our visits to Mina's family, stopping first in Baker at her aunt Nakeisha's. There, I heard more stories about Mina growing up as an above average child. If it wasn't her bringing home a stray cat, she was taking up for some kid who was being picked on by a bully. Even though the bully would be twice Mina's size according to the aunt.

Mina didn't mind the tomboy stories. It was when her aunt Nakeisha began telling stories about the boys Mina dated; then it was time to go according to my wife. Not before we received a big tin of homemade Pralines to take with us. We said our goodbyes and made promises to return with Mercedes.

Our next visit was to a small trailer home on an open piece of land in Zachary, Louisiana. That's where fifty-five year old William Albert Montague lived. The name William in Old Columbian Spanish is Quijelmina. William was Mina's father. This stop was the most solemn.

William Montague and a woman introduced only as Marbella were in the one bedroom trailer home. Mina's aunt referred to Marbella as an old school *gold digger* who was pinching off William's veteran pension and disability checks. The mention of this sent Mina into a protective rage. She regained respect for her elders' composure once we were seated on a couch before the older couple.

Marbella complimented Mina with, "Ooh *chile*, you are most definitely yo' daddy's girl. You are so pretty and you *sho'* got his cheekbone," said the woman who seemingly was older than Mina's dad. That's not saying anything in her favor.

Mina's father was in visibly poor health, from years of alcohol abuse and heavy smoking. He gets around the small trailer with the aid of a cane. The cane supports the bad hip injured in a trucking accident for which he receives a disability check.

Seeing her father in a debilitating and dependent condition put Mina through an array of demeanors and emotions. First she was *daddy's little girl*, doting over the man whom she's named after. In a soft cooing Tweety voice, she made general inquiries about him and gave updates about herself and us. My conversation with the man was mainly in responses to his questions.

Later, Mina became the *chastising mother figure*; getting on her father for still smoking, despite his doctor's orders to stop. His only defending response was "I know baby girl." From there, she quickly became the *criticizing caregiver*, blaming the "so called help" for his shameful condition and that of his home. Directly and indirectly she spoke her mind, with a sharp tongue, while straightening around the house trailer, ignoring the pleas from Marbella not to.

When it's time for us to leave, Mina gave her father a strong hug. I noticed the familiar gathering of his shirt material in her hands as she holds him. She does the same thing to me when we hug.

Sitting in the car to give Mina a semi-private goodbye moment with her father, he stands at the trailer doorway. From my vantage point, I could see Mina adamantly spitting words aiming them at Marbella who's standing behind William. His frail frame kept the two women from getting to one another. I heard Marbella's voice even with the car's windows being closed. Mina was walking toward the car throwing up a "talk to the hand" at the couple. When she opened the front passenger side door, I heard her parting words, "Whatever. You heard what I said." She climbed in and slammed the door.

It's a long and quiet ride on I-12 east toward I-55 north toward Franklinton.

"WHO DAT!"

It's Saturday, the big game day for the Bayou Classic. I kissed Mina and Mercedes goodbye. Their plans for the day were more visits with friends and family and maybe some Christmas shopping.

Uncle Raymond picked me up in his Ford Expedition at the hotel. Two of her brothers are in the SUV. I bought a round of coffee and crumb cakes for us before we got on I-10 East headed for New Orleans. The early start affords us time for me to get a tourist ride in New Orleans East, the Lower Ninth Ward, Congo Square, the West Bank, Uptown and the French Quarters. I got to see the famed Bourbon Street. Seeing the impact of Hurricane Katrina up close and personal gave me a more respectful perspective on the catastrophe.

The Thirty Third Bayou Classic between the Grambling Tigers and Southern Jaguars was more for bragging rights since they both had losing records for the season. You couldn't tell it by the hyped atmosphere of the city and in the Dome, from the excited mood of the fans. The Battle of the Band can only really be appreciated live and in person. Southern won the game 21-17. The cheering and boasting was maintained the nearly two hour drive back to the hotel.

The holidays with the family can reveal *the good, the bad* and sometimes *the ugly*.

"TRAIN UP A CHILD IN THE WAY HE SHOULD GO . . ."

Our first week back from Louisiana, I noticed a change in Quijelmina's behavior. She was a lot more focused and determined toward her care and treatment of Mercedes. Not that she has ever lacks in her dedication to our daughter. Mina's love for Mercedes was unquestionable. Her style in raising her was straightforward and sensible.

Mina doesn't teach Mercedes any fairytales or, as she calls them false doctrines. That means there is no Tooth Fairy, Easter Bunny or Santa Claus for Mercedes. Jehovah Witnesses love talking with Mina, up to a point of disagreement. The other things Mina instilled in Mercedes is to be self-reliant, and about the importance of saving money. By keeping her room clean and helping out around the house with chores, we give Mercedes an allowance. Twenty-five or 50 cents for every dollar she saves, we match it to help her savings to grow faster. It started as her personal 401-Kindergarden fund. She'll now understand the concept of personal investment when she works for an employer who will offer her the same program.

When Mercedes wants a toy or an animated DVD, Mina has taught her to save her money in order to buy it for herself. "Always be able to do for yourself. Never depend on *any man*, other than Matthew, to do anything for you," Mina instructs. I don't take offense to the "any man" reference because I come out of it as the exception.

Insisting on providing her the opportunity of getting the best education, we enrolled Mercedes in the Dekalb Academy of Technology & Environment. Part of the academy's mission statement . . . *to educate a student population about the essential need to consider environmental ramifications or technology and other business decisions, via a hands-on, community-oriented instructional curriculum. The Academy is to improve student achievement via a curriculum which: promotes a higher order thinking skills – critical thinking, problem solving, and decision making.*

Something else that kept Mina distracted since our return was her continuously being on her Blackberry cell phone. She was either calling or being called to manage some situation involving her father. I overheard Mina haggling with Marbella over what was best for William. For the woman that I would have given a character reference as "being respectful to her elders" had been anything but when it came to Marbella. Mina does not hold back when it comes to her father. With the aid of the legal staff at ASK ME, Mina applied for legal guardianship of one William Montague.

The other person whom she's constantly on the phone with was LaDessa. LaDessa had asked Mina to be the godmother of her unborn baby. Of course Mina said yes and had parceled out more of her time to seeing to the needs of her god child.

If it was not William or LaDessa; Mina received calls from long lost relatives who had a new found reason for getting in touch. They were under the impression that she was financially rich. With Mina tooling around her old Parrish stomps in my black CLS500 Mercedes Benz may have left a misleading sense of our financial status. Nonetheless, Mina was called and asked for money or some kind of support. And her kind heart always said "yes."

DECEMBER

"GOOD TIMES. AIN'T WE LUCKY WE GOT 'EM"
    IT WAS THE FIRST OF THE MONTH.

Mina called me at work to ask if I would pick up Mercedes from school. It gave me a chance to leave the office just a little bit early, so I told her it was "no problem." There was a serious tone about her voice. It's understandable; this was the time of year she tried to convince assisted living mothers to spend their money responsibly and not lavishly because of the holiday season.

Responsible spending is the crux of her efforts on "How to avoid Ghetto Tax" and Easy Credit Rip Offs," workshops for the underserved and low income residents of Atlanta and surrounding areas.

Most of Mina's clients are welfare single mothers or other government assisted living men and women; like Mina's father. At the first of the month, the inner city and neighboring-*hood* areas are the richest in the country. It's part of Mina's goal to help those riches go toward the needs of the recipients and not wants.

"Hey Sadie," I greet the little tike climbing into the backseat of the car. She's wearing her white Peter Pan blouse, Khaki Jumper, with white tights.

"Hello."

"How was school today?"

"Fine."

"What did you learn?"

"Um, let me think. We learned direction and signals?"

"Like what?"

"We learned how to tell our left from our right."

"But you already know your left from your right don't you."

"I know, but some of the other kids in the class didn't."

"So how did they teach you to know the difference?"

"All you have to do is hold your hands out in front of you, facing away. Then you stick your thumbs out. The hand that makes the capital letter L is the left."

"Oh, I see. That's pretty smart. Look at you."

"You silly," remarks Mercedes, repeating a phrase Mina often uses.

Before heading home, we went to Stonecrest Mall to do some Christmas window shopping. I had no intention on buying, not while I had the little one along. Mercedes enjoyed the ride and the music playing on the radio. She liked singing the local jazz station's call letters.

♪ *Smoo-oooth jazz, one oh seven point five, double-u- jay zee-zee* ♪ she chimed.

Mercedes was quite the little talented singer. We've been approached several times about entering Mercedes in to the National Actors, Models & Talent Competition. We have yet to decide whether we should.

By the time we arrived home, Mina was there. Once we're in the house, Mercedes runs through it calling for her, "Mommy." She finds her in the kitchen preparing dinner. "There you are," announced Mercedes.

"Yes, here I am Sweet Pea . . . and how was your day?"

"Fine, and don't ask me what I learned in school because I've already told Matthew."

"Well yes ma'am. How about you go and change out of your uniform so you can go with me to get groceries? We need to make out a list first."

"Okay." Mercedes runs out of the kitchen.

"So how was your day," I asked my wife who was cooking stove top Lasagna, my favorite food.

"Oh, let me tell you. Do you remember me telling you about Tanisha; the teenage girl that got pregnant by the twenty-five year old guy, who then moved in with her and her mother?"

"Yes," I didn't remember the girl's name *per se*, but I definitely remembered the gist of her circumstances.

"Now her mother is pregnant."

"Really."

"No, you don't get it. Her mama is pregnant by the same guy."

"What!"

"Oh it gets worse. Now the mama wants to kick Tanisha out, because there's too much drama in the house." Mina continues to tell me the sordid details of the perceivable next guests on some Reality Series, *My Mama's Baby Mama Drama*.

To be truthful, I enjoy listening to my *Bookie* tell about her day and about her social work. Her firsthand account of the *Ghetto Tales from the Hood* was my vicarious exposure to their colorful lives. The same black American urban dwellers I watch and read about in the news and receive email jokes about. The black Americans who because of their highly profiled media coverage; are the face of black Americans to most of the casual yet ignorant onlookers. Black Americans who are seen as a cluster of stereotypes.

Then there are those like myself, the stand alone achiever. I'm the embodiment of Ralph Ellison's *Invisible Man*. Socially, I'm mixed in the melting pot of the working middleclass whose income doesn't cause a blip on anyone's radar. On the landscape of America, I've blended into one of Atlanta's many suburbs. At work, I'm considered an assimilated African American, "typically meets" performer, unthreatening to the rank and file, safely tucked away in my corner office.

So it was with Mina and her colorful background and life[1] which brightened my otherwise safe and stable existence.

_____

[1] Read *Ghettoway Weekend* by Lawrence Christopher

Not many men can appreciate the rich fulfillment of the life that I found with Mina. She's sexy cute, street savvy, dedicated to family, determined and dependable to a cause. And what man wouldn't want a woman who was able to enter an Amateur Stripper's Contest and win. I had one, who was standing at the stove cooking me dinner.

"So what is, uh, Tanisha going to do?" I asked.

"If it comes to it, I have a shelter where she can go stay. I told her that she needs to take his ass to court for child support. I'm reading this book, *Girl Get that Child Support*. This lawyer wrote it. It's good too. Now I can help my clients get more money and start getting some of them paid from even unemployed *baby daddies* and get them other assistance."

"Look at you; becoming a social avenger."

"I am huh?"

"Yes you are. Come here." I grabbed my baby in a full body hug, wrapping my arms tightly around her. "Now drop it like it's hot."

"You watch too much *Bernie Mac*" she scoffed.

"THE EASYWICK A.K.A. E'WICK"

Two weeks later, Mina called me at work. I can tell she's upset by the tone in her voice.

"My car won't start," she excitedly tells me.

"Does it make any noise when you turn the key?"

"No."

"Will the lights come on? I'm thinking it's the battery."

"Nothing comes on."

"Okay. Where are you?"

"I'm at the *E'wick*."

"Okay. I will be there to pick you up as soon as I can. Are you going to be okay until I get there?"

"Yeah" she said with assuredness.

I was upset with myself for not adding Mina's car to my AAA Roadside Service coverage, as I had been meaning to do.

The Easywick Village Town House complex off Candler Road in Decatur, Georgia was known to be one of those seedy urban communities. Mina once lived there with her aunt and Mercedes. She still owns property there, which she now rents to tenants. Easywick Village, also known as the *E'wick* is only a fifteen minute drive from our Ellenwood home, but it might as well be worlds away from our suburban living.

Not intending to sound judgmentally uppity, but the *E'wick* was a known drug trafficking urban area. And for me to know this was saying something. The things I witnessed while visiting Mina before we were married caused me to plead with her to move in with me. But she wouldn't do it. Numerous visits to the area allowed me to spot the dope dealers and runners. I knew their faces so well that I could have described them to the police without drawing on any superficial caricature.

I drove through the opened gate of the *E'wick*. My black Mercedes Benz was no stranger to the young soldier guards standing watch. Still, they kept their eyes on me as I cruised through the complex in search of Mina's car. I heard an altered signal go out that was used to alert those who care that the police were coming. Though, instead of "Po-Po" being yelled, then echoed around by others, I hear "Benzo."

The "Benzo" alarm goes out across the bald yards and concrete playgrounds. I follow the aim of the echo until I drove up to Mina's car parked almost at the back of the complex. Pulling up along side of the car with fogged windows, I could make out two figures seated inside. By the time I park, Mina was out of her car and heading toward me. Behind her, I watch who was getting out of the front passenger side of the car.

The face was familiar, but his stature was a lot smaller than it was the last time we encountered one another. Mina's passenger was Tyriq, her old boyfriend or *what not. He was the father of her aborted baby*. The looks on their faces were contrasting; with Mina's was one of "glad to see me" and Tyriq's was "Yeah remember me, I used to own those *panties*."

"Hey *babe*," Mina spoke.

"Hey." I'm looking toward the man standing next to my wife's car.

"Don't trip. Tyriq came over to see if he could fix the car," she defended.

"Well, did he?"

"No."

"I see. So then he thought he would just keep you company until I got here."

"As a matter of fact, he did. He said you were going to *trip*, but I told him that you weren't worried about him. Right, *Bookie*?"

"Right . . . as long as he didn't put his hand under anything besides the hood of your car."

"You so silly."

Tyriq walked away with a confident stride and no sense of urgency. Something appeared to have changed about the man whom I once looked upon as a threat. His size seemed to have diminished. He still had the height but no longer the imposing mass. In fact, he looked drawn in, or shrunken.

He's joined by a couple of his boys. I recognized the one who was wearing an oversized t-shirt that had "I CAN'T SELL DRUGS FOREVER" printed on it. He's OG, short for Orangello. The teen was the one who gave me the nickname Mr. Benzo. He was just one of the handful of boys and men who weren't happy that I took away Mina, their ghetto princess. OG actually surprised me by showing up at our wedding reception at the house. I laugh now, because I remember having someone keep an eye on him if he ever went inside the house for any reason. While Mina may frequent the *E'wick* when dealing with clients or checking on her town home, I don't.

"*What'up* Mister Benzo," OG acknowledged me with an *uptick* of his head. I nod in their direction and give him a genuine smile. I actually like the teen. He returned a smile with a mouth full of gold teeth. I thought to myself, could he be any more of a stereotype.

I tried a few things with Mina's car, confirming that it indeed would not start. I called and made arrangements to have the car towed to a Pep Boy auto shop down the road. Mina and I sat in my car to wait on the tow truck.

"Are you alright," she asked.

"Yeah. What's up with your boy?"

"What?"

"He looks different."

"He's got Type two diabetes."

"Oh yeah."

"He hasn't been feeling well. He was telling me how he wants to get out of *the game*. He wants to go into business for himself selling hip-hop gear on eBay and leave the street hustle. He also has an idea to start a t-shirt design business, working with funeral homes. You know how every time there's an untimely death in the hood, the family goes and buys a R.I.P. t-shirt for their loved one."

"Tomorrow, we're going to get you a new car." I blurted.

"What!"

"You've been talking about that Chrysler Sebring you like. We're going to pick it out tomorrow."

"Are you serious?"

"Yes."

"I don't know if I can handle a new car payment right now."

"Don't worry about it. I'll help you."

"But why now? I'm sure my car can be fixed."

"I just don't want you stranded anywhere and have to depend on . . ."

"Is this about Tyriq? I told you not to *trip*."

You damn right it was about him. What did she expect? The man whose last words to me were "I own them panties" came to her aid. That's my job. I'm her man, her husband, her provider. This was my way of dealing with his potential threat and my insecurity.

"You need a dependable car." I tell her while looking at the increased gathering of guys with Tyriq.

"You're lying, Mister I Need a Dependable Car. I mean I do, but that's not why you're talking about buying me a new car. If you do that, then you can show them that you're *da man*, who can get me whatever I need. That's what it is, isn't it? It's a damn *man* thing, isn't it? And how are you just going to make a decision like that without us talking about it first? I don't need you to take care of me Matthew. We are partners, who make major decisions like this as a couple . . ."

She was partly correct about the man thing. What she didn't touch on was me having to face a street thug that didn't play by any gentleman's rules. The instant I saw him get out of Mina's car with that smug look on his face, my greatest fear revealed itself to me. That fear was the chance of losing Mina.

It was an emotional fear, a pain – an emotional hurt that we men aren't allowed to talk about. If I were to lose either Mina or Mercedes, it would hurt. One of the hardest things for a man to do is to say "that hurt me." That's not how we we're raised. If a man shows a woman his sensitive side, he's considered emotional or weak. I would rather appear stubborn.

"Think what you want. The tow truck is here." I got out of the car without having to defend my position any further. We had the car towed, then we head on to pick up Mercedes from the academy.

"So what time tomorrow?" asked Mina.

"What?"

"What time are we going to pick out my car?" She jibes, "Don't play with me, 'cause I'll call you on it." And she did.

She picked out a fully loaded, black Sebring with XM satellite radio. The first two weekends of having the car, Mina puts a thousand miles on it by driving to Chattanooga, Tennessee. She and Mercedes would go on road trips come rain, sleet, snow or hail, just to get one of Mina's favorite comfort foods, a Jambalaya or red beans and rice bowl from Bojangles restaurant.

Winter

"I'LL BE HOME FOR CHRISTMAS"
FOR CHRISTMAS MINA AND I TAKE OFF THE ENTIRE WEEK. It would be our longest time vacationing together since we married. It's also the first trip to my parent's for Mina and Mercedes.

Saturday morning we set out to drive to Odelot, Ohio where my parents live. Being the morning person, I took the first leg of the eleven hour road trip up I-75 through Tennessee and Kentucky. Mina insists that we take her new car. It was fitting that she was behind the steering wheel for the first speeding ticket registered against the vehicle.

"I was not driving fast" she protested.

"Whatever Mina."

"Oh, I bet *chu* just loving this aren't *chu*?"

"Um, somewhat."

"Are you going to jail Mommy?" Mercedes asked.

"No Sweet Pea."

"THE HOUSE SMELLS OF MEMORIES"
Mina was still fuming about the ticket when we pull in front of my parents' Scottwood Avenue three story, four bedroom house in the Old West End historic part of the city. It's 5:00 in the afternoon; the reported weather in Odelot is 42 degrees, mostly cloudy and windy. A major front is expected to pass through, bringing colder temperatures but maybe not so much snow. I was hoping for some snow, especially for Mercedes to see. It would be her first time seeing the white stuff. Big changes were in store compared to Odelot's recent balmy weather. Often I'm told by my mother, the weather conditions in Odelot are close to that of Atlanta's, with maybe a few degrees difference.

The smell of home was the most comforting and welcoming ever. Years of home cooked meals, nights of washing dishes with Liquid Joy and weekends of dusting with Lemon Pledge culminated to embrace us as we walked through my parent's home. Each distinct fragrance triggered a memory which took me to a comfortable place and time. Very little had changed from when I lived there, down to the same plastic runner laid over Forest Green deep pile carpet leading into the hallway.

Dad wasn't home. Moms was giving hugs all around and fussing over Mercedes, being the complete hostess as well as surrogate grandmother. My mom has been a homemaker all of her life.

"So how was the drive?" my Moms asked.

"Mommy got a ticket from the police for driving too fast." Mercedes announced. This leads to a thirty minute discussion on how police target female drivers or how on how they have to make their ticket quota.

"How long are you guys staying?"

"Probably until the end of the week" I answered, which draws a look from Mina because we hadn't actually discussed it. Now I'm sure we will.

"That will be nice." Moms tell us of a proposed agenda for us.

It involves going to a number of Christmas programs being performed around the city. For Mercedes, we are to go see "The Lights Before Christmas" display at the Odelot Zoo. Moms had also made plans for us to see the annual Clarence Smith Community Chorus, and Christmas Watch Night Service at Holistic Salvation Church, where Reverend Isaac M. Lowdown presides.

"But right now you can help me put up the Christmas tree."

I retrieved the boxed Christmas tree out of the basement. The aluminum tree was one of those assembly types, with fifty branches kept in paper sleeves. It's probably as old as I am. Mercedes helps me assemble the tree. Mina was sitting on the couch watching us while talking on her cell phone. There was no Christmas tree for

Mercedes in Georgia. Our wrapped gifts are gathered around the fireplace in the family room.

My little helper enjoyed her job of unsheathing the branches and handing them to me. As the tree starts to take shape, Moms is in the kitchen baking sugar cookies. The aroma comes in the living room and distracts Mercedes and we still had the tinsel to hang on the tree. She asked if she could go in the kitchen and I relieved her of her duties. I looked to Mina to lend a helping hand, who gave me a "Who me" look. I finished it myself.

Dad came in the house carrying shopping bags. He doesn't look happy. He hardly ever does, just satisfied at best. The Vietnam veteran and Odelot Scales Company retiree and I exchange verbal greetings and a handshake. Mina gave him a hug, which was her style. I can tell she has an effect on him, because of the revised more than satisfied look which transformed a smile on his face.

He hurried off upstairs with the bags.

After dinner, we're sitting in the living room watching television, an episode of *Law & Order: SVU*. My father was in his lounge chair. Moms was on the couch with Mercedes who was stretched out and asleep. Mina and I are sitting on the love seat. Moms wasn't actually watching the television, she was looking through the latest issue of *Ebony* magazine. That was until she heard something that piques her interest.

The scene is where a rape victim on the show is refusing to report her attacker. She tells the attending ER nurse to just issue her a "morning after" pill and she'll be on her way. Detective Olivia Benson was unable to convince the victim to cooperate.

"What did she ask for, a morning after pill?" asked Moms who raised her gaze from the magazine pages.

"It's a pill that prevents pregnancy." I provide the answer.

"*Lawd* have mercy. They got a pill for everything nowadays." Then seemingly out of nowhere she adds, "Now if they could make a pill that would bring me a grandbaby."

"What?" I asked without looking to Mina for her reaction.

"Myrtle," exclaimed my father, calling my mother by her preferred middle name. "Who do you think that is lying next to you?" He adds.

"You know what I mean. This angel is as precious as she wants to be, but she's not Matthew's flesh and blood."

"Mama; Sadie is my daughter, our daughter, so that makes her your granddaughter."

"I'm just saying that it would be nice to have a little grandson who looks like a King."

"Myrtle, leave it alone."

Without saying a word, Mina stood and picked up Mercedes from the couch and went upstairs. The rest of us watched in silence until we felt they were out of earshot. It was a tossup as to who came at her first.

"What was that about?" I asked, winning the toss.

"What? I just said that it would be nice if I had a grandbaby?"

"Where is this coming from? You never mentioned this before."

"Your father and I have talked about it."

"Dad?"

"Your mother talked. I just listened."

"But how are you just going to blurt it out like that? I don't believe you."

"I didn't mean no harm."

"Well you did. How do you think what you said made Mina feel?"

"She didn't say anything."

That's when Mina stepped back in to the room.

"Mrs. King; not that I owe you any explanation but Matthew and I have chosen not to have children. We have Mercedes and she's the joy and love of our lives." Mina spoke with conviction.

"Baby, I didn't mean no harm by it. I just think you and Matthew would make a pretty baby, though you are a little on the dark side."

"MA!"

"I'm sure your parents want a grandchild, don't they?" Moms asked.

"Myrtle!"

"My parents haven't said one way or the other. One, they respect the way I'm living my life. And two; you may mean no harm as you say, but I don't think it's any of your concern."

"Well, if you ask me I think that's rather selfish. '*Be fruitful, and multiply, and replenish the earth, and subdue it: and have dominion over the fish of the sea, and over the fowl of the air, and over every living thing that moveth upon the earth.*' Beside, you sure got you a new car."

"Mama."

"Myrtle, you're so heavenly bound, you're no earthly good."

"The car was Matthew's idea. Not that anyone *did* ask you; but anyone who thinks it's selfish that I don't want to have kids should think about all the parents that never should've had kids and about all the ones abandoned and abused in this world." Mina stated, as she looked to me then turned and went back upstairs. There was about a minute before anyone spoke.

"*Humph*, well I guess I'll go have a cookie and some eggnog. Would either of you like for me to bring you some?" My mother asked apparently unfazed by what Mina had to say or what had just transpired. "Probably don't want to lose that cute little butt of hers" she mumbled as she walked out of the room.

"Dad, are you going to talk to her?"

"And say what? Your mother wants what she wants, and that is a grandbaby that looks like you. I can't fault her for that. That's not to say that she's right or wrong."

"That doesn't give her the right to insult my wife."

"I think your wife can handle her own. I like her. She knows that you don't have to win every argument. That's one of the secrets to a successful marriage, son."

"I love mom, but this isn't right."

"Son, life isn't fair, but for the most part it's still good. You go on upstairs and make sure that wife of yours is okay. You don't want to lose a woman who will stand up to your mother."

"But Dad . . ."

"No one is in charge of yours and her happiness but you two. Now go on up there and listen to her. Don't talk, listen."

"Yes sir. Good night.

"I'D RATHER BE WITH YOU"

Mina was already under the covers when I entered the bedroom. The light in the room was still on. I put on my pajamas and climbed in bed to spoon up behind her. With her hair wrapped in a scarf to preserve its straightness, I am ever so attracted to her at that moment. But then wasn't the time for sexual affection, but rather emotional support . . . time to listen.

"You okay *babe*?"

"I'll be alright."

"I, I apologize for my mother."

"There's no need for you to apologize. She's the one who should apologize."

"You're right."

"And I don't want you to ask her to. If she doesn't know to do it on her own, then she won't mean it."

"I just want you to know that I didn't know anything about how she felt. My father says she just wants a grandchild."

"If you want to leave me and go have a baby with someone to make your mother happy, then go right ahead."

"*Whoa, whoa* hold up. What are you talking about? Are you *quazy*? I'm not going anywhere with anyone. There is no one I'd rather be with than with you."

I pull her closer, holding her tightly. In response, her body stiffens.

"NO." She pushes out and away from me. Now sitting on the side of the bed, "Do you want a baby?"

"I told you we have Mercedes."

"What if Mercedes wasn't here?"

"I don't like what ifs."

"That's what you do for a living . . . looking at peoples stuff and write contracts to protect them from what if somebody stole their idea or what have you."

"That has nothing to do with us. We have Mercedes, who's our daughter and no one is going to steal her."

"Whatever."

"Whatever hell. You need to believe that. Do you hear me?"

"Um hmm."

"Do you believe me?"

"Yeah, I guess."

My father once told me "What other people think of you is none of your business."

Mina returned to lay next to me, allowing me to nestle up behind her. If she doesn't know by now, then there was little I could do to have Mina believe that she was the only woman for me. For the time being, the best I could do was to simply hold her. I loved having her to spoon and cuddle with. It doesn't matter whether we're together watching a movie or sports on television, we are always touching – laying on one another's lap or our feet are pressed together if we're on opposite ends of the couch. When it's time for bed; it's the closest and most secure feeling in the world to have Mina in my arms.

"3:15 ANTE MERIDIEM"

"Matthew." Mina softly speaks just behind my ear. We've reversed our spoon position.

"Yeah *babe, what'sup*?" The LED clock displays that the time is a quarter after three in the morning.

"I want to talk."

"Okay."

"Do you want to have a baby with me?"

"Is this some sort of *trickeration*; because I told you *if* I were to have a baby or anything it is going to be with you?"

"But you know how I feel about this."

"Yes and I respect that. I might tease or joke with you, but that's all it is."

"What about your mother?"

"This isn't about her. She'll be alright."

"I don't want to come between you and her."

"Too late."

"Why?" Mina sat up on her elbow.

"You came between us the day you said 'I do.' And I accepted by saying 'I do' in return." She slips her hand beneath my shirt to have her warm hand next to my skin.

"I love you." A man doesn't need to hear those words every day, only when it matters. "I had a dream. That's what woke me up." Mina informed.

"Was it a bad dream?"

"I don't think so."

"Do you want to talk about it?" Her hand begins to softly and slowly stroke me just below my navel.

"Not really." The conversation pauses, while she continues to drag her fingernails across my abdomen. "You know what I said to your mother about parents abandoning their kids?"

"Yeah."

"I was talking about me."

"How so, your mother did a great job raising you."

"Yes she did, mostly by herself."

"Your dad . . . You know you need to make peace with your past so it won't mess up your future."

"Yeah. I was Sadie's age when he decided to leave us. Just like Sadie's father left her. My mother called my father a '*drive-by*' dad. The only times I saw him after that was on special occasions to him, birthdays, holidays and my high school graduation. For me, any time that I would see him was a special occasion.

"When he would walk away, he would leave behind an upset, scared, angry, heartbroken little girl. You know how people say that girls look for men like their fathers . . . well; I was looking for boys and men to do me like he did and leave me."

"Do you still feel this way?" I thought second about asking that question. I may not have really wanted to know the answer, especially since it took her a moment to respond.

"I guess not."

"You *guess*? You said 'I do' when we got married, not 'I guess.' So why did you marry me?" That was another one of those *don't ask, don't tell*, you don't want to know questions.

"I love you Matthew."

I can't say which was affecting me more; whether it's her impassioned words or the fact that her long fingers had reached my pubic hair and began combing through it.

"You aren't like any other guy that I've been with. You're cut from a different cloth. There's a big difference between love and lust. I can honestly say this is love . . . love of a friend and help mate. You have shown me and are showing me what real love is supposed to look like and act like. Thank you."

Mina's finger plowing left my hairy knoll and she took a determined hold of my root.

"LIKE FATHER LIKE SON"

Christmas Eve, Sunday morning my father and I are up before the crack of dawn. He's fully dressed and about to leave the house when I come down. Ever since I can remember it has been his routine to drive downtown and pick up his Sunday newspaper from Leo's Book store. He would then come home and read half of the paper while drinking a cup of coffee and waiting for my mother and I to dress for church.

"You want to ride with me to pick up the paper?"

"Yes sir. Are you going to church?"

"I guess. Your mother will be expecting us all to go."

"I was thinking of driving to Somerset Mall in Detroit and do a little Christmas shopping."

"Detroit. Why not go over to Franklin Park Mall? They've expanded it, you know."

"Maybe. I was thinking it would be a good idea for us to get out of the house for a while."

"You can do that without having to drive all the way to Detroit."

"I suppose."

Dad was a regular churchgoer before the founding pastor of our home church passed away. He's a no nonsense man, who goes to church to hear God's word, not to stand for hours during a praise worship service. Our church home went through a number of pastors before settling on the presiding, Reverend Isaac M. Lowdown. From what my mother told me, Reverend Lowdown was revered as young, energetic and sometimes as controversial as his name. Under his watch, he had made Holistic Salvation Church, Odelot's first mega-church.

The ride through Odelot city was like taking a tour guide. The downtown had been revitalized with new development of office buildings and a brand new baseball field for the city's minor league team right smack downtown. The city's downtown looked good.

"So how's your wife?" Dad asks.

"Quijelmina is fine. We talked it out and we're good."

"Good. You know, however good or bad a situation is it will change."

"The only thing constant is change."

"That's your mother, constant change. Today, that whole grandbaby talk will have been forgotten."

"You think so?"

"I know so."

"Is she gonna be okay?"

"As okay as she can be, I suppose."

"Do you still love mama?"

"Yeah, I guess."

"You guess?"

"I do."

"Why?"

"Breakfast and dinner is served to me every day. She washes and irons my clothes and keeps a clean home."

It would be a lie if I said that I wasn't disappointed in his answers. I see my mother as being a lot more than that. Moms had always been the guiding light of our small family, with my father being the strong silent type provider. There was a similar strong will in Mina as in Moms. If all that my retired father needed from her was a maid, then fine, because it's kept them together for 40 years.

"You don't have to mention this to her, but your mother is also my better half." My father admits reluctantly it seems.

Back at my parent's home, the women were dressed and ready for church service. Mom cooked breakfast. Mina and Mercedes were together in the living room watching television. After I showered and dressed we all sat at the table and ate. It was a quiet sitting.

"I FORGIVE, RELEASE, AND LET GO."

Second service at Holistic Salvation Church, had overflow attendance. While we stand out in the vestibule, my mother was in rare form introducing Mina and Mercedes as her daughter-in-law and grandbaby to her friends and other churchgoers. She even picked up Mercedes, hugging and kissing her as if she were her "own flesh and blood." My dad gave me an "I told you so" nod.

We made it in to the sanctuary just before ushers closed off entrance and began directing people to the churches' overflow auditorium where there was a video projection of the alter to a large screen.

The choir selection was *A Closer Walk*, before the Reverend Lowdown took to the pulpit and preached on forgiveness. I don't dare turn and look at either Mina or my mother.

"Good morning Saints," the pastor opens. "Just before I came out, the Holy Spirit put a word in my ear and said speak on forgiveness. Now you know I was ready to talk about the birth of Jesus Christ with Christmas being on tomorrow, amen. But the Holy Spirit said somebody needs some healing from some pain of their past. And It said that the past pain is still causing hurting *today*. Let me say this. In first Corinthians, one and ten '*... and let there be no divisions among you; but be perfectly united in one mind and in one thought.*'

"Let go of disappointments, bad memories and anger. All things happen for a reason even painful experiences. There are no accidents. Replace the pain with forgiveness. When you are driving a car, you can't move forward looking in the rear view mirror. Do you live your life looking in the rear view mirror? Past experiences are behind. They came to pass, not to stay.

"Have an open heart, be willing to forgive. At times, we hold onto old pain because it is safe to hide behind. It gives us reason not to move on. Nothing can hurt me unless I allow it. I release every disappointment. In prayer, I ask the Holy Spirit to help me practice forgiveness. The only person I am hurting by not forgiving is me. I release and live harmoniously with a renewed spirit of peace. I replace the seeming hurts with an inner calm. I allow God to be in the middle of every wound, replacing my old thinking with new vision and clarity.

"God has already healed the situation. I forgive, release and let go. Thanks, God. And so it is. Amen."

"T'WAS THE NIGHT BEFORE CHRISTMAS"

A fire was burning brightly in the fireplace. Dad and I were talking about current events in the news. This was the first time that he's had a chance to go through the newspaper. At that moment watching him, I learned that I've become my father. Like he has done since I can remember; like him, before I read the Sunday paper I make sure that I put it in order by section. Before then, I never thought about why I did. It stemmed from when I was a paperboy and dad and I would have to sort the large Sunday paper before delivering them to the customers on my route.

Mina and Mercedes are on the couch. Mina is on her cell phone talking to either a relative or one of her friends LaDessa or Synea. She's watching my dad sort and put the paper in order. She turned to me and smiles as if recognizing the similarity as I did.

Mercedes was watching *Merry Christmas Charlie Brown*. My mother comes in the room from the kitchen, where she has been busy baking Snicker-doodle cookies and mixing eggnog. She had a tray in hand presenting the fruit of her labor.

"Here you are. And Sadie, eat as much as you'd like. I have another plate in the kitchen for Santa Claus" Moms informs the wide-eyed little girl.

"Mommy says there is no Santa Claus." Mercedes says with assuredness.

Dad and I locked gazes on one another. I break the lock with closing my eyes, raising both brows and shoulders, as to say "oh well, here we go." When I opened my eyes, I'm met with my father raising his hand signaling for me to stay out of what's about to happen.

"*Lawd*, is you just going to steal all the fun from her childhood." Mom says, not directing it to anyone in particular.

"It's not about fun, it's about fact." Mina says holding the phone away from her mouth. Mom doesn't respond to her, instead she defiantly looks to Mercedes.

"Sure there's a Santa Claus honey. You just don't see him because he comes on Christmas Eve while you're sleeping."

"That's silly. Then if he comes tonight, then how come there are presents already under the Christmas tree?" Mercedes inquired as we all noticeably look toward the tree. Under the tree are gifts that my parents bought, with those that Mina and I brought with us.

"Well, I can see who you fashion after." Moms' replied, dismissing the little girl's astute observation. Bringing her husband a glass of eggnog and two cookies wrapped in a napkin was my mother's escape from the reality of a young child's truth and innocence.

In our bed, Mina turned to lightly pound my chest with one of her small fists and asked, "Why does your mother dislike me?"

"She doesn't dislike you."

"Then what is it then . . . why is she always *trippin'* about the way I'm raisin' Sadie?"

"The way *we're* raising Sadie; I'm in this with you on this remember."

"You know what I mean."

"I know that no matter what my mother says or thinks, it doesn't change how I feel about you or Sadie."

"Well I know she's got one more time . . ."

"What, you're going to jump on my mother?"

"You silly. I'm just *sayin'* . . ."

"Come here." I grab my feisty wife and pull her on top of me to receive a passionate kiss.

"What was that for?"

"Because you're so cute when you get like this."

"I'm serious; she needs to *squash* that *bull*."

"All right now. You are still talking about my mother."

"Do you think we're going to end up like your mom and dad?" Mina whispers.

"Like how?"

"I mean they don't sleep in the same bedroom anymore. Your mom says she got tired of your father always *poking* at her when he wanted to *get busy*. That's how she put it."
We chuckle.

"Then she said he has the *Jimmy legs* when he sleeps?"

"Yeah, that's where one or both of your legs kick wildly. Now they call it Restless Leg Syndrome. Anyway, that's her side of the story."

"What do you mean?"

"He said he had to get away from her because she kept coming after him. I do remember when I was younger, that my parents would go in the bedroom for a long time. Whenever that would happen, my mother would put *Mister Magic* by Grover Washington on the record player."

"YOU' LYING."

"Shh"

Mina buried her face in my chest to muffle her laughter. It was five minutes before she could gain her composure. In fact, she giggled herself to sleep.

"I SAW MOMMY KISSING SANTA CLAUS"

In the middle of night, I got up and went to the bathroom. On my way back to the bedroom, I bumped into my father coming out of my mother's room. Another toss up as to which one of us was more embarrassed or uncomfortable. He volunteered, "Just tucked your mother in," as we passed. Mina was awake when I climb back in the bed.

"*Babe*, you asked me if we will end up like my parents. I hope so. I'm looking forward to spending the rest of my life with you."

Sitting around the dining room table having breakfast, I can't look at my father and Mina can't look at my mother with a straight face or without snickering. After breakfast we gather around the Christmas tree to open presents. Mercedes is first to open her gifts. Mina and I had brought but a few of her gifts with us; one of them being a V Smile Electronic Learning game, and Sasha, one of the Bratz™ dolls.

My parents exchanged their gifts for each other; a sports coat for him and a bottle of perfume for her. For my father, I ordered copies of the front page newspapers of the *LA Times, NY Times, Detroit Free Press* and *Odelot Blade* from the day he was born. For my moms, we gave her a diamond necklace and *The Pampered Chef® Cooking for Two*

& More cookbook. Cooking was something my mother and Mina have in common, with Mina being a Pampered Chef consultant.

My parents gave Mina and me his and her matching watches. We didn't let on that by choice Mina doesn't wear a watch.

Learning a lesson from the Jimmy Choo gift giving fiasco, I put careful thought into the items I buy for Mina. Because I love her from her head to toes, I bought a collection of gifts to reflect that. I brought but a few of them with us; starting with a pack of silk scarf wraps for her hair, and a rose gold necklace with a precious stone heart pendant. At home, around the fireplace is the remainder of her from the neck down gifts.

In exchange, Mina handed me a small package which contained a pair of Mont Blanc® cufflinks. Back home she had waiting for me a pair of Waterford® brandy snifters.

The rest of the Christmas day was quiet and spent at my parents' home, with the exception of a short walk around the neighborhood where I grew up. Weather wise, it was a light snow shower with the temperature hovering around the freezing mark. Mercedes enjoyed the snowfall. Mina wanted to get out of the cold. Back to my parent's we were thankful for the comforting warmth of a fireplace with the fire my father had going.

That evening we were watching television. Mina was on her cell phone calling and texting friends and family, wishing them Merry Christmas. Moms and Mercedes were entertaining one another, with Mina keeping a watchful eye on them.

Dad and I watched a basketball game between the Miami Heat and Los Angeles Lakers. The local news had been announcing that one of the Lakers' cheerleaders was from Odelot and might be selected to represent the Lakers on an NBA All-Star Dance Team. My dad pointed her out to me every time a camera man had her in his sight.

Mina looked up from talking on the phone long enough to spot Shaquille O'Neal sitting out of the game due to an ankle injury. She watched a basketball or football game with more interest in the players than the sport. I've seen where one of her girlfriends would email her shirtless body shots of professional football players Terrell Owens or Reggie Bush. I can't complain, because Marcus voluntarily sends me everything from string-bikini-clad, to naked photos of women.

For dinner, Moms fixed my favorite, lasagna layered with three cheeses, cheddar, Pepper Jack and Ricotta. I made the mistake of comparing her oven baked lasagna to Mina's stove top cooked version of the dish, which can be cooked in half the time my mother takes. My father offered me no rescue to un-ring the bell that brings my mother out of her corner for the next bout.

"Well, it's not how fast you can get some things done. Haven't I always told you 'anything worth having is worth waiting for," my mother posed?

"Yes ma'am. I was just saying that this is just as good as . . ." My mother looked at me. "I mean Mina's is . . ." Now Mina looked up from her plate. "Excuse me; I have to go to the bathroom." I stood from the table and made a quick exit, not before hearing my father let out a rare chuckle.

FIVE EVENTS IN ODELOT THAT YOU JUST CAN'T MISS

For the next few days in Odelot, we were treated by my parents as tourists. We visited the Odelot Museum of Art, COSI Children's Museum, and Westfield-Franklin Park Mall. To give my mother a break we ate at Tony Packo's Café, and on the city's waterfront at the Old Navy Bistro. By Wednesday we had seen everything that there was of interest to see in Odelot. Mina was ready to return home.

As soon as I announced that we were leaving early, my mother made the snide remark "I bet I know whose idea that is." All packed and ready to go, Mina and Mercedes were getting in the car. My mother was giving Mercedes a last minute hug and kiss.

CHOSE YOUR BATTLES.

On the porch with my father, he offered me some advice.

"Son, you will always be your mother's baby boy."

"What exactly does that mean?"

"It means that she's not going to like anyone who she thinks is going to come between you and her."

"You mean Mina."

"I mean her, that little girl or your Sunday school teacher."

"Sunday School teacher?"

"My point is that it doesn't matter who it is."

"You know what would change things." I offered.

"What's that?"

"If you got me a little brother," I nudged him with my elbow.

"Boy, you are funny. You are too funny." My sixty-five years old dad seemed to get an honest to good laugh out of that.

"HAPPY NEW YEAR"

New Years Eve in Atlanta and the surrounding areas started with the sound of rainfall. The forecast called for rain on and off throughout the day, especially around the turn of the year. This would put an obvious damper on the dropping of the big Peach at Underground Atlanta.

Mina and I turned down invitations from friends and neighbors offering a place to bring in the New Year. We got a call from a member of Word of Faith, alerting us that the overflow rooms were standing room only for this New Years Eve Watch Night service. So instead, we decided to *chillax* at home with Mercedes. I bought a bottle of Krug champagne for Mina and I and sparking apple cider for Mercedes.

Mercedes doesn't make it past 10:00, having fallen asleep in our bedroom where Mina was on the computer sending instant messages to her girlfriend Synea who's in Detroit. She paused her texting long enough for us to put Mercedes in her own bed. One of us always puts her in bed, and read to her *The Tickle Fingers: Five Finger Prayer Handbook.*

If we both put her to bed, we have this tradition that we've started where I kiss Mina and say "I love you." Mina then passes the kiss to Mercedes and repeats, "I love you." To complete the circle of love, Sadie kisses me and says "I love you."

"I love you too Sadie Mae. When you wake up, it will be a new year." I alert the child.

"And we get to start all over again."

"Something like that. How about you just keep being the good little girl that you are, but only better." I suggest.

"Okay, and you too."

"What! I'm not going to be a good little girl." I tease.

"You silly." Mercedes teases back.

"Both of you are silly" Mina chides. Her attitude has had a slight edge since our return from visiting my parents.

Mina heads back to our bedroom. I go in the den and sign on to my desktop computer. I log on to the Watch Night Service internet streaming webcast from Holistic Salvation Church in Odelot, Ohio. Reverend Lowdown is speaking from the pulpit.

"*This is what the Lord says, 'Forget the former things; do not dwell on the past. See, I am doing a new thing! Now it springs up; do you not perceive it? I am making a way in the desert and streams in the wasteland.*

"*The year is gone, finished, past. We cannot reclaim it or undo it. We cannot rest on the great distance it has brought us. If tomorrow dawns, it will be another day, a new opportunity, and the time to show our faith in Jesus as Lord. Let's journey forward, knowing that God already inhabits the future and promises to provide us refreshment on our journey there.*

"*Let us pray. Lord of all eternity; please help me to learn from my mistakes this past year, but not to dwell on them. Please help me not rest on my accomplishments in this past year, but use them to further your work in me and through me. Please help me not quarrel with those who injured me yesterday, last month, or this past year. Instead, O Father, lead me in your paths and help me see your mighty works this next year. In Jesus' name and by his power I ask it. Amen.*" The reverend concluded.

I wished Mina was with me to hear the reverend's words; it may have brought healing of any ill will she may have had towards my mother. I go to the kitchen to retrieve the bottle of champagne from the wine chiller. With two tall flutes in one hand and the bottle in the other, I made my way to the bedroom. The sound of fingernails clicking and hitting against a keyboard greeted me. Mina was busily typing on her laptop computer, into the familiar instant messaging box. She doesn't bother stopping when I enter the room. It's 11:45 p.m.

"Mind if I turn on the TV?" I asked. She hunched her shoulders giving a non-committal answer.

I turned on the television and tuned in a local channel that was a simulcast the Peach Drop in Atlanta and the Crystal Ball drop in New York. The cork popped loudly as I opened the champagne. Mina jumped, with a startling "Ooo" escaping her lips. She signed off of MSN Messenger, and reached for her phone. She proceeded to thumb out a text. When she finished, a chime goes off on my phone and I'm sure on most of the phones in Mina address book. The text message from my baby reads: *"Have a Happy New Year!!! Make everyday count and enjoy the life you have been given. Peace and Love. Mina."*

After filling the wineglasses to the rim with champagne, I handed one to my wife. She's not as much of an alcohol drinker as I am. When she does drink, she gets silly. When she gets silly, she's sexy as well. A night of celebratory or social drinking almost always ends in a night of uninhibited love making. We're both aware of the aphrodisiac affect of alcohol on Mina; and I know not to abuse it.

With not nearly the fanfare that was being shown on the television, Mina and I say "Happy New Years" to one another as we clink glasses. We don't even kiss. Instead we whet our lips with the taste of the semi-dry champagne. For the next few minutes we sit and watch the revelry of the thousands of people.

"What's up Mina?"

"What do you mean?"

"You've been in a different place tonight. What's on your mind?" I refill her glass.

"We take life for granted."

"We, as in you and I, the world at large, who?"

"Everybody."

"Okay."

"Do you know that Chinese men are going to be in huge trouble because in China there is a gender imbalance?" She asks. Mina once told me that when she smoked marijuana with her old boyfriend Tyriq, that it didn't have the desired affect. Instead of lifting her to a state of euphoria, she would become pensive and critical. She said that this would agitate Tyriq, because he would often be on the receiving end of her criticism, mainly because of his life of hustling. So she stopped smoking marijuana, because it would always lead to a fight between her and someone in the group that may have been getting high with them.

"No *Bookie*, I didn't know that. Why?" I'm sniffing the air for any hint of *weed*.

"Because by two-thousand and twenty, there will be thirty million more men than women and since you can only have one child in China many couples had doctors control the birth process to ensure boys."

"And you know this how?"

"I read it on a blog."

"And what does this have to do with the price of tea in China?"

"What? I'm not talking about tea." She says with slight agitation inflected in her voice, not getting the joke. I look to see if the window in the bedroom is open to air out the room, allowing the smell of *weed* to escape.

"Never mind. Why do I care about the men in China?"

"It's about how we are trying to play God with life and children suffer for it." The theme of children is making me think that her line of thinking stems from my mother's desire for a grandchild.

"Who's playing God?"

"We are. God gave us life and the ability to create life. Who are we to decide who lives or die?"

"I don't know."

"Listen."

"Okay."

"Instead of making abortion about a moral issue, which is so opinion based, we should make it about money instead." She waves her empty glass in the air, for me to refill its content. I'm thinking the alcoholic beverage is not having in my opinion, the desired affect on her. I can now identify with Tyriq.

"Money?" I question.

"All the government has to do is declare that any woman who is pregnant at the end of the year, she can claim the child as a dependant on her taxes. That would take away the argument on when a baby is a life." Okay, she's being silly. "So what do you think?"

"It's a thought," was my safe answer. I'm actually thinking that it would be nice if Mina and I was butt naked, in fervent throes of making love. Especially if there is any truth to the superstition that the way you bring in the New Year is the way your year will be.

"You know what Synea thinks?" Mina poses, and then takes a swallow of champagne.

"No," I find it difficult to believe that we're talking about this on New Years.

"She thinks that some form of birth control is a good thing because our society is growing too fast and we're over consuming the environment."

"Over consuming the environment?"

"Helloooooo, global warning."

"Ah."

"I agree with her about the environment thing. I just don't agree that birth control is the way to fix it." Mina stopped talking and stares off at some invisible spot on the bedroom far wall.

This gave me a chance to study her. Her hair was wrapped in one of the silk scarves I got her for Christmas. On her face there was a dry beige spot on one of her black cherry hued cheeks. If I didn't know any better, I would think it was the evaporated remains of a salty tear. The corner of her mouth has a small crusty gathering. The view of the rest of her shows a cashmere camisole top and shorts, exposing ashy elbows, knees and chafed heels. Envisioning sex with Mina to bring in the New Year was becoming more difficult to imagine.

I grabbed a bottle of Martini and Rossi Asti Spumante to keep the libations flowing. It's not that I'm trying to get her drunk, but rather relaxed. We exchange another celebratory clink of our glasses to usher in the New Year. Just as I move in to touch lips, we both are startled when Mina's phone chimes, announcing the arrival of a text message. She turned her head and attention to the phone. A faint smile presents itself on her face.

"Who's that?" I ask. There was a noticeable hesitation before she responds.

"Just Tyriq." She admits.

"As in your old boyfriend?"

"As in now, he's just a friend."

"Did you send him your Happy New Year message?"

"Yes. What? I sent it to a lot of people. You got it didn't you?"

"Are you comparing me to your old boyfriend?"

"Why are you *trippin'*? He's just a friend. You're my man . . . my, my husband." Maybe it was just my imagination that she struggled with conjugating those last words.

"I don't want you texting him and vice versa."

"I thought you were more of a man than this." Questioning my manhood was fighting words.

"Being your *man*, I won't have it."

"You seriously *trippin'*," she accused.

"This is not up for discussion Mina. Either you can tell him or I can."

I don't know where the anger came from. Maybe it was fueled by fear, the fear of Tyriq trying to make good his boastful ownership claim.

"I can't believe you. You don't trust me." She shot at me.

"This isn't about trust. Okay, yes it is. But I do trust you."

"How can you say that?"

"I trust you. I don't trust him."

"No, I don't believe you. I can take care of myself and I can handle Tyriq. And if you don't believe that, then you don't trust me."

By those terms, she was right. I didn't trust her, because I didn't think she *could* handle a determined street guy like Tyriq. We don't say another word. Not in the mood for a fight, I move away from Mina's side.

I hoped a hot shower would ease my mind from the mounting jealousy. The steamy water pounded some sense in to my head. I had no reason to be worried about Tyriq. Mina was my wife; she loved me and gave me no reason to suspect her of cheating on me.

Mina had cleared the bedroom of the glasses and leftover wine. While she's in the kitchen, I climbed in bed, but sleep won't come. It was twenty minutes later when Mina comes and lies next to me. Our king size bed hadn't ever felt that big, as we stay to our respective sides.

Happy New Year. Yeah right.

"*NEW YEAR RESOLUTION*"

The worst thing that could happen to a creature of habit like me was to oversleep. Not to find Mina still in bed shook me awake, with her being the usual late sleeper. Neither of us had to go to work on that holiday Monday. Just as soon as my eyes focused on seeing that I'm alone in the room, my nose assured me that Mina was in the house.

The unmistakable sweet smell of bacon and fried home style potatoes draws me out of bed. She's still with me. After brushing my teeth and washing my face, I go to the kitchen. There I find Mina finishing breakfast. Mercedes was sitting at the table playing with her V-Smile handheld game.

"Morning everyone," I greeted the two immediate women in my life.

"Good morning," Mercedes says cheerfully. She followed with "Happy New Year."

"Happy New Year, Sadie Mae." I gave her a hug around her neck and then kiss her on the cheek. Mina was at the oasis counter in the middle of the kitchen. She's making Mimosa, mixing orange juice and the leftover sparkling wine from last night.

Inching up behind her, the scent of vanilla and brown sugar comes off her body and fills my nose. As much as a cliché that it is, she smelled good enough to eat. If I was lucky; maybe later.

"Hey baby," I spoke just behind her ear, following with a kiss.

"Morning Mister Jealous Man."

"I want to apologize."

"Um hmm."

"If I trust you, I should let you handle your business."

"I know that's right."

"At least you're not so mad that you're not willing to cook me breakfast."

"Oh, I'm not like that. I'm not your mother, like you're not my father. I'm not going to punish you by not cooking or withholding sex."

"Whoa, hold up. Where'd that come from?"

"I'm just saying. I don't have to play those kinds of games."

"Glad to know that. Look, I said I'm sorry. Do you accept my apology?"

"I do, but we still have some business to take care of. Now go sit down so we can eat." She tries to boot me away with her backside. I don't move. "Go on now." She urges.

I followed her urging and joined Mercedes at the table. We quickly ate breakfast, and then we cleaned up afterwards. Mercedes runs off to play in her room.

"You really hurt my feelings last night." Mina starts.

"How so?"

"By not trusting me."

"Mina, I said that it wasn't you that I didn't trust; it's that Tyriq."

"No matter who it is, I have to know that you trust me."

"I do and I'm sorry if I gave you that perception. Do you accept my apology?"

"Yes. I will not let a little miscommunication come between us."

"Still love me?"

"Always."

Mina called for Mercedes to come and join us in the den. Mercedes slides close to me on the couch. Mina went to the stereo and tuned in the Smooth Jazz radio station, 107.5 WJZZ, before turning to us.

"To start the year off right, we're going to set our goals." Mina announced.

"What's goals," Mercedes asked.

"It's something that you *wanna* be or something that you *wanna* do."

"Can it just be something you want?"

"I suppose. So we're going to write our goals for this year."

"I already know what mine is." Mercedes declared.

"Good, then I want you to write five things you're going to do better for yourself this year," Mina jots the categories on a notepad, "for our family, school and work."

"Okay."

"So for me; five personal, family and professional resolutions," I asked.

"Not resolutions; solutions," Mina confirms as she gets up and starts to leave the room.

"Hey, where are you going?"

"Why?"

"Aren't you going to do this?"

"I've done mine," she boasts.

"May I see?"

"No. That would be cheating *Mister Contract Management*."

Mina left the room with an exaggerated switch of her hips. Once she's beyond the door, she playfully throws a look back over her shoulder and sticks out her tongue. It brings a smile to my face. Mercedes was busily writing, until her pencil stops moving and she looked to me.

"How do you spell Disney World?" She asked.

For her, I spell the name of the place where I proposed marriage to Mina, while riding in a spinning teacup ride. Mercedes was sitting right alongside, when I held Mina's hand and presented her with a three carat, marquise cut cognac colored diamond engagement ring. The dark colored gem made a nice accent on her elongated bronze ring finger. She answered "yes."

Coming up with meaningful New Year Solutions, as Mina called them was somewhat of a challenge. After twenty minutes I'm still pondering. It was an easier undertaking for Mercedes, as she made known that she finished the assignment and climbed off the couch to show Mina.

"Hey, let me see." I asked.

"No. That would be cheating *Mister Contact Man.*"

I tossed a throw pillow after the little girl, chasing her out of the room.

"Moments in Love"

By mid-afternoon I'm mentally and physically tired, due in part to being up so late or early, and whichever way one wants to think of it. I'm dozing, stretched out on the couch covered to my waist by a throw, beneath which I have a hand tucked comfortably inside the waistband of my pajama pants. Lying on my chest is the notepad which has only few listed "solutions" for the year ahead. When Mina comes into the room, I'm slow to react. The sight, sound and smell of her stands by my side.

"I see why you're not finished." She guesses. "What are you doing under that blanket?"

"Staying warm," I reply, not moving my tucked hand, my eyes divert to its general area.

"Um hmm." She pulls back the cover, "Staying warm," remarking skeptically.

Removing the notepad, placing it on the coffee table, she climbs on the couch blanketing me with her body. She's warm and still smelling sweet of vanilla and brown sugar. Once she's nestled easily in place on me and between my legs, she pulls the blanket over us.

Both of my arms are wrapped around her and immediately my hands begin massaging her lower back and waist. A soft moan escapes. I make my way up the sides of her body applying pressure along the way. More moans seemingly come from deep within her. Mina isn't the softy type of woman who complains at pinches, pokes and squeezes. She enjoys a firm hand and I enjoy applying a strong massage to her back and backside.

"Where's baby girl?" I ask, feeling that maybe we should move to the bedroom.

"In her room sound asleep."

"Are you sure?"

"Positive," she punctuates with a slow grinding hip thrust.

Given her assurance, I'm able to relax and enjoy our *moments in love.* Her open mouth kisses with enveloping full lips causes my head to swell and swim. She's an incredible kisser, which is a lost art of romance. Dry - soft - hard – poised – passionate – wet. I quickly become intoxicated by her mouth juices. In response my hands ravish her body, in which she splays and contorts to allow ease of access.

With a leg bent erect in the air, Mina straddles my thigh and begins writhing against it. Hands on each of her gyrating hips, I'm controlling nothing, merely following the motion. Using both of her small hands she forces my head back exposing my neck. She begins covering it with kisses from one side to the other – from my chin to the throat. She licks my gullet. What almost sends me over the edge is when she focuses on my Adam's apple, suckling it in her mouth.

Artfully she raises and lowers her lips on the slight projection of bone. Her soft tongue traces the border of her grasp.

In an instant, she moves to one side and latches on to my neck, pulling in a mouth full of flesh. She keeps the soft tissue secure with biting teeth. I can't help but to emit a grunt, which proves satisfying to Mina, as she lets up on her vampire like clinch. She doesn't fully let go as she continues to pull my flesh into her mouth, with the skillful use of her tongue and lips.

I move one of my hands just behind her neck, with spread fingers combing up into her hair. Without letting go of my neck, she pushes my hand away guiding it back to her circling hips. With mounting pressure, Mina's strong thighs contract and release their grip on my erectile leg. In an attempt to keep it up and steady, a charley horse forms in my calf. I flex my ankle to fight off the muscle cramp.

In the meantime, Mina's ride is growing in momentum. Maintaining a firm hold on my neck with the help of piercing teeth she begins to whimper. Her thigh contractions are quickening. I assume as to what is shortly to follow. The stiffening muscle in my calf wants its share of my attention. No matter which way I twist or turn my foot, I can't abate the increasing pain.

"*Ump – ump – ump*," Mina gives off through quick and short nostril breaths.

By her thrashing, Mina is close to a pleasurable achievement. In my attempt to not disappoint her, I dug my heel into the couch cushion to stave off the painful muscle spasm tightening in my calf. She clamps harder onto my neck and my thigh, easily bringing my attention back to her. With her arms hugged around my head, she uses the hold to leverage herself.

Her whimpers change to grunts and finally into a drawn out, muffled squeal. I join her with my own anguishing cry as I kick straight my leg which gives Mina an extended personal buck ride. She skillfully holds on while burying her face into my chest giggling, sounding much like Mercedes when we wrestle playfully.

"What's so funny?" I asked.

"It tickles . . . but I like it."

"Girl, you *quazy*."

"Me. You're the one giving me a *horsey* ride."

"A *horsey* ride . . . I was trying to work out a cramp."

"For real." She giggles. "Oh *babe*, I'm sorry. Are you okay?"

"I am now."

She grabs my face and kissed me with the insides of her lips covering mine. "I love you."

We took a shower together followed by a short nap. Later, Mercedes jumped in our bed, waking us from a not long enough sleep. It doesn't take long for the rambunctious child to have us up and about.

I finished my assigned task of writing my goals for the year. To name just a few; relationship-wise, I want to strengthen my bond with Mina and Mercedes. Physically, I want to get back to working out at the gym. I've slacked off having become a domestic dad, with picking up Mercedes from the academy or taking her to extracurricular activities. Career wise, a salary raise would be nice.

In comparing our lists; we all had Disney World for our vacation destination. Mina wants to build a better relationship with Mercedes. Mercedes wants to win a talent competition so she can become rich so she can give Mina and me the money.

We type our combined list into the computer and save it for later retrieval. Mina has me order copies of our annual free credit reports from the three major credit bureaus. It's great to have a woman who *looks out*.

As I look at my wife and daughter, I'm looking forward to the year to come.

"GATOR FAN OR GATOR BAIT"

January 8th, the BCS National Championship football game between Ohio State Buckeyes and University of Florida Gators was televised during prime time to a national viewing audience. Marcus was sitting on my plush leather easy chair to watch his alma mater

Gators play against my home state Buckeyes. Mina was cuddled next to me on the couch.

"Who do you want to win, Mina?" Marcus asked.

"Ohio State," she replied without looking at him.

"I should have known. Well all I can say is, you're either a Gator fan or you're Gator bait."

"Then why are you over here? Don't you have a home with a TV?" Mina shot back. I generally enjoyed the verbal battles between my best friend and my wife; especially since she could hold her own with him.

"Yes I do. But your husband has a fifty-two inch HD plasma screen and he keeps Heineken cold for me."

"Excuse you. WE have a fifty-two inch flat screen; and yes he does keep beer in the fridge for your mooching butt. That doesn't mean you have to be over here all the time."

"If it weren't for me, he probably wouldn't have anyone over. I'm the only one of his *boys* who's not scared of you."

"You need to be scared."

"Scared of who, you?"

"Alright you two . . . Let's leave the rough play up to the players on the TV." I interject. Just then, Mina's cell phone rings.

"Hello. - Hey girl. - Sittin' here watching football with Matthew. - Naw, that's okay, come on over. I could use the company. - Okay then. Bye." Mina concludes her call.

"Who was that?"

"Synea. She's coming over." Mina offers. A look over to Marcus, he gave me a wide eye, eyebrow raise with apparent interest.

The games score is tied at seven all. Ohio State had a runback at the opening kickoff. The doorbell rang. Mina went to let in her anticipated friend.

"So, what does she look like and remember the *Man Law*," Marcus asks hurriedly.

"What *Man Law*?"

"You can't say that another woman is cute or *fine* unless she is as cute or *fine* as your woman."

"Oh. I must have missed the meeting when that law was passed."

"Come on, hurry up."

"Why, when you can see for yourself in a few seconds."

"I don't like surprises; especially if I might have to make a break for the bathroom to throw up."

The sound of voices started nearing the family room. Marcus looked at me and smacks his lips in disappointment. I hunch my shoulders in return. I keep my eyes on him as the women enter the room. As expected, his eyes widen as does the smile that grows across his face when he sees the attractive woman accompanying Mina.

Synea Jackson and Mina met when Mina returned to CAU to finish earning her BA degree in Finance. As a member of the professional organization The Financial Management Association, Synea offered to become Mina's mentor. Synea a Seventh Day Adventist has a good job as an independent financial consultant for non-profit organizations and churches. She is intelligent, personable, articulate, well-read, interested in everybody and everything. This is what makes her and Mina seem like soul mates. Visibly, she's cute, stands 5'10" and weighs around 125 pounds.

Mina mentioned her physical stats when she was telling me of Synea's failed attempt in becoming a runway model. With all that she has going for her, Synea's independently single. Not that there's anything wrong with that. This seemingly would be good news for Marcus, if it weren't for the fact that she's not looking to date.

There's something else about Synea; something out of the ordinary. She's not your typical academically accomplished and socially successful African American woman. There is a reverent, soulful, very spiritual side to her being. It's eerie.

When she greets me, she reverses my name, "Hello King Matthew," she offered with her customary bow and collapsed praying hands.

"Hello Synea," I offer in return with a stand and open hand covering my heart. It's all a part of our little ritual. The same goes for when she addresses Mercedes, whom she calls a Nubian Princess. "So what's going on?" I ask.

"It's the same *ole deal pickle*. I had to come over and rescue my girl from watching football."

"Hey, she's watching because she wants to."

"Um, hmm. Who's playing?"

"Ohio State and Florida."

"WHAT! GATORS? This ain't going to be no game."

"Don't tell me . . ."

"Yep, UF all the way baby" Synea cheers, quickly transforming from her reverent visage.

Marcus practically leaped out of the chair to give *dap* to Synea and join in the college chants and cheers. It was like they were still students and they were back on campus. Mina's sitting next to me on the couch watching the two of them. The look of disbelief on her face could be for one of two reasons. One, she can't believe the silly antics of her friend or two; she can't believe that her good friend is siding with her arch rival Marcus.

What made matters worse was that the highly-favored No. 1 ranked Ohio State Buckeyes, with their Heisman Trophy candidate quarterback, were playing their worse game of the season. The second half of the game was all Florida and Marcus' and Synea's boasting. I mean they carried their bragging rant close to the point of obnoxious to which Mina took exception.

"I can't believe y'all," Mina announced.

"Believe your eyes then. The score is forty-one to fourteen," Marcus quipped.

"Whatever," Mina weakly replied?

For the moment Mina and I were defeated, along with our sure bet team. Allowing Marcus and Synea time to bask in their glory, they took charge in the conversation, which eventually changed to travel destinations. Unlike Mina and I who have not traveled beyond the shores of the United States; both Marcus and Synea had been abroad.

Yearly, he travels to Kingston to visit his distant relatives and travels to the neighboring islands via a cruise liner. He also makes an annual trip to Rio to enjoy the Brazilian sex-tourism. After his return, I'm one of the first people he visits to tell of his *sexploits*. "*Bruh, these girls make you feel like a million dollars,*" he boasts. "*I'm talking about dimes who can cook, clean and not only stroke your ego, but they know how to stroke Mister Marcus,* he laughed as he tugs at his crotch. "*And the best part is I can jump on a plane and leave their asses right there until I come back,*" he states as his final note on the trip.

Interestingly, he doesn't mention Rio as one of his ports of call in his stories to Synea.

Synea on the other hand was a world traveler. She tells us that she's been to Vancouver, Canada; Bangalore, India; Paris, France; Ghana; Haarlem, Netherlands and several other European countries. She tells us that she was in Europe among a group of "emerging leaders" ages 28-40 chosen for the prestigious German Marshall Fellowship. Her storytelling of where she's traveled and what she's encountered was captivating. At least I thought so. Mina sat quietly.

"So what do you do?" Marcus asked.

"I'm a financial consultant for non-profit organizations."

"For non-profits, they must have a lot of money to pay to fly you all over the world."

"Other than the trip to Europe, I pay for my own travels."

"Oh, you got it like that huh?"

"Yes I do."

"So where to next?" I ask.

"I'm going to Darfur."

"What's in Darfur?"

"I'm going to stay for a few months as a volunteer to help the people there deal with the crisis in Sudan."

"What crisis?"

"Millions of Sudanese are going hungry, and have been displaced by violence." Synea reached in her huge bag and pulled out the book *Not on Our Watch: The Mission to End Genocide in Darfur and Beyond* by Don Cheadle, and hands it to me. "It's all in here. You can keep it. I'm finished," she offered.

"Thanks."

"Oh my gosh; look at the time. I've should be going." Synea recognizes.

"Yeah me too," Marcus follows with.

Mina and I saw our friends to their cars. The two women stood by Synea's Land Rover which was blocking in Marcus' Nissan Maxima. Being in earshot of the ladies, I overheard what I took to be a consoling response from Synea to Mina. *"Girl you know I wish you could go with me too. But I'm proud of you and King Matthew for doing the family thing."*

I couldn't make out Mina's response. The two of them exchanged hugs. Synea climbed in her SUV and drove away. Mina passed us without an utterance.

"Good night Mina," Marcus blurted.

"Goodbye," she spat.

"That woman is *hot* but deadly," Marcus remarks once she's inside.

"She's my girl."

"But are you *fo'* real happy?"

"Of course I am."

"So *bruh*, if you weren't with Mina, would you get with her friend?"

"I don't do what ifs when it comes to Mina."

"Nobody is saying that your girl isn't all that and a bag of *Flamin' Hot* chips. I'm just asking if she wasn't in the picture, would you do *ole girl.*"

"I don't entertain the thought of any other woman."

"Damn man; are you that *pee-whipped*? It don't hurt to look."

"It's not about being *whipped* and I do look, but that's as far as it goes. It doesn't go past my eyes."

"Okay Do Right Man. Can you get me *ole girl's* number?"

"I'll see what I can do."

"*A'ight.*"

"BIRDS OF A FEATHER . . ."

Mina was already in bed. Her clothes are on the floor at the foot of the bed. That told me that she was in a haste to get out of them. Her position at the far edge of the bed showed that she wasn't necessarily in a hurry to get out of her clothes for the wanton reason I hoped for.

"Hey baby, you okay?" I asked while climbing in bed and moving close behind her. My hand made it to her waist where it was immediately met by Mina's seizing grasp.

"I'm fine."

"Come on, what's up?"

"It's your *straight-up-trifling* friend."

"Who, Marcus?"

"Who else?"

"What did he do? This isn't about the game is it?"

"It's about him. I can't stand him."

"Why?"

"Do I need a reason?"

"To be fair, I think so."

"You don't want to know."

"If it upsets you, then I do."

"I don't like the way he is and because he's your friend; what's that that they say, *birds of a feather flock together.*"

"Marcus is my boy and all, but that doesn't make me like him. My friends are all types of guys who are cool, and some who are, well, like Marcus. You should know by now that I'm my own man."

"But he's the one over here all the time."

"Only to watch a game every now and again. Look, college football is over. The pros will be over in a month, and then it's March Madness." I stopped there, because the NBA season would be in full swing by then. "Maybe one of the reasons he's over a lot is because he doesn't have a steady girlfriend. What do you think about him and Synea?"

"OH HELL TO THE NO." She says and sits up in the bed. "ARE YOU SERIOUS?"

"Yeah."

"She wouldn't have anything to do with him."

"Are you sure of that?"

"Y – Yes."

"What do you think would happen if he were to give her a call?"

"She would laugh in his face and hang up."

"Really. I don't think so."

"Uh, Synea is my friend. I think I know her better than you."

"And I know Marcus and I say he might have a chance."

"Not a chance in hell is more like it."

"Bet a nickel."

"No. I'm not betting, because I'm not going to have any part of it."

"Afraid of losing?"

"Alright, bet."

"When you lose, I don't want any pennies. I want a case nickel."

"Whatever."

"1ST ANNUAL MLK WINTER SKI FESTIVAL"

When the email pop-up window appeared in the lower right-hand corner of my computer screen, announcing the arrival of a new email; it was the subject line that caused me to click on it. The *1st Annual MLK Winter Ski Festival* was what it read. All that I could do was shake my head in amazement that the recognition of Martin Luther King, Jr.'s birthday had fallen subject to commercialism. Out of disappointment and disgust just when I'm about to delete the forwarded email from my inbox I noticed the name of the sender, NatalieP-P@LawsOfficesofP&P.com.

"*I BELIEVE IN COPYRIGHT AND THE RIGHT TO COPY*"

It was cloudy overcast day in the city of Atlanta. Activities were slow in the office. To rescue me from boredom Mina called and asked me to meet her for lunch at one of her favorite stylish Midtown restaurants, Baraonda *caffé italiano* on Peachtree Street and 3rd. She arrived late, walking in carrying shopping bags from Shoe Studio. "What? You know what happens when Bobbi and I get to talking," is how she defended herself. Bobbi is the owner of the unique fashion clothing and shoe boutique.

We were waiting for our orders of *Penne Salsiccia*, a hot and spicy sausage with pasta and Alfredo sauce and cups of Harney & Sons Peaches & Ginger hot tea, when Curtis, a banking software developer stepped to the table.

"Hey Matthew, I'm glad I saw you over here," he extended his hand for me to shake.

"Why is that," I responded while receiving his hand. "Ah, this is Mina, my wife."

"It's nice to meet you. Matthew, I need to ask you something?"

"Okay."

Curtis pulled up a chair and sat to begin telling me about a software program he developed. He called the program LOC, which is a mnemonic for "Language of Choice." He went on to explain that the program allows a bank customer to choose their language of choice when they open an account. So when they call or access their account via an ATM or over the phone, the information will be given in the language chosen.

"They're implementing the program, because they see the benefit of the transaction time savings and the increased customer satisfaction. The bank did a sampling of customer's responses and it was all positive," Curtis boasted.

"That is a good idea. I know I hate having to choose English. They ought to know that." Mina chimed.

"So here's my question," he posed to me "can I take this idea to another bank or banks and get paid for it?"

"Well, without knowing the policy of bank that you work for, I would suspect that they have an intellectual property or proprietary rights clause in your employee agreement that you signed that gives them the rights to anything that you develop while being in their employ."

"Really," he stated with disappointment.

"That doesn't seem right." Mina offered.

"You might want to check with your HR department to verify if they have such a thing and whether you signed something that binds you to it. The intellectual property clause pretty much says that they own anything that you think of or dream up while taking a nap in their break room that pertains to your job."

"That's some *bull*." Mina expressed.

"You know Sadie's Bratz dolls? A federal jury reached a verdict in favor of toymaker Mattel in its copyright infringement lawsuit against another company which makes the dolls. Because the ideas for the Bratz characters were conceived while the designer used to work for Mattel, they're talking about getting ten million in damages."

"What?"

"Yep."

"Wow. So can I copyright my idea?" Curtis asked.

"You can't copyright an idea, but rather the expression of an idea . . ." I explained until our food arrived. Curtis thanked me for my advice and promised to look in to the bank's policy then he would get back with me if he needed help.

"So is this what you do?" Mina asked.

"Kind of, sort of" I answered.

"And you like doing it?"

"It's okay; I mean it pays the bills. It may not be as fulfilling as what you do. So I get that feeling by volunteering at ASK ME."

While we were dining, a flash flood rain hit the downtown area. It had not tapered off by the time we were ready to leave. Mina had a small umbrella only big enough to cover her and her recent shoe purchases, which meant that I was going to get wet. The rain that had reached the ground was whooshing by and in some cases up over the curb side, causing a several inch deep stream.

Mina complained because she was wearing a pair of her thin soled ballet shoes. After looking both directions, I saw no feasible way for us to cross the street without our feet getting soaked. So I rolled up my pants legs, looked at my wife, swept her up into my arms and carried her across. Drivers, who had stopped for the traffic light, blew their horns and gave me the thumbs up in response to my gallant act.

Once I reached the other side of the street and prepared to put her down, I was met with a protest.

"No, don't put me down yet?" She asked.

"A girl, you are not that light."

"No you didn't."

"I'm just saying."

"Well, do you think you can carry me over to there?" She pointed to the Hotel Indigo.

"Yeah."

"Then let's get a room and dry off."

And that we did.

"HAVING MY SADIE"

Mina's friend LaDessa in Louisiana called to ask how to host a baby-shower. Apparently she was attempting to throw her own. I was sitting on the couch next to my wife, while she spoke to LaDessa on the phone. During the course of the instructional conversation, Mina was asked that *we* be the god-parents of her high school friend's unborn child. Mina graciously accepts the honor, while reaching out and grabbing my hand to inform me that I've accepted by association.

Looking back on that day, I realized that I've never even spoke with LaDessa – never even heard her voice. Whenever she's called Mina, it's always on her cell phone. I know LaDessa only through stories told to me. Not that it matters, I don't expect our relationship to change.

With her newly appointed and accepted guardian role, in classic Mina style, my wife volunteers to coordinate the baby shower for her friend.

While Mina was gone for the long weekend spent in Louisiana, it's up to Mercedes and I to fend for ourselves. It's not a problem because I'm very hands-on when it comes to her. Because I have the standard set of holidays off from work, along with a generous amount of accrued paid-time-off, I spend a lot of time with her. Once we're given Mercedes' academy school's calendar, I match my vacation schedule to the time she's out of school. Then it's just me and her.

We often started our days together in downtown Decatur at the Starbucks store. If it's cold out, she'll have hot chocolate. During the warm months, she gets a Frappacino. We may have breakfast at a Huddle House and maybe take in a matinee movie. Other ways to spend the time while having fun together, we'll go to Dave and Busters or Kangazoom in Smyrna, which is like a Chuck E. Cheese's on steroids.

"Am I going to be a god-sister?" Mercedes asked.

"I guess you will be." I reply to the six-year-old.

"Good. "

"Why is that good?"

"So I can write my commandments."

"Commandments. What commandments?"

"The ones that the baby will have to do for me."

"What are you talking about?"

"God wrote Ten Commandments in the Bible for people to do, right? So now that I'm going to be a god-sister, I'm going to have some commandments for the baby to do for me."

"Honey, that's not the way it works. What made you think that you were supposed to write commandments for the god-child to do for you?"

"Oh, I was just thinking."

This is why parents need to talk to their children, to understand what they're thinking.

"IT AIN'T NO FUN UNLESS YOUR FRIEND GETS SOME"

"Where's Mina?" Marcus asked as he walks in to the house.

"She's out of town."

"Good . . . I mean we need to talk."

"Okay."

He heads for the den by way of the kitchen, where he grabs a beer out of the fridge.

"Where's the munchkin?"

"She's in her room. So what's up?"

"It's your girl's girl."

"Synea?"

"Yeah man."

"What about her?"

"Okay, don't *crack* about it, but I'm *diggin'* her."

"Say what?"

"Yeah man. We met up the other night at the Apache Café off of Spring Street to watch some band. Anyway, we had a good time and everything. Afterwards, she came over to my place and we had this long talk."

"Long talk?"

"Yeah, we just had this incredible talk, *knowhaimsayin.*"

"I'm finding it hard to believe."

"I'm serious. This girl could be the one." Marcus remarks with a glint of enthusiasm I've not seen in his eyes when talking about a woman. I can hardly wait to see Mina's face as she's handing me my nickel.

"She's the one, after a conversation and no sex?"

"That's the crazy part, *knowhaimsayin*. I knew that I could have *hit it* anytime that I wanted to, but I didn't."

"You mean she wouldn't let you."

"I could have got that *split*, but she came at me on another level *knowhaimsayin*."

"She hit you with the *three month rule*."

"Nah *bruh*, we didn't even go there. She asked me what my core values were."

"Say what?"

"*Seewhatimsayin?* She broke it down to me. What she wanted to know was what I believed in; what laws or rules do I live my life by?"

"And you said?"

"That, 'I would get back with her.' Then I just listened to her talk about Africa. Do you know what the capital of Djibouti is?"

"Djibouti." I answered.

"Yeah, she messed me up with that one. How'd you know that?"

"From watching Jeopardy."

"Did you know Africa ain't a country?"

"Yeah, it's a continent."

"Jeopardy?"

"Fulton Elementary."

"Anyway, I know I have to come at her on a different level, if *Mister Marcus* is going to have any chance of going panty dipping. So have you started reading that book she gave you?"

"Not yet."

"Why don't you let me hold it for a minute so I can do some homework?"

"What she's got you doing homework?"

"Hey, *a playa got ta do, what a playa got ta do*. Plus, she's makin' a brother work for it, *knowhaimsayin?* I'm like a lion in the forest."

"You mean on the plains."

"Wherever, and a lion likes the hunt, *knowhaimsayin*. I ain't for nothin' easy. No road kills for me."

I handed Marcus the book given to me by Synea. From under his shirt sleeve, a silver on silver Movado™ watch is revealed. The watch retails at $895 or higher. I was pricing one for myself. I have two material indulgences; fine watches and ink pens. Marcus teases me about it when he notices a new purchase of mine. He wasn't one who would spend a lot of money on a genuine Movado.

"Whoa, what do we have here?" I asked.

"Oh yeah; one of my *side pieces* bought it for me."

"One of your *side pieces*; are you serious. It would take two of your women working overtime to afford this watch. And what did you do to deserve this?"

He cut his eyes in my direction as if for the first time he's embarrassed to say.

"This *chick* is different than my regulars. She's a *Buckhead Barbie*, with style as you can see. And this ain't no knockoff neither, *knowhaimsayin*. She also took me to spend the weekend in a cabin in the mountains . . . all expenses paid.

"I thought she was going to be *Lazy Daisy* in bed, but it was a freaky sex wild weekend. I'm talking about with gadgets and shit. You would never know it to look at her. As a matter of fact, she turned out to be a *G.I. Jane* in the bedroom, giving me orders on how she likes it and where she wanted me to put it, *knowhaimsayin*."

"Say what?"

"Hey, don't knock it 'till you've tried it."

On his way out of the house Marcus thanked me. For the second time he asked about Mina.

"So when is Mina coming back?"

"Tomorrow."

"So you got one more night of manhood."

"Whatever."

"*GIRLFRIENDS*"

After putting Mercedes to bed, I'm lying in bed sipping on a cordial glass of sherry and television channel surfing when I come across a late night rerun episode of the sitcom *Girlfriends*. It's a show that I strongly disliked because I don't like the degrading, shallow, superficial and hyper-stereotypical portrayal of the black female characters. Yet, during its run, the show maintained a Top 10 ranking among African Americans, according to Nielsen Media Research. Mina said that the female characters are more realistic than I knew.

If what Mina said was true, about these women's characters being reflective of today's black women; that thought disturbed me even more. For that reason though, I secretly watched an episode from time to time to possibly gain some insight in the *world of black women*, in particularly Mina's. Surprisingly, what I learned was that I could recognize a little bit of Mina's behavior in all of the characters. Mina could be strong willed like Joan, a little too fashion conscience like Toni, manipulative like Lynn, and she definitely represents the struggling to success story of Mya.

The *Girlfriends* episode that was on was one where best friends Joan and Toni get in to a fight because Joan causes a breakup between Toni and her boyfriend. In retaliation, Toni attempts to seduce Joan's boyfriend. As I reached for my glass of sherry, I struggled to understand why they named the show girlfriends.

Just as my hand passed over my cell phone, it begins to ring. Displayed on the screen of my phone was Natalie's name. It had been at least six or seven months since the last time I had seen Natalie and even then it was a brief in passing encounter. To the casual observer, we exchanged friendly smiles, but I saw something lingering in Natalie's smirk. The speculation of what lied behind the leer may have caused my hesitation in answering the call.

"Hello."

"Hey. Guess who this is?"

"Natalie Pennington-Peel."

There was a delayed response, before "Very good. How'd you know?"

"I recognized the number."

"So you haven't completely erased me from your life."

"Of course not . . . not completely."

"So you've tried?"

"Mina . . . I'm sorry . . . Natalie, what's up?" An even longer pause hung between us this time, giving me the time to recall the last unfortunate incident when I called Natalie, Mina. *Natalie and I were in the passionate throes of hot make-up sex and she was being totally out of character. At the height of our passion, Natalie cried out for me to call her name. While my hands were on Natalie, my nostrils were filled with the sexual scent of Natalie, my eyes were fixed on Natalie, my mouth spoke the truth of who my mind's eye wantonly saw – "Mina."*

"Oh, I just had a thought about you, so I called." Natalie finally broke the uncomfortable silence. "Well actually, something came up at work which made me think of you."

"Really, and what was that?"

"Um, it's not important. I'm sorry for calling so late. Let me call you back at a decent hour, maybe at your office. Goodnight Matthew."

"Goodnight."

The phones didn't disconnect the calls right away. I remained on the line listening as I felt Natalie on the other end doing the same. Fifteen to twenty seconds elapsed before the "no call" signal appeared. I laid the phone on the nightstand, replacing it in my hand with the patiently waiting drink. In one gulp, I emptied the glass of the silky smooth, pure raisin sherry wine. My head quickly found the pillow and a sound sleep.

"WERE YOU SLEEPING?"

"Were you asleep?" Mina asked over the phone at 2:30 in the morning. It was an hour earlier in Louisiana where she was calling from.

"Yeah" I answered while trying to orient myself.

"I'm sorry."

"Are you okay?"

"Yes." She didn't sound convincing.

"What's the matter? What are you doing up?"

"I couldn't sleep.

"So you were asleep?"

"Yeah, but not for long. I had . . . never mind. How's Sadie?"

"She's fine. She's asks about you all the time. 'When is Mommy coming back' is all she's concerned with . . . Mina?"

"I'm here."

"Are you alright?"

"Yeah, I just love her and miss her that's all."

"Is she the only one you love and miss?"

"Quit being a *goober*."

"How am I being a *goober* when you call me at two-something in the morning to say that you love Sadie and not your husband?"

"You know I don't like it when you get like this."

"What, I wasn't being emotional or sensitive. I was just kidding with you, but now I'm being serious." I emphasized.

For the next few minutes we went back and forth with points and counterpoints about the acknowledgement of devotion. My point was that Mina doesn't say that she loves me enough, though I know in my heart-of-hearts that she does. So it's not about me being insecure. Mina's point was that she shouldn't have to remind me that she loves me, since I'm the one she married.

"All I'm saying Mina; is that every once in a while a man, this man, would like to be told that I'm loved, needed, depended on to give the love that I can give." I versed.

"You need to stop listening to them old school love song CDs of yours" she shot back. "Look man, I love you. Now can we drop this? I didn't call to argue with you about who loves who more."

"Right; and why exactly did you call or were you checking up on me?"

"I don't know. I'm sorry. Goodbye Matthew." She hung up.

In the short time of our marriage, I've learned that winning a point can be a loss cause.

"GOD BLESS THE CHILD . . ."

After a night of restless sleep, it was back to the morning routine. Getting Mercedes dressed and ready for school was easy now that she's adopted my habit of laying our clothes out for the week. Occasionally, my only challenge was with styling her hair. Mercedes has long hair, which offers too many options for style. The other challenge is as Mina puts it, the child is tender-headed. I've seen the two of them wrestle a bout befitting the World Wrestling Federation, with Mercedes often coming out the victor. In order to comb the child's hair without incident, Mina will wait until she's in a sound sleep.

To save me the fight, Mina would put Mercedes' hair in French braids for low maintenance. The only thing I have to do is to make sure to wrap her hair in a scarf before she goes to bed. Mercedes likes having the wrap on her head because it's like she's imitating Mina.

During the drive to the academy, Mercedes sat in the backseat doing her favorite thing of reading road signs along the street side or what comes across the display panel of my car stereo.

"XM-one, sixty-four, The Groove, Have you seen her? The Chi-Lites" read the little girl. The Groove channel is one that Mina listens to regularly in her car. Then the little girl began singing the soul ballad. ♪*I see her face everywhere I go, on the street, and even at the picture show. Have you seen her? Tell me have you seen her.*♪ "Matthew, is that how you feel when Mina is gone?"

"No," I answer, surprised by the probing question.

"Don't you miss her? I do."

"Yeah," purposely keeping my responses short.

"She's coming home today, right?"

"Yes."

Mercedes stopped asking me questions long enough to return to singing.

♪ *Why, oh why did she have to leave and go away? Oh, I've been used to having someone to lean on And I'm lost, baby I'm lost.* ♪

I drove in the parking lot of the academy to get in behind a line of luxury vehicles. Children were climbing out of Lexuses, BMWs and jumping out of SUVs to take off running to inside the building. After I pulled up in front of the school's doors, I caught a rarified candid glimpse of Mercedes being a child, being herself, which is a darling little girl. Just before getting out of the car she turned to me.

"You have a good day at work, *okay?*" She instructs.

"You have a good day at school, *okay?*" I mimic her.

"I love you," she added, which caught me totally off guard.

"Love you too, Sadie."

I really do love that child.

"THE OFFICE"

In the Law Offices of Buckmire-Williams and Maender it was business as usual for the early quarter of the New Year. My case load was extremely light and I was reading through email in my junk mail folder. Aside from the multitude of SPAM Viagra offers there were numerous emails of events promotions sent by Denice, a mutual friend of Natalie and I.

Denice is the consummate socialite and event planner. She either knows about a party in Atlanta or she's planning it. Natalie and I were regularly on her VIP list of attendees. Despite our breakup, I never asked to be removed from Denice's emailing list. Sorted by sender, I systematically hit the delete button on my laptop, until I came across a forwarded email titled *The Best Damn MLK Jr. Ski Weekend Celebration.* I hit the delete button with some emphasis.

My office phone rang. The call was on the inner office line.

"Hello.

"Mathew, you have a call," announced Ruby, the receptionist.

"Thanks."

"Wait; did you hear that we might be downsizing?" She asked and was telling to spread an office rumor.

"No I didn't."

"There's some foreign guy in Mister Kubiak's office. I think that's who's going to take over our clients."

"Really."

"Yes. Now you didn't hear it from me."

"Okay. Uh, my call?"

"Oh, right. It's *ahem*, Natalie Pennington-Peel." Ruby's "ahem" was a clue that there would be a follow up visit by her once I was off the phone.

"Hello Natalie."

"Hey Matthew. Were you busy?"

"Not really, just reading emails."

"Did you see the one about the MLK ski trip?"

"Yeah."

"Are you going?"

"Yeah right. I wouldn't be caught dead going to that resort on that weekend."

"I thought that's what you'd say. Still the same old socially conscience Matthew King."

"Damn straight."

It's one of the reasons I continue to perform *pro bono* work at the ASK ME Foundation, a non-profit organization. Natalie remarked that I was a future Bill Cosby, the activist, in the making. She said that she expected to see me on a panel with Cosby, Tavis Smiley and Michael Baisden and Cornel West solving the ills of the black community. Our thirty minute conversation carried on so comfortably that I hadn't realized how much time had passed.

"I guess that's what I miss most about you; that *do right* attitude of yours" she commented.

"Well, like around here I try to stay above the office gossip and below the company politics."

"That's my . . . . . . I mean, that's the Matthew I once knew."

"Well . . . so why did you call me last night?"

"Oh that. I didn't get you in any trouble by calling so late did I?"

"No. Mina is out of town."

"Good . . . I mean about not causing a problem. When does she come back?"

"This evening some time."

"Right. You know about AT&T's acquisition of BellSouth."

"Yeah."

"This is a huge deal as you can imagine. Millions of dollars being spent in contract negotiations alone. Pennington and Pennington won some of the legal work, representing BellSouth."

"Congratulations."

"Well it could be enough good news to go around."

"What do you mean?" I queried.

"Look, Matthew I have to go. How about I call you tomorrow with the details?"

"Sure."

"Okay then, tomorrow. Matthew."

"Yeah."

"It has been good talking with you."

"Yeah."

Not a minute after I hung up the phone, Ruby was standing in my office doorway. She was about the only person in the office that I spoke with on a personal level and still that was a divulgence of a need-to-know basis on my behalf. On the other hand, in regards to Ruby, "too much information" certainly applied. From her two failed marriages, her gay son and her daughter who never calls or writes, I knew far more than I wanted to about her troubles. Sadly, the only high point in her life was when her second husband, to whom she's still married but separated from, comes by for a booty call. That wouldn't seem so bad if he didn't manage to mooch a home cooked meal and some money off of her all in the same night. Then she doesn't hear from him again until he's in need.

"So what's the old married girlfriend calling about?" Ruby asked.

"Business."

"Um, what kind of business?"

"I don't have all the details."

"Really, after close to an hour of conversation . . ."

"We did some catching up if you must know."

"I see. I read in *The Georgia Bar Journal* that Pennington and Pennington is the fastest growing law firm in Atlanta. And just think; you could've been hitched to that gravy train."

"Is there something I can do for you Ruby?"

She handed me a business card of Satish Tatavarti, president of a law firm based in India.

"MY SENSITIVITY (GET'S IN THE WAY)"

My early morning fight with Mina was still weighing heavily on my heart and mind. Even the comfortable as an old shoe conversation with Natalie couldn't ease my troubled mind and heart's pangs. I needed to talk to someone. Marcus was out of the question to call. He wouldn't know what I was talking about when it came to being in love and the pains associated with it. Though Ruby shared with me everything that's going on in her life, I didn't trust her with the same level of information about me. That meant my next choice was my twin cousin Emily.

Instead of picking up the phone to give her a call, I opened an AOL Instant Messenger® window on my computer. After a couple of clicks, I checked my Buddy List, under Family and there I saw that she's online.

King_Matt: What's up *cuz*?

EMCEE: Who is this?

King_Matt: Who do you think?

EMCEE: I don't know. The cousin I know I haven't heard from in two months. I wasn't sure if he was still alive.

King_Matt: It hasn't been that long has it?

EMCEE: You damn skippy it has. I knew that marriage and the family life and all would bite into our time, but dayum. Kick a *cuz* to the curb, why don't you.

King_Matt: Okay, my bad. I promise to do better.

EMCEE: Yeah, right. So how is the family?

King_Matt: They're fine. Mina's been out of town for a few days.

I updated Emily on the whole LaDessa, the baby shower and with Mina and I being asked to be god-parents. I banged out on the keyboard how Mina is always there as a true friend to those that are in her life, while as for me, I don't feel any more special than they are. Then I mentioned our last phone conversation.

King_Matt: True, I'm more often the one to initiate the exchange of "I love you" between us. Her point was that coming from a man it makes me sound *soft*, to which I took offense.

EMCEE: She's right.

King_Matt: WHAT!?

EMCEE: Hey, I'm just saying. It is usually the woman who wants to hear that.

King_Matt: What is wrong with a man wanting to hear his wife say I love you?

EMCEE: Nothing. Just don't whine about it.

King_Matt: Who's whining, I just asked.

EMCEE: Coming from a man, it's whining. Look at it from her side. Wasn't she with some roughneck, dope boy before you?

King_Matt: Yeah, this guy named Tyriq.

EMCEE: Do you think she told him she loved him; or better yet, do you think he even cared. As long as he was getting respect and sex, which was all that probably mattered to him.

King_Matt: Did you have to go there?

EMCEE: Yes, to prove my point. In your case, YOU are married to Mina and you got her *on lock* . . . I hope. LOL

King_Matt: Whatever.   I thought of all people you would understand where I was coming from.

EMCEE: I do *cuz*. You happen to be that rare breed of man that women read about in fiction romance, but really wouldn't know how to handle once they had him. Women are more attune to dealing with the alpha *dawg* male than the nice and caring guy. Question, how did Natalie let you know that she loved you?

King_Matt: That's it see, Natalie and I bought one another Mahogany™ greeting cards and expensive gifts to express ourselves, and then we would confirm it with an act of perfunctory sex. That's what Mina fails to realize, is that I came out of a long term relationship where there was hardly any exchange of words of sentiments.

EMCEE: That sounds about right for most modern day couples. But Mina's got you feeling old school about her. I mean, I understand that too. When I met the girl, I was impressed with the way she carried herself for her young age. She is precious. But you have to know that she loves you. And *cuz*, it's not so much in what she says, but in what she does. So stop being so sensitive.

Emily was right as usual, which was why I turned to her for advice. We instant messaged for a little bit longer for me to tell her about the phone calls from Natalie. She cautioned me to be careful; calling me naïve like most men are when it comes to the deceitful ways of some women. She pointed out something that I had not given any thought. Why would Natalie call me on my cell phone late at night, unless she wanted to cause some trouble between Mina and me?

"GUESS WHO'S COMING TO DINNER"

Mercedes and I were in the family room watching the game show Jeopardy on television.

"In the category of before and after; the clue is 'this word grants the blank to live and the blank to die" Alex Trebeck read to the three contestants.

"What is *a will"* I said aloud, which was the correct $200 response.

"What's a will," Mercedes asked.

"Well, it means several things. One is the part of the person that makes decisions. Another is a document to leave somebody something after they die, which is called a will."

"Do you have a will?"

"Which one?"

"Ummm, the second one."

I was embarrassed to say, "No I don't. Why do you ask?" I made a mental note to call my lawyer to schedule an appointment to get a will started.

"Um, cause I want this house for me and Mommy" the little girl said as a matter of fact.

"Okay. Now you know for that to happen, I would have to die first."

"Un huh. But you can come back as a ghost."

"I see, and you wouldn't be scared?"

"Not if it's you."

During this exchange of words, not once did Mercedes look at me. Unexpectedly, the doorbell rings. Its sound acts as the firing pistol at the beginning of a race. Mercedes hops off of the couch, racing in the direction of the front of the house, shouting "MOMMY." I take chase after her making the sound of a haunting ghost, "Boooooooo waaaaahhh" while reaching after her. I grabbed the back of her shirt, which evoked a playful, yet shrilling scream from the child.

"Nooooooooo, let me get it" she cried. I let loose my grasp, freeing her to answer the door. Just as she begins turning the lock and the doorknob, it dawns on me that Mina wouldn't need to ring the doorbell. So . . . when the door swung open and Brianna,

Mercedes birth mother was standing on the other side it was made clear. All of us stood speechless, in response to seeing a woman that we had not seen in almost two years. For me, it hadn't quite been two years, since I realized that it really was Brianna that I saw begging for money outside of the Starbucks in downtown Baton Rouge.

Mercedes backed away from the door to stand close by my side. Mina came rushing up behind her aunt. There is a look of agitation on her face.

"I thought I said to wait for me," Mina stated.

"*Chile*, you move too slow. I couldn't wait to see my Sweet Pea. Hey honey, it's mommy." Brianna claimed. I had not realized that Mercedes had grabbed a hold of my hand and was squeezing it tightly. "What's the matter Sweet Pea?" Brianna stepped toward us with outstretched arms. Mercedes moved closer and behind me.

"Hey Brianna, what a surprise," I offered my hand for an intercepting handshake.

"Matthew" Brianna gives me a close body hug. I could feel Mercedes scooting further behind me. "How have you been?"

"I've been good."

"You *sho* still look good. Ooo, if I had of known ya'll was living like this, I would've came back to Atlanta a long time ago. Look at this place."

"Thank you."

"Now where's my baby girl?" Mercedes continued to elude contact with her mother by keeping me between them. "What's wrong baby?"

"How about we bring in the luggage?" I interjected. Mercedes now has a full grasp of my hand and forearm.

"Yeah, let's do that," Mina supported my suggestion and asked Mercedes to help, giving her reason not to leave my side.

Brianna becomes obviously and painfully aware of the intentional diversion. Mina placed a hand on her aunt signaling for her to stay in the house, while Mercedes and I went outside. There wasn't much more luggage to unload from the car, except for one large plastic garbage bag and a laundry clothes basket of odds and ends. We put Brianna's things in the guest room.

Mercedes doesn't leave my side for the rest of the night until I put her to bed. She only spoke when answering a direct question, and she gave no elaboration. After she said her five finger prayer, I gave her a kiss on the forehead. As I reached the door she called my name.

"Yes Sadie."

"Are you and Mina going to give me away?"

Returning to her bedside and gathering the girl in my arms, "Your moth-, Mina and I love you and we are not going to give you away and nobody is going to take you away from us. Do you understand me?"

She nods her head.

"What were you thinking?" I asked Mina in the privacy of our bedroom.

"I tried to tell you last night when I called."

"Well why didn't you? Never mind. Do you know what Sadie just asked me? She asked if we were going to give her away."

"Really?"

"Yes. Seeing her mother has probably traumatized her."

"I don't think so."

"I do. You saw how she was acting. What is Brianna doing back here anyway?"

She told me how Brianna showed up at her mother's house looking for something to eat and someplace to sleep. She had been staying at shelters when there was room and living on the street when there wasn't. By the end of her storytelling, Brianna had everyone who cared feeling sorry for her.

Mina's mother didn't have the room in her house for Brianna to stay with her. And no other relative came forward to offer any help. Somehow Mina was convinced that her aunt would have a better chance of getting back on her feet by coming back to the Mecca of opportunity, Atlanta.

"Did any of you think of Mercedes?" I stressed.

"Yes Matthew."

"Well."

"Brianna said she wouldn't cause any trouble."

"What does that mean?"

"What do you think it means? Look Matthew, I don't need this right now. Brianna is my family. I couldn't just leave her out on the street."

"So how long is she supposed to stay with us?"

"I don't know."

"I do. We give her three months."

"That's not long enough."

"Why isn't it?"

She knew that Brianna would be starting from scratch. The woman had no identification to speak of. So Mina would have to help her aunt obtain a birth certificate, state identification and whatever else she would need to reestablish herself.

For the remainder of the waking morning hours, Mina and I also came to an understanding about decisions being made without discussing it with each other, especially when it affected the household.

"Listen, I know she's you aunt; but this is our house. Inviting any overnight guests into it ought to be a joint decision."

"Like I said, I tried to tell you, but you started an argument because I didn't call to say, I love you."

"That shouldn't have kept you from telling me something as big as you bringing Brianna here to stay."

"You made me mad and I didn't feel like talking to you anymore. By the time I thought about calling you again, we were on the road and Brianna was always around."

"All I'm saying is that from now on, we need to come together on these types of decisions."

"You're right. I'm sorry."

"LET'S KEEP IT IN THE FAMILY"

With the late night into early morning talk with Mina, I overslept. Fortunately Mina was home to take care of getting Mercedes up and off to school. After I was almost dressed for work, I went to the bedside to wake my sleeping beauty. What a sight. Her mouth was open with a slight drizzle of slobber out of the corner of her mouth. Under the blanket, there was no hiding her pronounced, volley ball round behind. With a palm full of cheek, I gave her a knead awakening.

"Mina . . . Mina . . . it's time to get up. Will you take Sadie to school?"

"Mm hmm."

"Come on now *babe*. I let y'all sleep in."

"You ain't let me sleep in . . . like you somebody's daddy."

"Alright, but you'll get up and get Sadie, right?"

"Yep."

Not having to make the extra stop to drop Mercedes off at school, I was no longer in such a rush. I was watching the news when I heard the fussing coming from the back of the house. It was Mina.

"I DON'T BELIEVE THIS . . . YOU KNOW YOU ARE TOO BIG. WHY DIDN'T YOU GET UP AND GO TO THE BATHROOM." Mina fussed from a distance, coming towards the kitchen where I'm eating some buttered toast with apple butter spread.

"Do you know what that girl did," Mina asked.

"Let me guess. She wet the bed?" I surmised.

"Yes. Wait; you knew didn't you? That's why you wanted me to get her ready for school."

"No. Now why would I do that?"

"Did she wet the bed when I was gone?"

"No."

"What did she have to drink last night?"

"Some juice, but I don't think that had anything to do with it."

"Then what, then." Mina questioned.

Brianna walked in the kitchen, braless, dressed in a t-shirt and sweat pants. Her heavy breasts, strained against the material, swung noticeably, demanded attention. I gave them a wandering glance, just to say good morning. The t-shirt had printed on it "I suck heads and pinch tails." There's a crawfish at the beginning and end acting as quotation marks.

Seeing the aunt and niece side by side, the resemblance between them would have one believe them to be opposing attractive sisters. Brianna would be the obvious older sister, with her fuller, rounder and softer womanly body. In contrast, my wife's physique is a scale smaller, with the same satisfying curves.

"What's going on?" Brianna asked.

"Sadie peed in the bed." Mina offered.

"Is that all?"

"Is THAT ALL!"

"I mean she should have gone to the bathroom, but it ain't nothing but some pee." Brianna defended.

"She would have had to pass the guest room to get to the bathroom." I offered in the child's defense.

"What *chu* saying?"

"That she probably was afraid of possibly bumping into you."

"I don't see why."

"She was visibly upset last night. I think it's highly possible."

"Well she'll be alright as long as ya'll don't make no big deal out of it."

"No big deal. She has never peed in the bed before." Mina exclaimed.

"It ain't like you never pissed on yourself." Brianna divulged.

"What?"

"You don't remember that time at the club when you had too much to drink and the line to the women's bathroom was long. You ran out to go in the parking lot between some cars, but you didn't make it."

Mina who threw up her hand to her aunt's face, "You know what, now is not the time."

She stormed out of the kitchen. Brianna followed closely behind. I watched them both as they disappeared down the hall, wondering what was going to happen next.

"IT TAKES A CHILD TO RAISE A VILLAGE"

For the next couple of weeks, I became a quiet observer in our home. Outnumbered, out gendered and out of my mind if I thought that I was going to get in the middle of any dispute between Mina and her aunt. I would only step in when it involved Mercedes. Otherwise, the battle was not mine, it was the Lord's.

Fortunately, the bed wetting incident was a onetime occurrence. In fact, Mercedes warmed up to her cheerful self. She became the guide of the welcome wagon for her birth mother, making her feel at home by showing Brianna how to operate the numerous appliances, electronic devices and entertainment systems. Together they worked on the desktop computer in the den. Mercedes has regular access to child friendly websites like Qubo.com and PBSkids.org.

One notable issue that surfaced was the first time Mercedes called for "mommy" and both women answered. After a long and at times, intense discussion, Mina acquiesced to being called Mommy Mina. From what I observed, it was painful for her to concede.

It didn't take long after Brianna had become our house guest, that more of Mina's family, those close and distant began calling. What spurred them was Brianna's characterization of our living as "high on the hog." The news traveled fast throughout Mina's family village. As Mina relayed it to me the word being spread was that she had "made it." She was the first generation of Parkers out of Franklinton, Louisiana to do so. Mina was the proverbial crawfish who made it out of the barrel.

Because she possessed the open and kind heart that I married her for having, she began doing what she could for those who called for help. And they called for help for everything from stopping household utilities from being shutoff to bailing friends or loved ones out of jail. The first and only time I heard her openly complain is when a distant younger niece called asking for some money, the day before her cell phone was going to have its service cutoff. It had gotten to the point that Mina had online MoneyGram® and Western Union® accounts to send money or to pay someone's debt. Mina was able to be the family bank and bondsman because she had amassed a savings that she had not touched, which was a part of her financial planning.

Despite our comfortable combined income, Mina insisted on having a set aside savings. She said that it would be for inevitable emergency auto and medical accidents. Her goal for us was to save at least six months of income to cover our total household expenses. She opened a 529 Plan investment account to save for Mercedes college expenses. Lastly, Mina purchased life insurance coverage for Mercedes at eight times our annual salary. I married a smart woman.

With her head lying against my chest she laments, "Who do they think I am?"

I recognized this to be a rhetorical question. Women don't always want a man to provide an answer. Sometimes, we're just to listen. It took me a few times to learn that.

"Don't get me wrong, I love my family, but they're calling me for everything. My granny wants me to help her write a will. I don't know about writing a will. You can help me though, right?"

"Sure *Bookie*. We'll make it happen." I stated as a show of husband support.

Brianna and Mina were practically joined at the hip. What clothes that Mina didn't buy for her aunt; Brianna would borrow from her wardrobe and forced her body to fit in them. Sometimes the fit was right, and at other times the fit was tight. It didn't matter to Brianna, she wore the clothes proudly.

With Mina working three days of the week out of her satellite office at the Easywick Village Town House complex, there Brianna would go along to visit with old friends and acquaintances.

"DAY OF SERVICE"

It was one of those rare occurrences when Mina and I were both off of work. The day off for the observance for Martin Luther King, Jr. was one of those days. It made no difference to me; I'm awake before the alarm goes off at 6:00. I forced myself out of the bed and away from holding my wife. I go to my office in the house and boot up my computer. By the time I heat a mug of water in the microwave for steeping a bag of Earl Grey tea, the computer is ready for me to login to my email account.

I went through deleting several pages of junk mail before I came across one that the subject read "Matthew, wish you were here."

I opened the email, which had attachments to it. There was no text to the email. It merely contained JPEG photo images of Natalie at what appeared to be a ski lodge. Most of the photos are of her surrounded by people trying to get in the shot. There were a few of her alone where she seems to be sending a personal message with the come-hither look on her face and in her body language. In particular was the pose of her standing, wearing a ski suit that looked painted on, and she's playfully twisted with her behind to the camera. This wasn't the Natalie that I was in a relationship with for years. I scrolled back through the images to verify the notable absence of her husband Vernon.

It was the sound of the television in the den across from the office that gave me a guilty startle causing me to quickly hit the delete button to remove it from the screen.

In the den Brianna was watching the television ministry of Mason and Twyla Betha of SANE Church International.

"Hey Matthew. I'm sorry, did I disturb you?"

"No. So do you watch this often?"

"When I could, I would watch him in New Orleans. One morning I couldn't sleep and I saw that he came on here on CW. He has a church in Atlanta somewhere. Do you know where Cheshire Bridge Road is?"

"I can't say that I do."

"I wouldn't mind going."

For the remainder of the program, we sat quietly and watched. Pastor Mason Betha spoke of churchgoers having and demonstrating their faith through persistence, without fear and tithing over and above. After First Lady Twyla Betha gave the benediction at the close of the Save A Nation Endangered broadcast, a "be your own boss" SMC infomercial came on.

It offered me the opportunity to ask Brianna what were her plans for getting a job. Sounding like an infomercial herself, she proposed interest working as a dental or medical assistant.

"I can go to school for the therapist and assistant jobs. They're only like six or nine months." She noted.

We moved into my office so that we could go online to look at some websites on the training offered for the areas that she expressed interest. Her head was covered with a scarf. Brianna was wearing a housecoat that fell to her mid thighs, just covering the thin cotton shorts that she had on. She also had on a t-shirt, this time it had printed on it, "Good Girl looking for Bad Boy." I immediately thought of the influence it would have on Mercedes, who habitually reads whatever she sees.

Brianna sashayed around the room looking at my artwork and library of books. I questioned the innocence or not of her movements and exhibitionist exposure of her body to me. At one point she bent over, showing the obvious bunching of her shorts between her cheeks. Her plump thighs playfully pushed against one another.

"So you read a lot huh?" She asked.

"Uh, I wouldn't exactly say a lot."

"Oooo, you got Barack Obama's book. He is one fine black man. I can't wait. If he makes it to the finals, I'm going to vote for him. We haven't had a good looking president since Clinton. Clinton was cute, so I don't blame Monica for *kickin' it* with him. But Obama's wife better watch out if he gets in office."

She rambled some more while thumbing through the best-seller, *The Audacity of Hope*, where the Illinois senator proposes that Americans move beyond their political divisions. Astonished and embarrassed by her comments, I wondered if Brianna was even a registered voter.

She continued to move about the room, stopping and picking up the bottle of Navan liqueur that I kept stocked. Moving closer to me she stopped at my crystal clear beveled glass top, wooden twelve pen holder case. The brand of the pens' inside the case vary from Mont Blanc®, Pelikan®, Aurora®-Afrika, Retro Tornado®, Sensa® and my personal favorite Monteverde®; their cost range from $40 to $900 a piece.

"These are pretty. I know they must be expensive if you got them in they own box."

I don't respond to her, not wanting to divulge their value. Instead I usher her over to look at what resulted from the Google search on medical assistant training in Atlanta. Now maybe a *brother* is a little naïve about the ways of women and that's why I initially didn't think anything tempting about Brianna pressing her free swinging breasts beneath her t-shirt, against my arm. I could smell that she was wearing Mina's vanilla and brown sugar body wash as it permeated through her aunt's night clothing.

I offered Brianna the seat at my desk so she can move the mouse and click for herself. She declined and maintains her up close standing position. I minimized my movement to avoid initiating any misconstrued contact. It doesn't matter as Brianna inched ever closer with her heaving breasts climbed onto my shoulder and a hardened nipple poked me. I ignored it at first, then I imagined differently.

Studies and other infotainment sources say that men stereotypically and constantly think of sex. It just goes to show that you can't believe everything that you read or hear. Unfortunately for me, I'm living proof of that. It took me a while before I became acutely aware that Mina and I had not been intimate in the weeks that Brianna had come to stay with us.

Without any warning, my chair was swung around and I'm facing Brianna with her t-shirt pulled up exposing breasts the size of honeydew melons. Before I can react to the sight; in one fell swoop she was straddling my lap and the t-shirt was pulled over my head. I open my mouth to protest but it's crammed full of tender flesh. Words are forced back with my head against the high back leather chair. Despite my presumed height and weight advantage, Brianna had me pinned.

With amazing skill and swiftness, she crammed her hands down the top of my pajama pants. Chilled fingers grabbed hold of my jones and began pulling and jerking. It was a feeling of pain before pleasure; that which Tina Marie and Rick James sung about in 'Fire and Desire.' Forced to an aroused attention, my jones responded in kind. My mouth was suckling at Brianna's teat. Divided between my two heads, I was stupefied.

Nothing was clear to me. No decision made sense. Start. Stop. Continue. Enjoy, enough, insane. Then a small voice broke through the madness.

"So what are you two up to?" Mina asked, standing in the doorway of the office, looking like her aunt's twin. She too wore a t-shirt, pajama shorts and her head wrapped in a scarf. Brianna straightened up and pulled her housecoat closed.

"Your *Bookie* is helping me look for a job on the computer." Brianna offered.

"Oh, for a minute there, I thought y'all were looking at porn." Mina quipped. Brianna and I gave a nervous laugh. Mina added "Don't let me disturb you" then she walked away.

"Hey Mina, hold up." I cried out, again offering my seat to Brianna.

Not waiting for her to accept, I left the office to follow my wife. I found her returned to our bedroom standing at the doorway of her walk-in closet. I closed the bedroom door behind me, which drew Mina's head around. There was undoubtedly a look of fire and desire on my face.

"Matthew, what are you doing? MATTHEW. *MATTHEW!*"

"ELUCIDATE"

Later that morning Mercedes wasn't feeling well. That slightly changed our plans of attending a service honoring MLK, Jr. and non-profit community organizations. The event is hosted by the United Way *African American Partnership*. The executive director of the ASK ME Foundation paid for a table at the event. He rarely attends events that honor the great work his foundation does.

Mina wanted to stay at home with Mercedes, until Brianna volunteered to watch her so that we could go. It took some convincing before Mina accepted the offer. I saw clinching jaw muscles as we drove westbound down I-20 toward Atlanta.

"You okay?" I asked.

"Yeah. What about you? What was this morning all about?"

"What do you mean?"

"You know what I mean."

"Oh that. Let's just say that 'I had a daydream.'" I purposely misquoted and in doing so using a poor impression of Martin Luther King, Jr.

"What?"

"Never mind, it was a bad joke."

The guest speaker at the luncheon was the dean of the Civil Rights Movement, Dr. Joseph Lowery. He said that the day of observance honored the man and the country for recognizing him for what he stood for. He challenged those of us in attendance to "make a difference in our time, as the participants of the movement did in theirs." He sighted that it took courage and a touch of crazy to do what they did.

"There is good crazy and bad crazy" he exclaimed "and God looks after his good crazy people."

Dr. Lowery said that America is experiencing growth. "The growth is the disparity between the richer and the poorer, not the haves and the have nots, but rather the haves have so much and the have nots not enough," he announced. Continuing, "There are CEOs in this country who are being paid 200 times the average wage of their employees; being paid millions in stock options for resigning or being fired. The rich get richer and the poor get poorer or stay the same.

"If we expect to see a change, we must get involved and bring it about as the Civil Rights movers did. Politically, it would likely take another movement. But there was and is another approach, individually."

That was Mina approach in her effort to liberate the welfare dependent and working class poor who she works with through her FREE program. As we left the venue, attendees are handed a copy of Martin Luther King, Jr.'s "Letter from a Birmingham Jail."

"WAY TM I"

A week and a half later LaDessa goes in to labor. Mina packed an overnight bag and she and Brianna are gone to Louisiana. It was Mercedes and I on our own again.

"Man, yo' girl be boucin' back to hometown on a regular don't she. You sure she don't have a man back in the sticks?" Marcus suggested over the phone line.

"As sure as I need to be."

"So how long is she going to be gone this time?"

"A day or so."

"I don't know how you do it *bruh*. My girl wouldn't be dipping on me like your girl does."

"I love and trust my wife."

"*Bruh*, if you don't sound like a . . ."

"Like a what?"

"I'm just sayin' *bruh*; no one can be trusted a hundred percent *knowhaimsayin.*"

"That's what you're saying."

Marcus' view of relationships was broadly indicative of most black men today. When it comes to women, they are guarded and taking them for granted. In fact, many black men still play games as we put sexual conquests ahead of our women's desires to have a monogamous relationship. As for black women, realizing black men are shy to commit, they are expanding their field of play and venturing to the other sides; racially and same sex wise. I tried to explain this to Marcus.

"I ain't trying to hear that *bruh*," he defended. "I got too much playa left in me. Anyway, I haven't met a *ho* that I would trust in my house alone. They still play games too, like leaving shit in my car like makeup or panties in the bathroom in my crib so they can come back to get it or to mark they territory. I throw that shit out as soon as I find it."

"Why not return it?"

"I might return it to the wrong one." Marcus laughed.

"What about Synea, I thought she was the one?"

"Nope. Don't trust her, she's too good. So when is your girl coming back?"

"I said in a day or two, why?"

"I was just asking, *knowhaimsayin*, to see if she was going to make it back in time for the Super Bowl party."

"She'll be back. Do you have Anthony's, Michael's and Antae's email addresses?"

"Yeah, but you know you're going to have to call Anthony *cuz* he reads his personal emails about once a month."

"Send them to me anyway so I can send them the invite. It's been a while since we all hooked up. Michael's married and I heard he's got a kid."

"Word."

"Yep."

The Super Bowl party would be at our house. It's usually a couple's event. Which beg the question; "So who are you bringing" I asked.

"Synea is going to meet me there."

"Right. Mina owes me a nickel."

"What?"

"Never mind."

We ended our call and I took the time to check on Mercedes. She was doing her homework. Without speaking, the little girl looked up from her desk and smiled. She returned to her studies. I could hear my cell phone ringing. The ringtone was strangely familiar.

"Hello" I cautiously answer the phone.

"Hey, what are you doing?" Natalie asked.

"I was just checking on my little girl."

"Oh. How is she?"

"Fine."

"I need to talk to you about something." I noted that there was no follow-up to her inquiry about Mercedes. That told me that it wasn't a genuine concern.

"Okay."

"We've been married about the same amount of time right; about two years?" Natalie asked a question to which she fully well knew the answer.

Days after our break up and I proposed marriage to Mina, Natalie became romantically involved with Vernon Peel. A mortgage broker, Vernon is the nephew of Jamison Peel, one of the prominently successful businessmen among "One of Atlanta's Most Influential" people. Jamison Peel has an office in the Bank of America building on Peachtree Street and North Avenue, where we both work. The marriage between Natalie and Vernon was a grand affair. It was well publicized in the local and national publications.

"I suppose."

"Is it still the same for you as it was in the beginning?"

"What do you mean?"

"Is it all that you thought it would be?"

"I guess."

"You don't sound too convincing."

"Who do I need to convince?"

"Nobody I guess." She fell silent for a moment.

"What's up with you Natalie?" thus led to the divulgence of way too much information.

In so many words, her marriage was in trouble. Among other things, one of their problems was finances. While Natalie was still bringing in her high end six figure salary, Vernon hadn't sold a house in months due to the mortgage crisis in the country. Apparently, Vernon brokered sub-prime loans for individuals with sub-standard credit histories, which had been defaulting in record breaking numbers. It was reported in the news that the foreclosure rates had reached a feverish pitch with Georgia rising to fourth in the nation in the number of foreclosures.

Natalie said that it wasn't so much that Vernon wasn't brining in any money, but that he was still living and spending her money - like he had money. She said that he was still buying suits, accessories, and treating himself to salon visits. He claimed that he had to maintain an image. That's when she mentioned the possibility of another problem.

"Matthew, sometimes the charges from the salon are double what they should be."

"Double?"

"Like, he might be treating someone else to a massage and mani-pedi."

"You think he's cheating on you?"

"I don't know what to think. I . . ."Natalie's voice was interrupted by the incoming call from Mina.

"Hey, I have to take this call."

"Okay then. Call me back."

"Uh, sure . . . when I can. Gotta go."

"Bye," she says in an almost breathy voice.

"ANOTHER MOUTH TO FEED"

"Hello god-father." Mina greeted after I released Natalie's call.

"Hello god-mother?"

"You silly. LaDessa had her baby. It's a boy and guess what, she named him after us."

"Please tell me she did not name that child Matt-Mina."

"No silly. She named him King."

"King is his first name?"

"Yep. Before you say anything else, *I did* try to talk her out of it."

"Um hmm."

"I did."

"So when will you be home?"

"Day after tomorrow. Why, you miss me?"

"I think of you on two occasions, later days and nights."

"I miss you too *babe.*"

"TOO MUCH INFORMATION, MORE"

Late the following night, Natalie called again. She picked up where she left off, telling me of the woes of the relationship with her husband. There was a possibility that Vernon would be the subject of a criminal investigation due to his real-estate brokering. His uncle may be linked to a number of improper lending practices. One of which was misleading first-time homebuyers to accepting higher interest rates, when they qualified for lower rates and two, giving loans to people without documenting that they had sufficient income. Lastly, he may have also negotiated loans based on false appraisals.

"What does he have to say about all of this," I asked.

"All he says is 'not to worry, that uncle Jamison says it'll be okay.'"

"Was his uncle his financial backer?"

"Largely."

"So what's you guy's plan?"

"I don't know. We can't seem to get to that point in our discussion. We argue about the mess and his exorbitant spending."

"And his only excuse for the spending is so to keep up appearances?"

"Right, like I'm some kind of fool. I know that there's someone else."

"Have you asked him directly?"

"Yes, and he just denies it."

"What about the credit card charges?"

"He claims that they must have made a mistake and that he'll fix it. But he never does; because he can't fix it. You can't fix a lie." Natalie's voice drifted off.

This wasn't the strong and confident woman that I once knew. Marcus once called her the "Buckhead Black Barbie." She's the doll that only shops at Lenox Mall and Phipps Plaza, driving her Lexus SUV with a custom Eddie Bauer child car seat. Nothing in her life is below standard. Either by her will or her money she can correct any predicament that presents itself. At least, she could.

"Do you have any idea who the other woman might be?" I asked which was met by a delayed response.

"Not really. I just know something is not right. Instead of having sex with me, he'd rather watch porno."

"Say what?"

There was a strain in her voice, "Yes. If I don't initiate the sex, then we don't have it. But he says that he has to turn to watching the porno to get what he wants. I mean, I wasn't no prude in bed was I Matthew? Our sex was good, wasn't it?"

"Yeah, I guess."

"You guess. I mean, I might not have been a pole dancer like . . . . I'm just saying, I made you feel good didn't I?"

I felt that I was being baited into a trap. "Look, it doesn't matter how things were between you and me. Vernon is the one you need to please."

"*Hmph.* What about my pleasure? You know what I did for that man."

"No, and you don't have to tell me either."

"I don't mind. I don't have any secrets from you Matthew. We have too much history. I mean we are still friends, right?"

"Yeah but, maybe we don't need to be sharing everything."

"Like I said, I don't mind. Anyway, one morning I wake up and I see that he has a hard-on. So I take advantage of it. I climb on him and ride him until we both *get off.* After I come out of the shower he's sitting on the bed like he's got an attitude. I ask 'what's wrong.' You know what that *punk ass* had the nerve to say to me – that he felt violated."

I laughed first, at hearing her curse for the first time and then at what she said.

Natalie joined in the laughter. "That shit isn't funny," she chastised.

"Yes it is."

"Well I'm glad you think so. I mean, you wouldn't have felt like I violated you would you?" The trap was sprung.

"No I wouldn't. First of all, that doesn't seem like something the Natalie I once knew would've done." In a flash, the question came to my mind; "what would Mina have done."

"Well I've changed. I've learned some things."

There was silence. It's one thing to be trapped, but teased and tortured is something wicked.

"I'm not sure of what's going on with your husband, but you keep trying those things you've learned on him and I'm sure he'll come around."

"You're a lot more optimistic than I am. That's something I miss most about being with you Matthew. You always made me feel like the princess I am."

"They say a good man like me is hard to find."

"Tell me about it."

"SUPER BOWL PARTY"

We were next in the rotation of couples for hosting the Super Bowl Party. I made sure that the fridge and bar was stocked with *Heineken, Miller Chill, Corona, Mike's Hard Lemonade, Bacardi Mojito, Patron Silver,* liqueurs *Limoncello, Frangelica.* Mina and Brianna spent the first part of the day in the kitchen filling the house with the aroma of numerous food dishes. It would be the second Super Bowl Party with Mina and without Natalie. However, there would still be that chance that Natalie's name will come up in the course of conversation.

Our expected guests were Antae and *Felecia, Anthony* and Tiffany, *Dennis* and Melissa, *Michael* and Teri, Ontorio and *Sherhonda, Tone'* and Schveka, *Willie* and Sandea and Marcus and Synea. To this group of friends, Mina and I are affectionately referred to as M&M or M3 when including Mercedes. Mercedes was with our neighbor Sheryl. We believe in children being separate from adults when it's appropriate. The odd person out at the Super Bowl party would be Brianna.

The game was entertaining, but the topic of conversation was far more entertaining and combative than that taking place on the football field.

"What does it say about the moral compass of our society that celebrates a man who impregnates two women at the same time and isn't married to either one of them?" Teri asked.

"It says that there is no moral compass," Synea opinionates.

"I know you aren't talking about my boy Mr. QB MVP. That man has made me a lot of money." Marcus offered.

"AND that's the moral compass of America, money." Synea noted.

"Aren't the women that he got pregnant, super models?" Felicia asked.

"Yep."

"And isn't he modeling underwear for somebody?" Sherhonda followed up.

"Yes, that's what I mean about him being celebrated. Not only does no one publically speak out about his behavior, but he's plastered across magazine pages in his underwear, literally putting the nature of his transgression in our faces." We guys chuckle

"First it was movie stars jumping in and out of bed with each other, marrying and divorcing like they are going through revolving doors. Now it's sports figures, who are supposed to be role models."

"If you ask me, it's a double standard."

"How so?"

"If a woman gets pregnant by two different men, she's labeled a tramp."

"Today's baby's mama."

"But a man is a playa."

"Not just a playa, a Most Valuable Playa." Marcus one lined.

Most of us laughed.

"Seriously though," Marcus continues, "there is something else to consider. If he was a black man, he wouldn't be celebrated and getting underwear endorsements."

As if choreographed, everyone except his wife Teri turned to look at Michael, the only white man in the room. With his hands thrown up in the air as in self defense, Michael stated, "What, I've got only one baby mama and nobody's paying to see me in my underwear."

We erupted with laughter.

"That's an interesting necklace." Schveka noticed the sterling silver pendant around Teri's neck.

"Michael gave it to me. It says 'I love you' in Braille. When he gave it to me, he quoted Shakespeare, 'Love looks not with the eyes but with the mind, and therefore is winged Cupid painted blind.'" Teri proudly announced.

The women delivered "Awwww" in unison.

"HALF-TIME SHOW – TRUTH OR DARE"

The game's half-time entertainment show and showcased commercials were okay. It led us to review our ratings of the best and most memorable Super Bowl commercials of the past; from the Budweiser frogs to the "Wassup" guys.

We played an adult version game of "Truth or Dare." None of the couples opted for a chance at "dare." The "truth" had to be something revealed that the spouse or significant other didn't know. It was our turn. We followed suit and chose truth.

"When Mina's not around, I sometimes watch *Girlfriends*, a show that I swear that I can't stand," I admitted to. The ribbing from the guys began immediately. Mina gave me an "um hmm, I knew it" look. It was then her turn.

"Okay. Now don't be mad, okay." She prefaced her truth confession. "When you're not here, I use your precious ink pens." She playfully hid her face between my shoulder and the couch. This led to an affectionate game of slap and tickle. Mina screamed with laughter.

The doorbell rang. I got off the couch giving Mina one last goosing. She slapped at my hand. Just as I reached the doorway I heard Mina say, "I mean really, who keeps ink pens in a wooden box. He even bought a Mercedes Benz pen to match his car, and don't get me started on his watches." Laughter erupts from our guests.

"I heard THAT." I shot back.

Just before reaching the entrance door, I wondered who it could possibly be. All of the guests we invited had arrived. On the other side of the door, was Tyriq.

"Tyriq," I posed more as a question than a greeting.

"Mr. Benzo."

"What do you want?" I asked of my wife's ex-boyfriend.

"I was invited to the Super Bowl party. Sorry for being late."

Hairs stood on end in places on my body that I didn't know that hair grew. The look of discomfort must have shown on my face. My mouth went dry and my nerves ignited.

"Uh, uh, *bruh*, not by Mina – by her aunt, Brie." He clarified.

Just then, Mina came up behind me. *"Babe*, who is it? Ty?"

"HUDDLE-UP."

"How could she invite Ty to the party, to our house?" Mina lashed out. All of the guests were gone and we were getting ready for bed. "I mean there are some things that you just don't do, especially to family. What the hell was she thinking?" Her rant continued as she stripped and tossed clothes about the room. "Oh, as soon as she is able to get on her feet, she is on them and the hell out of here. Do you hear me?"

Behind Mina's back, Brianna had been getting reacquainted with Tyriq. The two of them would see each other when Brianna would tag along with Mina on the days she worked out of her satellite office at the Easywick. When her aunt wasn't around, Mina assumed that she was visiting with female friends that she knew in and around the complex.

In her defense, Brianna posed to Mina a challenging question, "Why are you worried about me seeing Ty? You got your man."

"BITTER OR BETTER"

The relationship between Mina and Brianna had become obviously strained. Mina felt disrespected by her irresponsible aunt who had abandoned her daughter. She's the same disrespecting woman who we took in and were providing room and board. She's wearing either Mina's clothes or those that Mina bought for her. Now she had broken some unwritten societal rule that 'you don't date the "ex" of a girlfriend of close relative.' The only thing that kept me from getting involved was advice from my cousin Emily "to let it work itself out and not to worry that it was just a woman thing."

Days shortly thereafter Mina's friend Synea dropped by with a surprise.

"I wanted to speak to both of you because my surprise will involve you both." Synea introduced. She continued with, "I'm going to Africa this month."

That announcement took me back to the night when Mina and Synea exchanged hugs and kisses and when Synea consoled Mina over the sacrifice made by adopting and raising Mercedes and not being able to be a world traveler. The thought of Synea inviting Mina to travel with her to Africa immediately entered my mind. What would be my reaction, my response? True; we were still within Mina's two years of my support of her personal development. Did our agreement have fine print that covered a voyage to the motherland?

"Depending on how you guys want to handle this, is why I have you both here." Synea offered while she dug in to her purse to retrieve an envelope. She handed it to Mina. Inside the envelope was a ticket to the annual *Black Enterprise Women of Power Summit*, along with a three day itinerary for the event. "Obviously, I can't go and I think you would benefit from the opportunity. All you would need to do is pay for your travel, everything else is paid for."

It was one of the few times my sweet jawbreaker was visibly emotionally moved. She kissed and hugged her good friend before saying goodbye. Synea left us with the information to get back with her with our decision.

Mina and I spoke of the opportunity for her to attend the networking summit. The only question to be answered was whether we would go to LaQuinta, California as a family, a couple or would Mina go alone. I had to check to see if I could get off work and we had to make a decision whether to take Mercedes out of school. Mina made it clear that she did not want to leave Mercedes with Brianna, which brought up another question. Could we leave Brianna in our house?

"WHEN ONE DOOR CLOSES . . ."

Though I had the accrued paid-time-off to take, the operations partner of the firm denied my request due to some initiative that was expected to take place during the same time as the summit. I called Mina with the disappointing news, which made our decision for us in regards to who could go and what we could do. That meant Mina would travel alone to the summit. That would leave me in the house with Mercedes and Brianna. Mentioning this to Marcus was a mistake.

"Damn, she's leaving you to babysit again" he exerted.

"I'm not babysitting. I'm looking after our daughter."

"You *wanna* talk about a dysfunctional household. Ya'll don't want the girl's real mama to watch her own daughter. And ya'll are taking care of the girl's mama. And now you basically are babysitting the mama and the daughter. *Bruh*, you are getting used."

To add insult to injury, Marcus pointed out that the summit would be held during Valentine's Day and that I saved on having to do anything special with Mina being out of town. Mina was not the sentimental type who stood on ceremonial or traditional pomp and circumstance. As an example, she doesn't like to be given cut flowers because she considers them a dead or dying gift or gesture.

The second week of February while Mina was out of town, every lawyer in our office was attending a week long briefing on the Multi Polar World. Multi Polar World is an analysis of global macro-economic and geopolitical events and trends. It's a broader look at the global economy.

The buzz around the office was that the firm was looking to outsource some of our work to a company in Bangalore, India. That would ultimately lead to position cuts for us. I had been reading in *Business Week* magazine that legal services were being performed in other countries in an effort to cut cost. So I couldn't say that I didn't see it coming.

Mr. Kubiak held the position of operations manager for the firm. He called me in to his office and had me close the door. He started our impromptu meeting with complimentary, even glowing remarks about my work and rapport with clients. Then he said something that I took as a backhanded compliment; "no wonder your billable rate is so high." He followed his statement with a light ingenuous chuckle which made me uneasy. It shouldn't have. The law firm makes a lot of money from my bill rate and customer satisfaction. I thought that would be in my favor.

He continued as an aside, "Do you have any best practices documented on how you review contracts? You know - any personal techniques you could share."

"Not really."

"Sure you do. Don't be modest. Go back to your office and jot down a few things. Create something and be ready to review it with me by the end of the week."

"What would be the purpose?"

"He put on a plastic smile, "let's just call it knowledge sharing."

After ten comfortable years with the firm, I felt an urgent sense of concern about my job and my income being in jeopardy.

"SOMEBODY'S KNOCKING AT THE DOOR"

Brianna stepped right in to Mina's shoes while she was out of town. Actually, Brianna could afford to do more, with her not having to leave the house to go to work. When Mercedes and I came home, dinner was waiting for us. Mercedes helped in setting the table, where she used her etiquette class training.

"Well, look at you being a little helper. Where'd you learn how to set the table?" Brianna remarked.

"Saturday school," Mercedes replied.

"How do you know what goes where?"

"To remember the order of the dishes and utensils, just say BMW; bread, meal and water," instructed the little girl to her mother.

Brianna's dinner table conversation was daily updates on her viewing of reality television shows like *Flava of Love,* and *Keyshia Cole: The Way It Is.* She was very animated and passionate in her storytelling which kept Mercedes and I entertained. She made our evenings relaxing and fun.

In fact, playing house with Brianna was almost too comfortable. Between all the women in the house; they looked alike, they talked alike and at times they even smelled alike.

The second night Mina was away Brianna came knocking on the door to the den while I was watching *The News Hour with Jim Lehrer*. The news report was on the growth of the global economy.

"Are you okay?" She asked, "It seems like something's on your mind."

"Life is all."

"I heard that. Anything specific?" Brianna pried as she came and sat next to me on the sofa, within the boundary of my personal space. The scent of her own caramel and butter cream lotion mingled with my breath of air. She placed her hand on my knee.

"Nothing that I feel like sharing."

"Oh. If it has to do with my niece I understand. Just *cuz* we family don't mean we always get along and see eye to eye on everything. Sometimes she can be a little full of herself. She forgets who's the oldest and she don't respect who I am. You know what she had the nerve to tell me?"

She didn't wait for me to answer.

"She said she forgave me for messin' around with Ty. The only thing that she want is that I 'don't have him up in y'all house when y'all not here.' Who does she think she's talkin' to like she's MY mama? I'm an adult. Can you believe she said that?"

"Yeah, because that's what we agreed on."

"I see." The knee-jerk pulling of her hand from my leg let me know what was to follow. "Well I guess I see who runs things. No wonder she gets to go wherever she wants, leaving you at home." She stood and began walking away, stopping and turning back toward me as she reached the door. "You might want to thank me you know."

"For?"

"Think about it. If Ty and I weren't messing around, who would he be trying to get with?" Again, without waiting for a reply, she left and left me with something to think about.

Not wanting to call Mina to tell her about my possible job loss and to learn if there maybe any truth to the threat of Tyriq trying to get back with her, I called my cousin Emily instead.

"*. . . A WINDOW OPENS.*"

I told Emily what I suspected was happening at work.

"So what are you going to do about it?" She asked.

"What do you mean, what am I going to do about it? What can I do?"

"I mean you do have options and this didn't just sneak up on you. This has been happening in almost every industry."

"This I already know."

"Then you shouldn't be at all surprised."

"I'm not surprised. I am worried about not having a job."

"Well, worrying will get you nowhere."

"And to think I called you for support."

"I am supportive. I've seen this happen here too. I have a team in India and Brazil that I'm responsible for. Those teams replaced workers here. You don't think that bothered me at first?"

"At first; you mean that you condone off-shoring?"

"Matthew, I don't agree with it as a public policy. I do understand it from a business perspective. Businesses are doing this to stay in business and to make money. For some it's a cost saving, for others, sure it increases their financial margin by using lower wage resources."

"All the while they're putting American's out of jobs."

"That is an unfortunate byproduct, true."

"Well your cousin may be an unfortunate byproduct."

"Like I asked, what are you going to do about it? Are you going to wait for them to tell you that you're out of a job or are you going to get ready for your next opportunity?"

"What opportunity?"

"I don't know Matthew. It's either the next one that comes along or the one that you make for yourself."

"That' a lot easier to say, than to plan for."

"No it isn't. That's your problem, you haven't planned for this. You weren't prepared and you should have been. Hold on for a minute."

When Emily came back to the phone, she read to me two book titles, *Dig Your Well before You're Thirsty* and *Good is not Good Enough*. She recommended that I read them both. She then told me about a professional networking website Linkedin.com.

"You might also think about getting some additional certification or getting your Master's degree, she offered. Then lastly, "have you told Mina."

"No I haven't. You're the first person that I've mentioned it to. I haven't even told my parents."

"You know Mina and I are planning to hook up while she's out here."

"And don't you mention anything to her, okay?"

"Oh you don't have to worry about me saying anything. But as soon as you know for sure what's going to happen, you need to tell her."

"Right."

Valentine's Day morning, Mercedes handed me a handmade card when she got out of the car as I dropped her off for school. In the office, Ruby the office socialite and cheerful inspiration came around delivering Lindt® chocolate to each of the lawyers. She had on a red dress, with a sparkling jeweled heart broach.

"So what romantic plans do you have for your wife," asked Ruby.

"My wife's out of town."

"Aw, that's so sad. How'd you let that happen?"

"She's on a business trip."

"That's such a shame. Well, I'm sure you'll make it up to her when she comes back."

"I suppose."

Waiting for me in my email inbox from Mina, was a blind copied email with Subject: "Holy Valentine's Day" which I'm sure she sent to a number of people. That was her way, to include others in her giving. In the body of the email, it read:

"For God so loVed the world,
   That He gAve
      His onLy
         BegottEn
           SoN
              That whosoever
     Believeth In Him
      Should Not perish,
     But have Everlasting life." John 3:16

When my cell phone rang I was hoping it was Mina, but the ringtone immediately let me know that it wasn't. The caller was Natalie. I didn't know how I felt getting the call from my ex on Valentine's Day, especially before getting a call from my wife.

"Hello."

"Happy Valentine's Day, sweetie" Natalie greeted.

"Thanks, same to you."

"You don't sound like a happily married man on the most romantic day of the year."

"I could same the same about you or you wouldn't be calling me, now would you?"

"*Touché.* But let's not spar on this lover's holiday."

"Need I state the obvious?"

"What, that we're not each other's lover? Of course we're not. I figure that since we're both in the same situation, we could provide each other a little comfort."

"How are we in the same situation?"

"Well, my man is out of touch. And your woman is out of town."

"How did you know Mina was out of town?" There was a pause before, "I . . . called your house and the woman who answered the phone told me. She thought I was calling for your wife and volunteered the information. I didn't bother to correct her."

"That would have been Mina's aunt."

"So, with that, does that make you available for lunch or dinner?"

"I don't think that would be a good idea."

"Oh, I'm sorry. This would be about business."

"Business, what sort of business?"

"I'd rather talk about it over a plate of pasta."

We met for an extended lunch at Peachtree Center's *Azio* Italian restaurant. It had been at least six months since I had last seen Natalie. It was an unseasonably warm day in February, even for Atlanta. This allowed for her to wear a slimming dress, showing that she had retained some of the weight she gained from when she was pregnant. The extra pounds on her didn't look bad. I didn't let on that I still found her attractive. Nor did I respond to the kiss she gave me on the cheek when she greeted me.

Despite the opening; the rest of the lunch went without incident or a hint of any romantic overtone. The business that Natalie wanted to discuss was the possibility of me working for Pennington and Pennington Law Firm as a contractor, on the AT&T and BellSouth acquisition. She said that I could earn up to $5,000 a week working in a premerger Clean Room, reviewing the propriety contract discussions involving logos and trademarks.

A Clean Room is where proprietary information is shared between companies undergoing an acquisition or merger. No documents or information is allowed to leave the room. There is security and officials who monitor the coming and going of anyone assigned to work in the room. Natalie had all but assured me that I would be selected to work with her firm. If I took her up on her offer, I would need to take time off from work at my office. I didn't know how I would swing that.

"Quiet Storm"

It's a warm night and the rain is falling steadily. I have the bedroom windows open, no lights on in the room, listening to the raindrops find rest wherever they land. There is no rhythm to the drops. I'm desperately searching for something to keep my mind off of my job, Natalie and Mina. I don't want to think about anyone or anything. I simply just want to be brain numb. At 10:30, the phone rings. It's Mina.

"Hey *Babe*. Happy Valentine's Day." She cheerfully greeted.

"Same to you."

"Wow. What's up with you sounding all dry?"

"Long day."

"Miss me?"

"Yeah. It's raining here."

"Oh it is? I wish I was there."

"I wish you were too. So how's the summit?"

"It's great!" Mina exclaimed followed by a rundown of the notable and influential women she's met.

"I'm glad you're enjoying yourself."

"Aw, you don't sound like you're glad. You do miss me don't you?"

"I said I did."

"Maybe this will make you feel better. Look in the bottom of my nightstand."

Doing as asked, I found in the nightstand on her side of the bed a box wrapped in heart decorated paper. Inside the package were a stylish Kenneth Cole® watch and a single pair of Hanes® cotton boxer briefs. The one pair of briefs was what remained from a two pair package.

"Thanks."

"You're welcome. I bet you thought I didn't get you anything didn't you?"

"The thought had crossed my mind."

"Well I know you better have something nice waiting for me when I get back."

"I will, me" I joked. Actually, I bought Mina an exquisite 18-inch strand cultured black pearl necklace from Danbury Mint.

"Yeah right."

"Uh, what's up with the open package of draws?"

"You don't like them?"

"They're cool, but there's just one. Who did you give the other one to?"

"Guess?"

"Tyriq."

"WHO? Why you say him?"

"You said guess."

"That's not funny."

"I'm not laughing."

"Are you serious?"

"Nah. It was just something . . ."

"What?"

"Never mind."

"Un uh. What?"

"Something that Brianna said . . . about Tyriq still being interested in you."

"SHE SAID THAT?"

"Not directly. She implied it."

"You know what; she's going to have to get her ass up out my house if she's going to be trying to bring shit up in it."

"Maybe I took it the wrong way. But that doesn't explain where the other pair of draws is. So where are they?"

There was an uncomfortable silence. Even the rain had stopped I was beginning to feel sorry that I asked.

"I wanted to have you near me on Valentine's Day."

"Then you should've . . . Mina . . .?"

"Yes."

"What are you wearing?"

"Guess?"

Mina had me hold on the line when a message came across with a photo file attached. It was a reflection shot of her with her back to a mirror, wearing nothing but a pair of boxer briefs. I will always remember our first act of virtual intimacy.

"THE WRITING IS ON THE WALL"

By the end of the week I had met with the firm's operations manager, Mr. Kubiak. The meeting was frustrating at times with Kubiak being a pedantic individual. He wanted a detailed explanation of everything he didn't understand, which was practically everything with him not knowing anything about what it was I did in researching and reviewing the terms and conditions in the protection of logos and trademarks. After the long meeting his remark was for me to flush out my documentation so that someone with the same level of knowledge as he would be able to benefit from it.

I presented my best company smile and said, "Sure."

As soon as I reached my office I looked on the firm's intranet website at our extended leave of absence policy. The policy stated that I was eligible to take three months off without pay. I was looking at my options if I were to work under contract in the Clean Room with Natalie.

"DEY KNOW"

Mercedes and I were wrestling on the floor when the house phone rang. When Brianna answered, it reminded me that I didn't ask her about Natalie's call. Then again, Natalie said that she didn't leave a message. Brianna handed me the phone with a disapproving look on her face. I trapped Mercedes in a leg scissor hold while I took the call.

"Hello." I initiated the call.

"Hey *cuz*," Emily responded.

"What's up?"

"I just dropped Mina off at the airport. She wanted me to remind you to pick her up."

"Yeah, like I'm going to forget."

"Hey, don't shoot the messenger. Matthew, I really like her."

"She's okay.

"I mean I really do. We were up all night just talking. She was being herself from what I could tell; being open and honest about her life. She was funny and down to earth. I really like her."

"Uh, do you want to marry her?"

"I'm just saying that she is nothing like Natalie."

"You got that right. Hold it a second.

'Sadie, do you give up?'"

"No" answered the little girl barely making an effort to get loose.

"Okay Emily, I'm wrestling with a munchkin."

"Tell her I said hi. How is Sadie? Mina told me things are a little tense around there now with her mother staying with you."

"It's been interesting." I dart a look at Brianna who was looking right back at me as if she sensed that she was being talked about.

I released my willing captor from my leg hold. Mercedes actually protested as I began to let her loose. I tell her that I'll be back as I get up off the floor and finish the call in another room. There was a look of obvious disappointment on her face.

"I'll be right back." I assured her.

Leaving Mercedes in the den, unhappily with her mother led to my next point of conversation with Emily. I told her Mercedes was always under foot and had become clingy to me since her mother arrived - even when Mina was present. Emily said that the girl saw me as a neutral and safe choice instead of having to choose between the two women in her life. That way she didn't have to disappoint either Mina or Brianna. I agreed.

Emily returned the conversation to her praise of Mina and how far she had come in progressing her life and career. She had gone from college dropout, working as an office mail clerk to going back to school and getting her degree and now operating her own non-profit program. Then Emily joked that if I didn't watch out, that I would have a little Natalie on my hands.

"That's what I'm afraid of."

"Oh come on, I don't think you have to worry about that. Mina is too down-to-earth for that to happen."

"Well I hope she stays grounded."

"Hey but you know what *cuz*. I know you think of her as a jawbreaker, showing little emotion. I just want you to know that she does have feelings."

"Why, did she tell you something?"

"Like I said, we were up half the night. We bonded."

"What did she tell you?"

"I'm not going to say exactly. Did she mention having dreams?"

"Not recently."

"Then I didn't either."

"Emily."

"I will tell you this, she's worried about Mercedes."

Just then I looked up and spotted Mercedes peaking around the door frame at me in the kitchen. I give her a head nod to come in. She runs and jumps in to my arms.

"WE'RE IN THIS LOVE TOGETHER"

It's raining, cooling the breeze blowing through the open window. I'm sitting up in bed pretending to read a magazine, when I'm stealing glances at Mina who's lying width wise across the foot of our bed. She's wearing the other pair of cotton boxer shorts that she bought me for Valentine's Day. The actual sight of her in the tightly stretched material is better than what I had imagined while we were on the phone. I'm looking forward to the expected "Smurf Sex" we will soon be having. That's the kind of sex we have until we are both blue in the face.

Mina is shuffling through papers she brought back from the summit. She stops at a free sheet of paper and reaches for a pen. Then I hear, "*Dayum!*"

"What," I inquired.

"I'll tell you in a minute. Let me ask you some questions first."

After she asked me a series of lifestyle and health related questions about me and my family's history, she performed some calculations on the sheet of paper. Then she looked at me with a worried stare. I return the look, dumbfounded.

"What?" I asked.

She tells me of this life expectancy survey she took at the women's summit, which she just gave to me. According to the U.S. National Center for Health Statistics, the average life expectancy in the U.S. for people of all races is 76 years. The first variable of the survey is a plus or minus of years based on race and gender. For black males, there is an initial subtraction of 11 years. That was what brought about the "*dayum*" remark. The only group that received an addition of years was the white female. Mina's survey result was that she would live until she was eighty. I on the other hand would die at 60.

Mina balled up the survey and tossed it in the trash. She climbed on to my lap, straddling and facing me.

"*Babe*, I want you to make a doctor's appointment and get a complete check up." She directed.

"Honey, I'm fine."

"I don't care. You are not going to leave me, do you understand me?"

"I hear you."

"*Babe* I want you around until we are old enough to have Social Security sex."

"And what is that?"

"That's where *you* get a little each month."

We laugh as I pulled her close to me and gave her a passionate kiss. In return, she gives as good as she gets. Mina is one who isn't to be outdone. Our mouths slide across one another's. At one point our teeth hit. We stop and laugh again.

"So let me ask you something." I interrupted. "Are you saying it's okay for you to die before me?"

"Hell yeah."

"SHOULDA BEEN THERE"

We were eating lunch at Mable's Barbeque and Smoked Meats restaurant on Snapfinger Road in Lithonia. I was having my favorite dish on their menu, the BBQ Ribs, with Texas toast and banana pudding. Mina and Mercedes were sharing a BBQ pulled Chicken sandwich and fries. The two of them love the restaurant's Uptown drink, which is a mixture of tea and lemonade. Brianna was stuffing her face with wingettes from her platter order.

We were all enjoying our meal when I noticed a couple of young women sitting at a table across the room were eyeing us. I nudged Mina and asked her if she knew them. She said no, but that didn't stop them from coming over to our table.

"Hi. We're sorry for interrupting you, but my friend and I wanted to know if this is you?" The one who was speaking showed Mina a photo in *rolling out* magazine. The photo was a group shot of women at the Black Enterprise Women of Power Summit.

"Oh my God, it is!" was Mina's reaction, settling the curiosity between the two women. Mina went on to point out some of the influential women in their community, who asked her to join them in the photo opt. She then told the young women about her financial education program, and they signed up on the spot. The topper was when one of the women asked Mina to sign their *rolling out* copy. At first, she giggled at their request until she saw that they were quite serious. She signed it.

Maybe Emily was right. Maybe Mina was another Natalie in the making. The good aspect of that possibility was that Mina could achieve whatever goal she sought. The bad side was I had already experienced how success can change a person as it did Natalie. When we first met, Natalie had aspirations to becoming a lawyer to champion the ills of our society, especially for the underclass. It didn't take her long to learn that handling corporate A&M law pays more than civic lawyers get paid championing causes for justice. Her becoming an acquisitions and mergers lawyer hardly does anything for the man on the street. In fact, the results of some of the work that her family's firm performs, puts people out of jobs and out on to the street looking for new jobs.

Unlike Natalie, Mina has always desired to work for or head her own non-profit agency as she is on track to achieve. My fear would be that Mina's success would make her lose focus on what she initially intended to do with working with the underserved. Maybe there was another fear of mine. With the way things were going, she would continue to achieve and grow in opportunities. While I was on the brink of losing my job, I would no longer be the respected bread winner.

"GUILTY PLEASURE"

It was a welcomed night out for Mina and me. We were getting dressed for a black-tie event. Here, I'm going to admit to a guilty pleasure. I enjoy watching my wife put on clothes. One would think that I would like the opposite, meaning watching her strip. That's okay too, but to watch her dress is more of a turn on for me, because of the finicky care she takes to make sure everything is just so.

After a long hot shower, she stood naked before the full length mirror. She began smoothing cocoa butter gel body oil over her arms and legs. Her medium brown skin reflected wherever light hit it. I became envious when she slathered hands full of the gel over her butt cheeks, igniting her natural moon glow. Her over the shoulder glance revealed an impish smile on her face, saying more than words.

She went to her dresser drawer and pulled out a matching black lace bra and panties. Before putting them on, she took her underarm deodorant and stroked it under her armpits then across the pubic hair just below her navel. She then slips on her undergarments. A few spritzes of Hanae Mori perfume on her inner thighs, across her midriff and up to the nape of her neck.

This night, for the first time, she would get to wear the luxury black pearl necklace I bought her. To match the pearls, Mina had her fingernails and toenails tips painted black, instead of her usual white French tips. To top it off, she puts on a knee length black cocktail dress with a plunging neckline. She's glamorous and gorgeous.

To accompany her, I wear a double breasted black tuxedo, white French cuffed shirt and a black bow tie.

"DON'T ASK. DON'T TELL."

The ASK ME Foundation had reserved a table for ten seats at the Atlanta's Business League's Women of Vision Annual Dinner and Midnight Ball. The event would feature recognition of Atlanta's Top 100 Black Women of Influence. After the fine dining and the evening's program, the night would end in a DJ orchestrated dance ball.

Mina was in rare form all dressed up and feeling the effects of two white wine spritzers. When she's being her natural self, is when I find myself most in love with her. She's not always as gentile or politically correct as she could be. She's the one I want at my table at a boring event.

"*Babe*, look at that." Mina pinches me on my arm to get me to look in the direction of a woman in a green sequin dress. "Now she knows that she shouldn't have tried to get in that."

"I know you aren't going to sit here and talk about people," I rebuked.

"I'm just saying that she should have known before she left the house that that dress was too tight. Look, I can tell if she's an *innie* or an *outie*."

"A what?"

"Look at her navel. She's an *outie*."

I had to laugh at my *baby's* observation.

"Do you think she look good?" Mina points out a statuesque woman with a pretty face, down the back hair, in a fire engine red body hugging dress.

"Now why are you asking me if she looks good? If I answer either way, I could be in for a long night of more questions. If I say 'no,' then you'll know I'm lying because she obviously is attractive. If I say 'yes,' then you'll ask what I like about her and if I would go out with her if she asked me. Then you'll be tripping . . ."

"Hold up Mister King." Mina interrupted. "I don't have to play games. It wouldn't bother me one bit if you like her - well, maybe it would - because that's a man."

"Get out of here."

"You get out of here."

"How do you know?" I ask with an equal amount of astonishment and skepticism.

"Adam told me."

"Who's Adam?"

"Adam's apple," Mina let out a burst of laughter and began pounding the table.

Upon closer inspection, she turned out to be right. The person in the red dress was indeed a man in a red dress. I was impressed with my wife's keen eye of observation, at the same time I was disturbed by being fooled.

At that point, Mina would playfully nudge me with, "go ahead tell him that he's attractive," she says with a husky voice.

"You're silly."

"It's okay *babe*. Now I know what I have to worry about with you."

"And what's that."

"Well, not that you'll get caught cheating on me with another woman, but with a . . ."

"Shut up. No more wine for you."

"Don't be mad at me."

"Whatever Mina."

"Hey, isn't that your ex over there?"

Following the direction of Mina's gaze, I find Natalie and her husband being seated at a table across the room from ours.

"Yep."

"Wow, she looks nice."

"Don't start Mina."

"What? She does."

"You women kill me the way ya'll always complimenting each other."

"And what's wrong with saying that she looks nice?"

"Nothing."

"She does, doesn't she?"

"Yeah."

"Yeah . . . would you get back with her if you weren't married to me?"

I look at Mina to read her face.

"I'm just kidding," she said right before punching me.

"I hope so, because you don't have to feel threatened by Natalie." I offered.

The toothy grin quickly left Mina's face. I immediately knew that I had said something wrong. When her eyes narrowed before she spoke, I braced myself.

"Threatened by her! Why would I be threatened?"

"Nothing. That's exactly what I . . . I . . . was just saying . . ."

Mina leaned in to me. "I'm getting ready to go to the bathroom. You *watch me* as I walk across this room. Then you tell me what I have to be threatened about, okay."

She didn't wait for an answer before she stood from the table. With every deliberate step and accentuated swing of her hips, she reminded me of how fortunate I was to be with such a confident woman. Sitting two tables away was a guy who was watching Mina's exit from the room. He turned to look back at me. When our eyes met, he offered a sheepish grin.

"MOVING ON UP"

The latest honoree as one of Atlanta's Top 100 Black Women of Influence was Mrs. Natalie Pennington-Peel, Esq. The Atlanta Business League presented her with a glass sculpture titled *Moving Up* from the famed Frabel Studios. As it was read by the presenter; "This abstract sculpture called 'Moving Up' was fashioned in molten boron crystal glass to denote the perseverance and indomitable spirit required for the achievement of difficult goals.

"I've known Ms. Pennington since she was a little girl. She's come a long way from Stuttgart, Arkansas. As the pretty face and talented mind of your family's law firm, you serve as a beacon of light to encourage and inspire other young women to strive to achieve. We present you with this sculpture as a show of our appreciation. Thank you."

Natalie said a few words in acceptance of the crystal statuette She returned to her seat, where her husband was noticeably missing With the formalities of the event out of the way, it was time to party The DJ got it started with Cameo's *Candy*, to get the hustle crowd on to the dance floor. So to the dance floor Mina went, with a few of the ladies from our table.

Mina loves to dance, where I'm more the wallflower. She studied dance in college. Since we are now married with child, we hadn' many chances to go out on the town dancing; maybe to a wedding reception every now and then.

On the dance floor, Mina steps, twists, turns and when it's called for, she takes a dip to rapper Flo Rida's *Low*. It's difficult to take my eyes off of her. After a round of the *shuffle*, the *electric slide* then came

the *Cupid Shuffle*. Mina and company came to the table and pulled
me out on to the dance floor. They got me in line to learn the steps.

♪*To the right, to the right, to the right, to the right / To the left, to the
left, to the left, to the left / Now kick, now kick, now kick, and now kick /
Now walk it by yourself, now walk it by yourself / (Let me see you do) /
Down, down, do your dance, do your dance (yeah yeah yeah yeah)* ♪

The DJ slows it down a taste with Snoop Dogg's *Sensual
Seduction*, giving Mina and me a chance to dance one on one. To an
even slower pace comes the duet between Cheryl Lynn and Luther
Vandross, *If This World Were Mine*. I place my arms securely around
my baby's waist and hold her close to me. She in turn accepts the
move in close and lowers her head in the crook of my neck. We sing
to one another each respective part of the song.

At some point we stopped singing and stopped dancing. We
stood in the middle of the dance floor holding one another so tightly
that we could feel one another's heart beating. Hanae Mori perfume
filled my nostrils.

We kissed. We're pressed, pushed penetrated the other's
opening. Mina's tongue was exploring my mouth. My tongue was
giving directions. Tongue met tongue - tip to tip - darting in and out
between the lips. We were lost in the moment and in to ourselves,
until a light tap found my shoulder.

"Excuse me. Mind if I cut in," asked Natalie.

Before I could speak, Mina offered "Um, sure. Congratulations
on your award."

"You'd thought that they could have afforded a bigger one,"
Natalie scoffed. Oh my, what a beautiful pearl necklace," she
complimented.

"Thank you. My husband gave it to me."

"Matthew always did have good taste."

"And *that's* why he's *my* husband." Mina wiped her thumb
across my lips as if to remove lipstick that she doesn't wear. While
in my direct line of sight, she mouthed "Watch me" before she walks
off.

With Natalie in my arms, I think to myself that men will never fully understand women.

"Cute girl," Natalie offers.

"Yes she is."

"On one hand I can see why you like her, but on the other, she's nothing like me."

"You're right, she not." She pulled back from me to look me in the face. "I see that her smart mouth is infectious."

"Whatever Natalie. You're pretty bold to cut in on our dance you know."

"Yeah, I thought about that as I was walking over. You only see stuff like that in the movies, I said to myself. Then I decided what the hell. Life is one big movie."

"Where's Vernon?"

"Around."

"So are you trying to make him jealous?"

"Not exactly."

"Then what exactly?"

"It will be interesting to see what his reaction will be. So what will . . . I'm sorry, what's her name again? "

"Mina."

"Mina. So what will Mina have to say about you dancing with your old girlfriend before she stole you away?"

"Trust me, if she would have had a problem with it, we wouldn' be having this conversation."

"I see. So, let's change the subject. Have you given any though to coming to work with me in the Clean Room?"

"A little. My job at the firm may be going away, offshore."

"Oh really. I'm sorry to hear that. How's Mina taking it?"

"I haven't told her yet. It's still not definite, but I can read the writing on the wall. It's getting to be about cost, margin and cheape bill rates. But I need to look after my family."

"Maybe this is a good thing. Coming to work with me will show what you can do on your own, either working as a contractor or an independent consultant. Maybe it's time for a change."

"DON'T ASK. DON'T TELL II."

In line at the coat check room to retrieve our coats, I noticed Natalie and Vernon near the door leaving the hall. Vernon was on his cell phone and Natalie stood by impatiently waiting. The look of annoyance on her face was easily readable. I wondered if the hold up phone call was payback for Natalie taking time away to dance with me. While standing off from his wife and talking on the phone, he still managed to keep his eyes fixed on Mina and me.

Vernon was one of those pretty boys. I mean almost too pretty. I know it's wrong to think this way, but I didn't like him because of his looks. His type is given chances and opportunities handed to them largely because of their appearance. They don't have to work hard for anything, especially when it comes to having whatever woman they want. Ironically, it's the women who want these pretty boys more than they "the pretty boys" want the women.

I don't know what that said about Natalie.

"So what did your girl have to say out on the dance floor?" Mina asked as she looks at the landscape along I-20.

"Not a whole lot. She did say that you were cute."

"I mean she's not blind."

"You're something else."

"Yes I am and I'm not stupid. I'm a woman first and I know she still wants you."

"What *chu talkin'* about?"

"You know."

"No I don't. I thought you weren't threatened by her, Miss Watch Me."

"I'm not. I'm just telling you. Men are so naïve about this kind of stuff. When something goes down, then all you can say is, 'I'm sorry or I don't know what happened."

"Now what are you talking about?"

"I'm just saying, *whatchoself.*"

"I'll admit that Natalie is bold and goes after what she wants, but she's married. I'm married . . ., we're married."

"Like that means anything; especially with that man of hers."

"What about Vernon?"

"He's not right."

"Not right how?"

"Did you see his cell phone?"

"Not really."

"It was a red Blackberry."

"So."

"How many men do you know have red cell phones?"

I could only count one.

Spring

MARCH

"HOPE SPRINGS ETERNAL"

"PEOPLE ALWAYS HOPE FOR THE BEST EVEN IN THE FACE OF ADVERSITY." This saying is from "An Essay on Man," by Alexander Pope. Hoping for the best is the expectation that each spring season will bring about new life, when in most cases it is the same old situation just warmed over. Nothing has changed much, just started anew for another go round.

That was my mindset as I stood in the shower, washing away the remains of the night's sleep and mentally preparing for the work day ahead. True, it was a new workweek, but the work was still going to be the same. As you can imagine, safeguarding corporations from intellectual property, copyright and trademark infringements isn't something that you go in to work kicking up your heels about. And in my particular case, that responsibility of my job was slated to be moved to some person half way or more around the world.

I still had not told Mina. The stability of my job was who I was for the past ten years. I went in to the legal field because Natalie suggested it and I knew that it was for sure a part of her future and that possibly meant that I would be too. I did choose contract law over litigation because I didn't care for the confrontational aspect of fighting a case in court.

My job established the comfortable living and home that my family and I enjoyed. Other than volunteering at the ASK ME Foundation once a month, I didn't know what else in life to do.

Standing at my dresser, I catch the sight of Mina asleep reflected in the mirror. From there, I can hear a light snore. From beneath the blanket and hanging over the side of the bed is her shapely calf. I found myself fixated on it. So much so that I walked over to her side of the bed and sat on the floor next to her dangling leg. In an impromptu moment I leaned in and planted a kiss on the front ball of her foot, close to the toes.

I can't say that I didn't see it coming, because I did. Mina's leg quickly recoiled like a snake preparing to strike and then she did. With the same swiftness that she pulled away, her foot returned with a kick that landed flatly on the bridge of my nose. It was an animated cartoon moment as I saw twinkling lights about my head.

"Oh baby I'm so sorry. What *were* you doing?" Mina sat up in the bed addressing me.

"I don't know. I had this crazy idea and . . . well."

"What idea?"

"Never mind, I said that it was crazy." The stars began to fade.

"Oh, are you okay?"

"Yeah."

"Are you sure? *Com'ere.* Let me kiss it." She leaned down and planted a soothing kiss where her foot last was felt. I supported her upper body weight in my hands. Cupping my face with her hands, she tilted my head upward to receive another kiss, this time on the lips. I allowed the support of her body to give so that she fell into my arms and on top of me on the deep pile carpeted floor. From there we both gave in to a crazy idea and made early morning love.

"SEX IN THE OFFICE."

I guess I should have been embarrassed that Ruby could see that there was something different about me when I walked into the office. Instead, I was pleased that someone saw evidence of unpredictable, carefree sexual romance in my life with my intelligent, pretty, sweet-tempered wife. For a while there, our bedtime activity had been less than thrilling. That's if we had time for it.

Since returning from the women's summit, Mina began online studying for certification by the International Coach Federation

Someone she met at the summit convinced her that in her line of work that she should become a certified life coach. This would help the ASK ME Foundation to receive more federal grant money for her program. So after spending all day at work, she'd come home and get on the computer to conduct her studies.

So yes, I was delighted in the chance carnal encounter to start my day.

Natalie called to tell me that she sent some legal documentation for me to review on BellSouth's registration protection of the bell symbol and the associated blue color trademark. Though she assured me that I would get the contract to work in the Clean Room, a brush up on the company would be just in case someone wanted to put me through an interview. She sent the information to my personal email account using "Cinnamon Red," a new address and screen name of hers. Cinnamon Red was the color of the last bra and panty set that I saw her wearing, the only thing that she wore under a raincoat the night she came over and seduced me. She claimed creating a new screen name was to help maintain the subterfuge of sending me the proprietary information. Her electronic signature in the email was "talk to you later sweetie."

"A SUNDAY KIND OF LOVE"

After returning home from early church service, it was lazy afternoon time. The weather was a fair 71 degrees and we had the windows open in the family room. Brianna was asleep on the love seat with a blanket over her. Mercedes was lying on the floor with headphones on, watching *The Goonies* movie on a portable DVD player. Mina and I were laying on the couch, at opposite ends, heads to toes, her back to my front. Her footie covered feet are tucked beneath my side. While she's reading one of her study guides in preparation for an online exam, I'm watching Game 7 of the Celtics and Hawks first round playoff series.

It was one of those afternoons that most don't appreciate until it's long past. My job worries weren't on my mind, because Bishop Bronner's message on *The Anatomy of Success* temporarily put my mind and spirit at ease. Seemingly we were in the calm, with no threat of a storm on the Doppler radar.

"UNQUIET STORM"

It's Monday morning and the first day of school Spring Break for Mercedes. I've taken paid time off from work to stay at home with her. Even though I don't have to go into work, I'm wide awake. At 5:00 in the morning a streak of lightning cracks the black sky causing rain to escape. It's followed by a loud and jarring boom. Mina lets out a gasp.

I'm lying on my back with an arm behind my head. I feel Mina's hand reach across the bed in search for me. She grabs a hand full of my pajama shirt and pulls herself over. Throwing one of her legs across both of mine, she then props her body against me. With her near hand she begins to pat my face like a blind person trying to make out features. She grips my chin then slides her hand to my throat, gripping it in a gentle choke hold. I place my hand on the naked thigh that's draped across me and start to firmly massage it.

"I knew you were awake" she says.

"Sure you did."

"I did."

"And if I wasn't?"

"I don't know." She tightens her grip around my throat with her long slender fingers.

"So what, now you're going to choke me to death?"

"Why would I want to do that," tightening her hold again.

I grabbed her by the wrist and pulled her hand from my neck and we begin to playfully wrestle. Mina doesn't easily give in to being penned to the bed. Our fingers are locked together and we straight arm joust. I was upright on my knees with Mina's legs around my waist with a scissor hold. The bedcovers are being tossed about and pillows fall to the floor. To the unknowing observer, it would appear that we were fighting, which accounted for the loud SCREAM from Mercedes. The little girl's shrilling cry scared the *bejesus* out of both Mina and me.

"STOP HURTING HER!" Mercedes shouted.

Like track sprinters out of the blocks, Mina and I raced to the little girl's side, who was noticeably trembling. Mina threw her arms around Mercedes and embraced her into a loving hug, pulling her head to her. Mercedes returned the hug.

"It's okay Sweet Pea. We weren't fighting. We were playing, that's all." Mina tried assuring her.

Just as I turned on a nightstand lamp, Brianna rushed into the room.

"What the hell was that? And what the hell happened in here?" Brianna demanded, looking past me and at the tossed condition of the bed.

"Matthew was fighting Mina." Mercedes answered.

"Honey, I told you we weren't fighting. We were playing."

"PLAYING?" Brianna says with skepticism.

"Yes playing" I say for all to hear but directed at Brianna.

"What are you doing up so early?" Mina asked Mercedes.

"The rain woke me up. I mean the thunder."

"It's okay baby. It woke me up too. Oh sweetheart, everything is okay . . ."

While Mina comforts Mercedes, I begin straightening the bed and picking the pillows off the floor. With her arms folded across her chest, Brianna's stare shifts between her niece and daughter hugging, to across the room at me. There is a look of doubt in her eyes and a judgmental look at that. Mina pays her no mind and brings Mercedes to our bed and climbs under the covers with her. I sat on my side of the bed, not wanting to crowd them at the moment.

A look back to the bedroom doorway, I see the look of contempt that was on Brianna's face has changed to a softened sadness. I could only imagine that the gaze of sadness stemmed from seeing the child she gave birth to, being motherly comforted by Mina. Without an utterance, she turned and left the room.

"RED LIGHT, GREEN LIGHT, STOP LIGHT, GO"

Due to the success of her FREE program, the executive director of the ASK ME Foundation asked that Mina incorporate the other social advancement programs into one. The *Dress for Success* and *NOW (Needs over Wants)* program will be under her direction. The health and legal programs would remain stand alone. Along with this reorganization, the ASK ME director was positioning Mina to be the spokesperson for the foundation. That meant Mina's absenteeism from home would become more noticeable. It also meant that Mina's visits to her satellite office at the Easywick Townhomes would be cutback.

Following one of my vacation day routines, Mercedes and I ride into downtown Decatur to enjoy a Starbucks beverage and brew. Brianna asked if she could tag along. Quite naturally, I say "sure." With my fortune, I find a parking spot near the Decatur Library on Sycamore, adjacent the town square. We get out and walk to the city's downtown square. We come to the corner crosswalk.

"Remember; look both ways before crossing the street, be sure to watch for the light." I tell Mercedes.

"Sadie baby, forget watching the light. Like my mama used to tell me, 'you better watch for the cars *cuz* a light won't hit you.'" Brianna emphasized with a smirk.

Our eyes met and reluctantly agreed. I conceded that Brianna's mother's wisdom was correct, though I didn't appreciate the challenge. Continuing on our route through the courtyard Mercedes went right and Brianna and I were going left around a lamp post.

"Sweet Pea, don't split the pole. It's bad luck. Come back around, this way." Brianna warned.

"We don't teach her superstitions."

"It's not a superstition."

"Then what is it?"

"It's bad luck."

After getting our drinks, we go to the courtyard square where Mercedes plays in the water mist sprayed from a fountain. We watch Mercedes from our seats on a bench.

"Brianna, we need to get something straight. Mina and I are raising Sadie with our beliefs and our morals. So I would appreciate it if you would not interfere with your superstitions."

"Interfere. I don't care what you or Mina thinks. I gave birth to that child. If I can tell her something that might save her life, then I will."

"We have legal custody of Sadie."

"That's a piece of paper. We have blood between us."

An elderly woman walking her dog comes by and stops to speak.

"Isn't it going to be a beautiful day?" She forecasts.

"Sure looks like it." I respond.

Looking over at Mercedes, the woman remarks, "Oh what a cute little girl. Is she yours?"

"Yes, she is. She's our little Sweet Pea." Brianna answered. Then she took her hand and stroked my arm.

"What a lovely family. My children are all grown and out of the house. It's just my husband and I. Oh, and Sebastian here." The woman went on with remarks about the Pomeranian, but my mind was on Brianna's comment and hand gesture.

On the way to drop Brianna off at Easywick, a light rain began. The sun was still shining through the sparse clouds. Just before getting out of the car, she turned to Mercedes who was sitting in the back seat.

"You know when the sun is shining and it's raining, the devil is beating his wife." She said to the child, while looking at me.

"Why does it rain when he beats his wife," asked Mercedes.

"He's whopping her so hard, that he's working up a sweat. Hey sweetie, do you want to come with me and hang out?" The woman asked in a saccharin sweet tone.

"No ma'am. I want to stay with Matthew."

"You sure?"

"Yes."

Brianna put on a playful pout, "Okay then *pooty* head." Turning to me, "You are a good man Matthew King. Where were you when I needed a good man?"

"I suppose I was somewhere waiting for Mina and Sadie to come along."

"I see. Remember, what goes around, comes around."

"Meaning?"

"She took you from somebody. The same could happen again."

"I don't think so. No one is going to take me away from my family."

"Oh really, and what about vice versa?" Brianna posed, before opening the car door. "There's no such thing as happily ever after, except for in fairytales," she taunted through the open car window, while tugging at her blouse to cover her exposed muffin top hips. Hips overlapping the top of her size too small sweat pants with the word "Juicy" printed across the back of them. She walked toward a few guys standing on the sidewalk. Tyriq was among them. When she reached him, his welcome was slapping a handful of one of her flabby butt cheeks. In response, she pretended to object and swung on and misses him.

I didn't bother to look toward Mercedes to sense her reaction. Instead, I put the car in gear and drove away. Through the rear view mirror, I could see Brianna following the car pull out through the gates of Easywick Village, left on to Candler road. The only sound from Mercedes during the short ride to South Dekalb Mall was her singing the call letters of the jazz station.

♫ *One oh seven point five, double-u- jay zee-zee* ♫ , she crooned. My heart swelled with fatherly pride each time I heard her perfect pitch rendition of the radio station's tag. We went in the mall and watched a movie at the Galaxy Funplex 12. Afterwards, we had something to eat in the malls' food court. Sitting across the table from me, Mercedes was dunking her chicken nuggets in her barbeque sauce.

"Hey, can you keep a secret?" I asked.

"You mean about mommy Brianna." There was no innocence in her voice.

"Uh, no. With Mother's Day coming up, I want to buy some things for Mina and I want you to help me. But I want to keep it a surprise, that's why I need to know if you can keep a secret."

"Oh sure, I can keep lots of secrets. Yep, like when Tyriq kissed Mina, because he says she's going to be his girlfriend again."

"WHAT KIND OF FOOL AM I?"

Jealous thoughts raced through my mind, playing out scenarios of Mina and Tyriq engaged in a kiss and whatever else may have followed. The image of him grabbing her behind brought on an instant headache. Did she object or did she playfully swing at and miss her old *bad boy*. Was that it?

Despite the fact that I loved and provided for Mina and Mercedes, did she still desire the thrill of the street life that she once lived? Because she still worked out of the Easywick Village, she had not left the sometimes dangerous environment and its crime element. While I know that she respects my nine-to-five job, it didn't have the often romanticized excitement of Tyriq's street hustle.

Mina would often defend the hustle lifestyle that many of her clients lived, especially those of the women. She pointed out that a woman may do some *shiesty* and socially degrading things, just to feed and take care of her children. She stated that "everyone is in pursuit of the American Dream of happiness. It's just that some people will have to go through a hellish nightmare journey to obtain it."

That being said, I asked myself; what dream was Mina pursuing that would cause her to throw herself back into the arms of a street hustler. Did Brianna know? To avoid the answers I went through with my gift buying with Mercedes. I didn't want to let on to her how upset I was over the news of the kiss.

"THAT'S NOT WHAT FRIENDS ARE FOR"

"SAY WHAT," Marcus yelped in to the phone, when I told him the news. "How did you find out?"

"Let's just say a little bird told me."

"Do you believe this little bird?"

"I don't know what to believe."

"Do you know the guy?"

"Her ex, from where she used to live."

"Wait a minute; isn't he *splitting* the aunt between the thighs?"

"Yeah."

"Oh, he's a *bad dude*. I mean I've done sisters before, but not at the same time, *knowhaimsayin*."

"That was very noble of you."

"You know." He missed my sarcasm. "So are you going to fire her?"

"Man I'm having a hard time getting my head wrapped around this whole thing. In my heart, I just don't think she would do something like this."

"Ask her ass and find out *fo'sure*."

"And if I'm wrong?"

"What if your little bird is right? I'm going to be *fo'real* with you *knowhaimsayin*. I always thought ole girl was too much *pork chop* for you to *bite off*."

"Oh really, and you failed to mention this because . . ."

"You didn't ask me."

"I think the preacher did when you were standing next to me as my best man at the wedding."

"It's too late then, *bruh*. Look, I was proud of you for being able to *hit it* in the first place. But to make her *wifey*, you took it too far *knowhaimsayin*?"

"I'm listening."

"*Dawg*, I'm your boy so I got to tell you. I never really cared for her ghetto-bourgeois ass. Just *cuz* she's cute, she thought her shit didn't stink, *knowhaimsayin*. I mean she makes a good *Baby Girl*, *knowhaimsayin*, the next best thing to a *wifey*, but . . ." Marcus went on about his issues with Mina and women like her.

The women like her all turned out to be those who wouldn't give him the time of day even if they were wearing a watch. I listened to him, not really finding any positive or useable advice, until the very end of his diatribe.

"Just promise me you won't go out like your boy from the building by killing her, then *yo'self*. No woman is worth that and there's plenty of fish in the sea. And not all of them have to be a catfish. Hey, a sardine will do in a pinch, *knowhaimsayin*." He offered and laughed.

"No worries about that," I confirmed. "I don't know what makes guys snap like that."

"I'll tell you what it is."

"Oh, please do."

"You ought to already know. It's being a black man; the hardest job in America. I'm talking about getting up every morning, going to work for life; being a black man with no time off *knowhaimsayin*."

"Maybe."

"This is what I'm *sayin'*. The man is against the black man, society is against the black man. The last straw will be when his woman turns against him. If he loses her respect then what else does he have? With her power alone, she can turn family and friends against him." He testified.

In Atlanta there had been reported in the news a rash of murder-suicides involving women and their husband or boyfriends. One of them took place in the very courtyard of the Bank of America building where I work. Around 3:30 in the afternoon, a man killed his alleged girlfriend, then turned the gun on and shot himself. I remember Mina calling me on my cell phone wanting to know if I was all right. She obviously cared about my well-being. Then why would she cheat on our relationship?

"THAT'S WHAT FRIENDS ARE FOR"

"SAY WHAT," my cousin Emily yelled in to the phone, when I told her the news. "How do you know?"

"Mercedes let it slip that Mina and Tyriq were kissing and that he wants her back."

"This took place in front of the little girl?"

"I don't know. I didn't question her any further."

"Have you confronted Mina about this?"

"No."

"Matthew, I don't believe it's true. If it did happen, I'm sure Mina squashed it."

"Marcus didn't have any problems believing it."

"Marcus. He's an idiot. What are you listening to him for? Do you trust Mina?"

"Yeah."

"It doesn't sound like it."

"I do."

"Then act like you do. And trust *me*, I've talked with Mina and I know she loves you. If you got issues with her being around this Tyriq, then ya'll need to deal with it. Who you need to be worrying about is . . ."

"Hello. Emily."

"I'm here. You need to get Marcus out of your ear and keep him out of your house. As long as I've known him, I've not heard you mention him being in a serious or long-term relationship. So by what authority does he have to speak from?"

"Um, so Emily; how's your man?" I quipped.

"Excuse me? Oh I know you didn't try to call me out. You know what; I'm going to let that one go."

"I was only joking Emily."

"Funny, ha-ha and that is the problem with *you men*, you take relationships with women as a JOKE. And another thing; it's not my fault the men who are interested in me aren't secure enough with themselves to deal with me. Yes, I am pretty, with two degrees, with a six figure salary. Men are afraid to step to me because they don't think they can compete or measure up. And I don't intend to lower my standards to make a man feel good about himself."

"Are you finished?"

"You pissed me off with that remark."

"I see. But I think there's something else going on with you."

"There may be. I really like Mina and I can't believe she would cheat on you. I see you guys as hope for successful black relationships."

"And I hope you don't take this the wrong way. When you say that you see us as hope, do you mean hope that you will find someone?"

"Not everyone in life is meant to have a mate."

"You don't believe that do you?"

"Maybe. Maybe not. What I do believe is that you need to find out what's going on with Mina."

"Yeah."

"I mean it Matthew and the sooner, the better. *'Be angry, yet do not sin, and do not let the sun go down on your anger, lest you give the devil an opportunity.'*"

"You sound like my moms when you go quoting scriptures."

"Good. I've been hearing about those killings down there in the ATL and I don't want to hear about you on the news."

"Not a problem."

"I mean it's because you men are emotionally immature. Y'all don't deal well with rejection and being hurt."

"It's not about being hurt. It's about being disrespected."

"Same thing."

"DON'T LET THE SUN GO DOWN ON ME"

Mina strolled into the bedroom where Mercedes and I were watching television. She spoke, displaying the high cheekbones that run in her family. She presented a grinning smile below a cute pug nose. Though I recognized all the familiar facial features, I didn't see Mina in the same way.

She asked Mercedes how her day was and what she did. I nudged the child with my foot and gave her a look to remind her to keep our shopping spree a secret. She mouthed "I know" and performed a hand gesture buttoning her lips. I said to myself, "yeah you know." From there, the child runs down our day's activity mainly giving details to the movie that we saw, *Chronicles of Narnia*. Mina climbs on to the bed and lies against me and strokes her hand across my stomach.

Brianna walked into the room and plops herself on the end of the bed. As she sits, the sweats that she's wearing pull down and expose the crack of her behind. Mercedes reacts with "Ewww."

"What, like we all don't have one" Brianna retorted.

"We all don't go around showing it to the world." Mina responded.

"Don't hate."

"Oh, from where I'm sitting, it ain't cute."

"Somebody thinks so."

No one remarked. It was time to change the subject.

"So how was work today," I posed to Mina.

It was a good day for her. She helped two of her clients to become employed agents with LiveOps. LiveOps is a virtual call center, hiring people to work out of their homes taking merchandise orders over the phone and entering them using computers. Through the programs of the ASK ME Foundation, Mina helped the clients pay the enrollment fees for the background check and with supplying them with refurbished computers.

"Why don't you get me one of those sit down jobs?" Brianna asked.

"Because you never asked," answered Mina. "The last time you talked about getting a job, you said that you wanted to go to school to become a medical assistant or was it a dental assistant. No, I know; you were going to be a massage therapist."

"Listen up Miss *Shitdiddy.*"

"It's *siditty.*

"That's exactly what I'm saying. I know what it is, and when it comes to you, it's *shitdiddy.* I'm getting sick of you thinking you're better than me and throwing it in my face."

"Nobody's throwing anything in your face. And I don't think I'm better than you."

"Because you ain't."

"That's what I just said."

"All of y'all can kiss the crack of my ass." Brianna announced before she got up and stormed out of the room. Mercedes laid at the end of the bed with her hands covering her ears. Mina looked to me with a "can you believe that" look on her face. Neither facially nor verbally did I offer any comment.

"IT'S ALRIGHT"

It's the Friday morning before Mother's Day. I'm dressed for work and about to leave the house. Mina is in the den, from where I can hear music playing. The song being played over and over is *Alright* by Ledisi. I've heard the song enough to know that the lyrics are of a woman confused, overburdened and struggling with her current life's situation, yet she says that it's "alright."

Mina is sitting in front of her laptop, with a stack of papers next to her. She's sighing heavily. That told me that she was either balancing her checkbook or paying her bills online.

"Hey, I'm about to head out." I announced.

"Okay."

"Don't forget Sadie's after school Mother's Day program tonight."

"Um hmm. Wait, say what, when?"

"Sadie is having a program after school today, at seven o'clock."

"Right."

"When is your mother coming to town?" I asked.

"Is today Friday? Damn. She snatches her cell phone and began clicking away. "Dang." She threw her phone on the couch seemingly, out of frustration.

"What's wrong?"

"My mother's flight arrives at four-thirty and now this after school program."

"You should be able to make it from the airport by seven."

"It's not that."

"Then what is it?"

"I'm supposed to go to this small business networking mixer at the WAMU banking center on Edgewood."

"For what?"

"My friend Dominique, she's a senior business banking specialist there and she's going to introduce me to one of the staffers at *rolling out* magazine. She's recommending me to write a financial management article that will appear weekly."

"And that's more important than attending Sadie's program?"

"Yes, I mean no. Matthew, they're going to pay me for each article."

"Is that what this is about, money?"

Mina went on to tell me about the drain on her finances since Brianna moved in. We never talked about it in details, but Mina had been financially supporting her aunt for the past four months. Whether it was buying her clothes or slipping her an allowance so she would have some money of her own. Obviously, our shared household expenses increased, but we just contributed what was needed to cover the higher grocery and utility bills.

For Mother's Day, Mina was flying her mother to Atlanta for an all expenses paid weekend of pampering. That included a Mother's Day brunch, where singer John Legend was performing, followed by treatment at Spa Sydel and then dinner at P.F. Changs restaurant. Brianna was expected to tag along.

"And every time I turn around, Mister Faulkner is asking me to be somewhere for him. Rumor is that he's going to make me the assistant director."

"But you were just promoted." I pointed out.

"I know." There was a long pause. "You ever feel like you're just . . . going?"

"What do you mean?"

"I mean that you're just going and doing?"

"And?"

"That's just it; *and* I don't seem to be getting anything done, *and* if I do, there's someone else who wants something else."

Not wanting to do the obvious man thing and try to provide a solution to her problem, I offered her my own view of having a lot to choose from on my life's plate.

"Mina, sometimes I feel like a man responsible for four or five kids on a swing set. Each child wants me to push them higher and higher. I had to realize that not all of them will be as high as the other at the same time. At times, one will not be as high as any of the others, until I get to them. The reality is, one of those kids is going to be sad, but it can't be helped."

She looked at me oddly, before saying "Thanks so much, *Bookie*. That really helped and I understand that fully. I . . . I, just thought that I was the only one." She stood up from sitting on the couch and walked over to me. She draped her arms about my head and neck.

"No *babe*, we all have a lot on our minds." I spoke to her.

"So can you pick my mother up from the airport?"

"What about Sadie's program?"

"Take my mama with you. I'll be there as soon as I can make it."

Mina didn't make it to Mercedes' school recital. She texted me that she couldn't get away from her meeting, because she was being video interviewed, on behalf of the ASK ME Foundation. Mercedes was disappointed, along with the rest of us. After the program, I took Mina's mother, Brianna and Mercedes to dinner at Depeaux Cajun restaurant in downtown Decatur. The two sisters, had crawfish and catfish Po' boy sandwiches. Mercedes and I had plates of grits and shrimp. It was good eating.

Despite her absence from the table, Mina was the topic of conversation. I began with trying to impress upon her mother how busy she'd become with work. Her mother followed with stories of Mina always being one who went out of her way to help others. She acknowledged that her compassion for others stems from way back. She also went on to tell stories of how her daughter was a scrapper when she was a child.

"Tweety didn't back down from a fight. Oh no. And it had nothing to do with her having big brothers at home. She went in to a scrap with the intentions of winning. That's how she is about whatever she comes up against," remarked the proud mother.

"If you ask me, she was just bad," Brianna interjected.

"How are you going to call her bad? My baby could always stand on her own when she needed to," said Rosemary, the older sister.

"What *chu* trying to say?"

"I'm not trying to say nothing. I said it."

"Said what?"

"That my child knows how to take care of herself and handle her business. But this isn't the place or time to talk about this. Not in front of the child." The matriarch sister ended the conversation without missing a chew.

Mina climbed into bed at 1:00 in the morning. She cuddled up next to me after spending the last few hours talking with her mother and aunt. I was watching the USA Channel and one of the original episodes of *Law & Order* from its first season. "*In the criminal justice system, the people are represented by two separate yet equally important groups: the police, who investigate crime; and the district attorneys, who prosecute the offenders. These are their stories."*

"Ooooo, which one is this, it looks old?" Mina asked.

"It is."

"Who's the *brother*?"

"I call him the *brother* with a scowl. His character name is Paul Robinette, one of the original ADA's."

"Oh look, he wears his pen on the outside of his suit coat pocket like you."

"That's where I first saw it. I liked the look. He's sort of the reason I started collecting pens."

"So you've been watching *Law and Order* for a long time."

"Yep."

"Hey *babe*, I want to thank you for today."

"No problem."

"I mean it. I really do."

"Okay."

"What's wrong, wrong with you?" She asked, I supposed from sensing my indifference.

"Nothing; I'm just watching TV."

"Okay." She moved over to her side of the bed and eventually went to sleep.

"HAPPY MAMA DAY"

After church service at Word of Faith, we drove back to the house. The women had plans to go out to dinner. I was invited along, but respectfully declined. They begged and pleaded, except for Brianna. It didn't make a difference. I was looking forward to lying on the couch, watching a NBA game. I did call Marcus to see what he was up to and told him that I had the house to myself. He had plans to do the same as me, so he invited himself over. Just before he arrived at my door and at the end of the first quarter of the game, I received a text message from Natalie. The message read, "I miss you." The cell phone was still in my hand when I answered the door.

"Yo' what's up boy?"

"You tell me. You're the one who's been MIA." I reminded Marcus. The last time he had been to the house, he and Mina had one of their verbal bouts that left Marcus leaving with his proverbial dog's tail tucked between his legs.

"Man, I've just been where I'm wanted . . . and that ain't around here, with your girl. So what did she say about messin' around?"

"I haven't asked her yet?"

"What *chu* waiting on?"

"Proof."

"What about your little bird?"

"Hearsay."

"What I hear you saying is that you're scared of your girl and the possible truth."

"No, I think that's you."

"Yeah, whatever *dawg*. Let me show you something."

I followed Marcus into my office where he turned on my computer without saying much about his intentions. As soon as the system was booted and I grant him access, he quickly types a mySpace.com address and there is my wife, with the screen name "Q' Mina." The music of Goapele's *Closer* played. Marcus pushed back from the desk to give me full view.

"Is this the dude?" Marcus pointed out Tyriq's photo among Mina's Top Friends.

"Yeah, that's him." I confirmed. I did not let on that it was my first time seeing Mina's MySpace page and learning of its existence. Besides Tyriq, I recognized a few others of her Top 12 Friends, which included her friend Synea and some of her Clark Atlanta alums. A quick browse of Mina's photo albums I found plenty of her and me and of Mercedes. Those of us had varying captions from our pet names of "Bernie and Wanda," "My *Bookie* and his *Boo*," "M&M" to

"King and Queen." Mercedes was appropriately identified as our princess.

Clicking to go to Tyriq's page, it featured his online business of hip hop gear, products and t-shirt designs. As his wallpaper, models are wearing a t-shirt with "Obama '08 for All Our Sake" printed on it.

Of course, Q' Mina was in Tyriq's Top 12 Friends.

"Soooooo, why ain't you on your girl's page?" Marcus asked.

"Because I don't have a MySpace page."

"LOOK WHAT THE COP BLEW IN"

Loud voices were coming from the front of the house. To be heard over all of them was Mina, "*I AM NOT TRYING TO HEAR THIS RIGHT NOW.*" Marcus sat up straight in the chair, as if his mama just came home and he was caught watching porno. His eyes transfixed on me as if asking, "What do I do." I chuckled at the worried look.

"What?" He asked.

"You should see the look on your face."

Mina rounded the doorway into the den. She took one look at Marcus, "Oh *GREAT.*"

Her attitude was obviously hot and bothered. She had on a pomegranate, pink and gold puffed-sleeve blouse and a tight fitting denim pencil skirt that accentuated her curvaceous hips. The pink, jeweled-toned T-strap stilettos gave a flattering defined form to her calves. She was hot looking in more ways than one. In her new outfit she was looking sexy.

Coming right behind her were the rest of the women, including little Mercedes, who came in and hopped on the couch next to me. She spoke to Marcus. It was clear that Mina was upset and her mother and aunt were trying to console her. Their attempts were failing.

"What's going on?" I asked.

"Mommy Mina got a ticket," answered Mercedes.

"Thanks tattletale." Mina smiled at the little girl, who giggled in response.

"A ticket, for what?"

"Her cell phone," Brianna offered up. "But why did he have you get out of the car?"

"He was just being an ass." Mina defended.

"Watch your mouth in front of the child." Rosemary instructed her daughter. Marcus seemed to like seeing someone have that kind of authority over Mina.

"Sorry Sweet Pea. But he was."

"I told you that you ought to fight it, because I didn't understand why he pulled you over in the first place. And he didn't write you up for any moving violation. I think he was just working on filling his quota. He saw a car full of black women and took a chance that he would see a cell phone sitting out. I mean, I think it's a good law and all, but not if they're going to abuse it."

The cities of Atlanta and Decatur passed an "In Plain Sight" law, citing drivers if pulled over for a moving violation, for having their cell phones in plain view without evidence of a hands free device. The first ticket is $100, with an additional $200 increment for each subsequent ticket.

"How much was the ticket?"

"Five-hundred dollars."

"Damn, five-hundred." Marcus exclaimed. All eyes became directed at him. "My bad."

"Mina, we've talked about this. I told you . . ."

"Matthew, I'm not trying to hear this. I don't need 'I told you so, not right now."

"You know what, you're right. I have something better. Sit down." I asked my wife.

"Matthew!" She protested, rolling her eyes.

"Will you just sit down? Mercedes, come with me?"

We returned with a gift wrapped box that I kept hid in the shed behind the house. Inside were a number of items that I thought would reflect on her personal, private and professional life. The items ranged from gift certificates to Spa Sydel and to another one of her favorite restaurants, an 18kt gold-plated Tweety Bird pendant with Swarovski® crystals, to a Bluetooth hands-free device. Both Mina and her family partook in rejoice as my wife opened individually gift wrapped packages to learn what was inside. I included something for Mercedes as well, because she is as every bit a part of my life as Mina.

Marcus sat idly by, with an occasional headshake of disbelief, I supposed.

"When did you do all this?" Mina asked.

"When Sadie and I were on vacation."

"Oh Sweet Pea." Mina reached out for the child to give her a hug. Then she came over to me, "I love you *Bookie*. But why?"

All eyes were focused on me. Mina's and Mercedes' sparkled. Brianna's were squinted. Rosemary's were wide. Marcus looked on with one eyebrow raised.

"Just because."

"Priceless"

Everyone had gone to bed, or so I thought. I was in my home office filling out a $20 rebate form for Mina's Bluetooth device, when she walked in with a big toothy, gum showing grin on her face. She was wearing the t-shirt and the men's undershorts. The light perfumed scent of clean musk invited itself in my nostrils. It was welcomed.

"What are you doing?" She asked, coming to a stop at the side of my desk.

I told her.

"But you put your name on the form. They're going to make the check out to you."

"Uh, that's because I bought it."

"Yeah, but you bought it for me."

"Right, what was I thinking?" I was being beyond sarcastic, but then wasn't the time to pit men's logic versus women's. Not with her standing there with raised nipples pressed against the t-shirt's cotton fabric. "When the check comes in, I'll sign it over to you."

"*Alrighty* then," she quipped.

We moved over to the couch and began a marathon conversation, like we used to as best friends.

"Matthew, you always go over and beyond. – Jimmy Choo shoes five-hundred dollars, Bratz dolls twenty-five, dinner at Benihana's thirty-five dollars, massage package at Spa Sydel two-hundred and fifty, but you *babe*, PRICELESS.

"The highest expression of love is to give without expecting, and to accept without exception. Not just things and/or money, but rather the best of you, your heart. Because too often people fail to really understand true expressions of love. – Remember, people don't care how much you know, until you show how much you care I love you, *babe*." She devoted.

We climbed under a blanket slung over the back of the couch Held tightly and closely in my arms, she felt safe enough to confess.

"You know the cop that gave me the ticket? It wasn't the first time I'd seen him. He's *hit on* me before. The first time was when was coming out of P.F. Changs and I hear this loud grunt and I look up and it's him. He follows me to the car trying to run his game and when I *floss* my wedding ring in his face. He says 'then I'm going to have to write you a ticket.' I say for what. He says, 'for carrying a concealed weapon in those pants,' talking about my *behind*. I tell him that he needs to go. He waits until I get in the car, still trying to run game. I pull out my cell phone to pretend to call someone and then he walks away. As soon as I pull off, here he comes behind me with flashing lights. That's when I got my first ticket." Mina's body stiffened as she came to this point in the story. She mentioned that after the incident, she stopped going to one of her favorite eating spots for a while for fear of running into the cop.

I wondered why, if she could confess the unwanted advances of the cop, why she couldn't come clean about Tyriq; which made me think that the operative word would be *unwanted*.

"Did you pay the ticket?"

"Yes."

"Do you have a copy of it?"

"No. I threw it away once I paid it. Why?"

"This officer needs to be reported."

"It ain't worth the trouble."

"I think it is."

"Babe, I want to be able to tell you stuff without you wanting to try and fix it. That's why I am so grateful that you are my friend so that I can talk to you about things."

"Like?"

"One of my clients called me because her teenage daughter was picked up for prostitution. Did you know that if a girl born in America is picked up for solicitation, she's hauled off to jail? But if a girl the same age is from another country and not a US citizen, they will take her to some child protection shelter and find someone to adopt her. Our system is "*F'd*" up." She stated distressed.

At the conclusion of our conversation, Mina climbed on my back and I carried her to our bedroom. Under the bed covers, we wrapped around each other.

"Mama told Brie that she needs to get a job and move out. Brie told her that she was waiting on God to bless her with a job and she was going to remain strong in her faith. Mama hit her with '*Even so, by itself, faith without works is dead.*' She said that 'Faith is an action word. It means doing something, taking action, moving and staying the course until it is done. It always requires waiting and patience. But you must walk the walk.'" Mina repeated her mother's words.

"What did Brie say to that?"

"She said that we were ganging up on her. I've decided to let her move in to my townhouse."

"She doesn't have a job, how is she going to **pay** the rent?"

"I'll get her on with LiveOps. That will get her some money coming in."

"You're good people."

"Whatever." She commented, punctuating it by giving me a shove.

"TOUGH LOVE HURTS EVERYONE"

Once the news was given to Brianna, our house became a lot quieter. Conversations were on a must-have basis. The oldest person in the house walked around acting as childish as the youngest one in the household. She pouted. She mumbled comments under her breath, enough to be heard, yet not understood. She had issues with not having things her way.

Despite her aunt's attitude, Mina gave her tenant at the time, a 30 day notice to vacate the property. In my office, we setup a workspace with a computer for Brianna to begin working as an agent for LiveOps, taking orders. Our efforts were met with a little appreciation from Brianna. As told to me by Mina, her aunt didn't see us as merely helping her, but as helping her move out of our house. The reality of the situation was, it was a little of both. Mina felt badly about the turn of events. I reminded her that tough love hurts both ways; the giver and the receiver.

"DIG YOUR WELL BEFORE YOU'RE THIRSTY"

At work, Mr. Kubiak called me into his office to tell me to immediately begin working with a lawyer in India on some of the contract reviews that I had sitting on my desk. In a month, he wanted to have all contract reviews handled by the India law office, which had a New York office. We would maintain the client facing intake role, explained Kubiak. He eluded that eventually we could just facilitate conference calls with clients and the offshore lawyers.

"The objective is to have only the most valuable people in Atlanta or New York, and the others in India," said Kubiak who is obviously a proponent in sending low-end work to the cheapest labor locations. "Lawyers are service providers. We are not gods" he added.

I said "okay."

As soon as I returned to my office, I called Natalie, who was more than glad to hear from me.

"Oh my God, I thought the receptionist was mistaken when she told me who was holding on the line. How are you doing sweetie?" Natalie embellished. I immediately felt like I had made a mistake.

"I was wondering if that work in the Clean Room was still available."

"Your timing is perfect. There is a stack of resumes of candidates being considered. But there's no reason why yours couldn't make it to the top of the pile. Or I can make the whole pile go away. You know I'll make that happen for you."

"I wouldn't want you to do that, though I think I'm ready to apply."

"You don't sound like you want it."

"What do you mean?"

"You sound like you don't care one way or the other. I don't hear eagerness in your voice."

"What's to be eager about?"

"Matthew, attitude counts for a lot when it comes to applying for an opportunity. I'm sure your resume is impressive, but so are a lot of these sitting on my desk. Your attitude could make the difference between you and the next person."

"Then maybe I don't want it that badly."

"Look Matthew, I'm just offering some constructive criticism that's all. Times are getting tough in the job market. If you are going to start looking for work, you have to have the right attitude going in. What's going on over there at Buckmire-Williams and Meander is happening all over."

"How do you know what's going on?"

"I have sources. Like I said, what's going on there is happening at other firms. The thing is how are you going to react to it? Are you going to wait for them to send your job offshore, and then show you the door?"

"I don't think I'll have a problem finding a job."

"I'm sure you won't Matthew. But will it be doing something that you want to do or will you have to settle for a job just to pay your bills?"

"It doesn't make a difference."

"You say that now. Good things might come to those who wait, but not to those who wait too late." Natalie went on rationalizing why I should act right away and to be proactive about taking control of the direction my career. She sounded as if she genuinely cared what happened to me. Not once did she mention my family.

"Okay, I'll send you an electronic copy of my resume. If it makes it to the top of the pile, then so be it."

"Oh don't worry. You'll be on top, where you belong."

I sent Natalie my updated resume. She replied with a smiley face in her email and a request for us to have lunch. I responded with "sure."

I began choosing contracts to transition to the partnering law firm in India. I worked on the script to begin conversations with their lawyer. I filled out my request for an extended leave of absence readied for submission to Mr. Kubiak.

Now that I had a plan, it was time to tell Mina.

"HUSTLE AND FLOW"

The bedroom television had *The Game* on, another one of those drama-comedy shows that I don't care for, but that Mina likes to watch. She was sitting at her vanity applying Tea Tree Oil to her chin, which is prone to reappearing pimples. The strong scented oil permeated the room like bug repellant. I moved on.

I began emptying my pockets and placing my personal belongings on my dresser valet. It was at that last minute I was trying to think of how to tell Mina about what was happening at work and that I might be working with Natalie for several weeks in an isolated room. There was always the "good news, bad news" approach.

"Honey, I'm about to lose my job, but, I've got a new one working with my ex-girlfriend." I introduced.

"Say what?" She calmly responded.

I gave her the whole "Multi-Polar World is Flat" economic business spin in explaining why I might be losing my job. While Mina is a very intelligent woman, well read in the area of personal finance, she doesn't pay much attention to what's happening in the world at large. Most of her news updates come from the internet and sites like EURweb.com and NecoleBitchie.com. She may be in the room while I'm watching *The News Hour* or *This Week*, but she's not necessarily listening. Mina relies on me to keep her posted on current events, while I rely on her to keep me up-to-date with who's doing who in Hollywood.

It was her response to my news of working with Natalie that threw me.

"And you're going to be making how much," she asked while she inspected the recent eyebrow arching performed by her stylist.

"Possibly up to five-thousand a week."

"Oh hell yeah, you should get your *hustle and flow* on."

"And you don't have a problem with me working with Natalie."

"Un uh. Why, should I have a problem? Do you have a problem with it?"

"Weren't you the one who told me that she wanted me back?"

"Yeah, and?"

"Well, what if she does and she wants more than a working relationship?"

"You tell her that you have *more* than you can handle at home and I'm taking good care of *mines*. That's more than I can say for her." Mina went on with her suspicions about Natalie's husband. She then followed up with encouraging words about me working with Natalie and possibly starting a new journey in my career.

"*Babe*, I think you're going to do an awesome job working with *Miss Thang* and then that's going to open doors for you. You'll see." She stated.

"LUNCH AND LEARN"

It was a strange nervous feeling that I had meeting with Natalie for lunch. We met at the prestigious One Ninety-One Tower office building in downtown Atlanta, which is also where the Law offices of Pennington and Pennington is located. There was a recently opened upscale eatery in the building, where Natalie had reserved us a table.

I arrived early enough to see her come in the door of the restaurant. Natalie wore one of her signature Brooks Brother's skirt suits. This particular one had an unusually shortened skirt, exposing her shapely athletic legs.

When I extended my hand for a customary shake, she pushed it aside and hugged me instead. I should have recognized that action to setting the tone of our meeting. Instead, I enjoyed the comfort of being in her arms again.

After we ordered our food, Natalie handed me a leather portfolio, pulled from her attaché'. I recognized the portfolio's hand tailored leather stitching. It was the same as her Mawhobbi® *Sac de Femme* designed business attaché. I recalled her ordering it on the internet and it cost $600 plus.

"Nice." I complimented on the ledger.

"I'm glad you like it. It's yours."

"No, I can't."

"You can. The question is whether you will."

"This must have cost . . ."

"No more than one of those precious pens of yours. Go ahead they deserve each other."

I ended my protest and accepted the lavish gift. It would stay on my desk in the office. Inside the ledger was a copy of my resume with editing red marks and notations.

"It needs some revising," she offered. "I have a stack of resumes on my desk of applicants who are just as, and to be honest with you, more qualified than you. At least they present themselves that way."

"What do you mean?"

"Sweetie, you need to put on paper what sets you apart from the rest. Quantify your skills in a way that translates into dollars. Show how, through financial profit and loss prevention, you can be of value. If you can generate billable hours by increasing client revenue or show how you've saved your firm or clients from losing money, this will demonstrate your ability to add value. To just list your qualifications doesn't cut it anymore." Natalie went over the recommended edits she made to my resume.

During the course of eating, I was campaigning for a pity party about me losing my job to someone half way around the world. Natalie was having no part in it and rejected the invitation. She basically told me to *man up* and not take it personally.

"Honey, this is about cost management. Is Kubiak still the Operations Manager; because he's just doing his job for the partners to increase the profit margin with reducing the billable rate – for the same amount of work." She commented.

"But . . ."

"But nothing Matthew. This isn't about you, it's about money. Instead of being upset about it, you need to make yourself indispensable or more valuable to the firm. Show what you bring to the table that some lawyer in another country doesn't. Like when I passed the bar . . ."

"What? When did you pass the bar?"

"It's been about a year now. I thought you knew."

"Not a clue. Congrats."

"I guess Mina keeps you so locked up out there in Ellenwood that you don't have the chance to know what's going on in the rest of the world."

"No one has me kept locked up. I choose to be where I am." I said defensively.

"Okay. Anyway, I was tired of always being introduced to clients as 'here's our female lawyer' as if I were nothing more than a diversity token. I wanted to be recognized for more than being a woman. I've added another layer to my worth, being able to litigate."

"I'm sure your family is proud of you."

"They are."

"And your husband?"

Her facial expression changed drastically. "Who cares what he thinks?"

"I just thought . . ."

"He only cares that my making more money takes the pressure off of him to step up and be the man of the house." She laughed at what appeared to be a private joke.

"If you don't mind me saying, you don't sound happy in this marriage. The Natalie that I once knew wouldn't tolerate being in a situation where she wasn't happy."

"I'm not happy, but what else am I supposed to do? He's the father of my child. I want my son to have a male influence in his life. For whatever it's worth." Again she laughs.

"What about marriage counseling?"

"You know what . . ." she paused. What came next were teary eyes.

"I'm sorry. I didn't mean to get all in your personal life."

"That's just it Matthew, you're the one who belongs in my personal life. I know. I know. You've moved on and I should have to."

"Natalie . . ."

"No, I know it's wrong for me to still feel the way that I do about you. But I just can't help it. Whenever he used to touch me, I always pretended it was you."

"Natalie . . ."

She grabbed my hand that was on the table and began stroking it.

"I mean he was very attentive at first, making sure that he satisfied my needs. That seemed important to him. I'm not saying he's a better lover than you. He was . . . different." Natalie went on with intimate details of their sex life, all the way until the lack there of. The waning turning point seemed to have begun not long after the birth of their son. Natalie confessed that she had lost interest in sex for a while, but when she tried rekindling the fire, Vernon wasn't ready or willing.

"Could it be . . .?"

"What?"

"Could it be this other woman is offering him something that you aren't?"

"Yeah right. I'm sure she is; but I couldn't tell you what it could be. Then again, I have asked myself that question a few times when it comes to your wife. What does she have that I don't have?"

"Me."

"Okay, smart ass. Can you make the same claim; that you *have* her, exclusively?"

People kept posing this question to me as if they already know the answer.

"YOU CAN'T REPLACE FACE-TO-FACE"

Over the ensuing weeks, I sent my updated resume to Natalie, and put in my request to take a month-long leave of absence (LOA). Upon receiving my LOA request, Mr. Kubiak's line of questioning was motivated by whether I would complete the transition of my Quality Assurance review work to my Mumbai counterpart. I assured him that I could and would. Then I asked him about the future of my position with the firm.

"India has very talented lawyers," he said. "But it's a misconception that you can just send work there and it gets done. You need proper supervision and security. That's where you come in."

For two weeks I emailed a guy named Satish, who worked for a law firm based out of New York and Mumbai. I also held late night and early morning conference calls with him going over my process documentation.

Satish, 26, a lawyer in the litigation and research department in Mumbai, says he makes three times as much as he would at an Indian law firm. He was eager and hungry for advancement. Like anyone else should be thinking, Satish wanted to be successful in his job and career. He made me realize that somewhere along the way; I lost that drive and determination within myself as it came to my own career. I had become complacent and settled.

Buckmire-Williams and Maender's first client meeting where our Mumbai lawyers were engaged was a cultural challenge. The client was your classic southern style living grandmother and granddaughter tandem who were starting the Straight to the Heart Foundation and they wanted trademark registration for their logo. The logo consisted of overlapping hearts connected by a piercing arrow.

The conference call took place in our conference room where the two women, Mr. Kubiak and I were present. On the phone were two lawyers, Signesh in New York and Satish in Mumbai. The biggest challenge was the language barrier. Kubiak took the lead for the meeting, and then handed it over to Signesh. I was told to sit and quietly observe, to lend support if and when needed. Though Signesh sounded quite Americanized, because of his quick speech Indian accent, the two women kept asking for clarification and repeats of his descriptions and explanations. He clearly knew the legalities and technicalities of trade marking words, names and logos. But from my observation, he wasn't connecting with the clients and losing them with too much detail. Kubiak sensed it too.

When Signesh pointed out elements of the women's logo, I noted something while observing the two women. The younger woman Mary Elizabeth Levenger was holding in her hand a Parker brand pen. I recognized the brand from the distinctive arrow clip. The pen style I remember seeing featured in one of my Colorado Pen catalogs. The elder woman wore a sweater vest with a prominently embroidered arrow on the upper left breast area. I remembered something from my days of logo research and studies.

"Excuse me," I interrupted. "Miss Levenger, I couldn't help but notice your nice pen. It's a Parker® *Pearl and Black* model isn't it?"

"I suppose. My nana gave it to me for a graduation gift," the young woman admitted.

"Matthew now is not the time." Kubiak interjected.

"He's right," commented the elder stateswoman.

"And Ms. Rutherford, you wouldn't happen to be a member of the Pi Beta Phi sorority?"

"Why yes. We both are. How did you know that?"

"It's the arrow on your vest. If I'm not mistaken, it's a symbol of the sorority."

"Why yes it is."

"The arrow is always aimed up and worn on the left to represent the sorority's permanent place in a member's heart. I recall in my study of logos, that two of the members of the sorority used the arrow in logos of their companies' Parker® pens and Wrigley's® gum. So I'm guessing the arrow connecting the hearts in your logo is a representation of Pi Beta Phi for your foundation."

"Well mister . . ."

"King."

"Mister King, I'm impressed. You're absolutely right."

That was the extent of my knowledge of either the sorority or and the arrow connection. To keep their interest, I threw in the trivia knowledge that Wrigley's gum was the first product sold with barcoding, that Americans have chewed Juicy Fruit since the late 1800s and the added tidbit of the subliminal arrow between the "E" and the "X" in the FedEx company logo. After that I was empty, but it was enough to leave them all impressed.

At the conclusion of the meeting, Kubiak gave me a celebratory pat on the back. The young woman with the three hundred dollar pen and probably didn't know it, gave me a flirtatious wink. While shaking Kubiak's hand the grandmother commented, "you have a bright young man there. I look forward to working with him."

Later, Kubiak stuck his head in my office doorway with a thumbs-up *attaboy*.

After he left I was on a personal high. I called Mina, but it went straight to voicemail. I called Natalie next and told her what happened. She was overflowing with accolades and kudos.

"DADDY'S GIRL"

The house was quiet. Brianna was away, spending more time at the Easywick. I located Mina in Mercedes' room after one of their shopping trips to the mall. The room smelled sweet of Pink Pomegranate Punch body oil, I was told. The scented oil was part of the storyline of *Pinksta & the Polka Dotted Pinstriped Pants Wearing Princess*. Once they put away their purchases, Mina laid across the bed while Mercedes read the book aloud.

Pinksta is a little girl who is seeking to gain the attention of her father. To do so, each day she wears a pretty pink dress and matching tights to school. When she comes home she sits eagerly by the window waiting for her father to come home from work. The pretty pink dress is to get her father's notice, but what she really wants him to notice is that she is "smart too" and does well in school. Though he does adore Pinksta, her father spends more time with his sports car and her older brother. While patiently waiting for her father, Pinksta drifts off into a "Wizard of Oz" or "Alice in Wonderland" like fantasy.

As I listened to Mercedes read the story, I wondered if she and had any father daughter issues. I never tried to stand in as her father, other than by being part of the household and family provider. She calls me Matthew, where she used to call me "two daddy." I love her like she was my own. Lost in my own train of thought, I almost missed Mina's mood change. By the time Mercedes gets to the end of the story where *Pinksta wakes up and her daddy comes home and reads her report card*, Mina is sitting up on the bed rocking. As soon as the little girl finishes, Mina abruptly excused herself.

I remained in the room for a bit, discussing the mission from Pinksta's diary to *"Provide peace. Protect people and places on this planet."* The book promotes girls' empowerment. I smiled at how the mission symbolically aligned with the mission statement of and what essentially is what Mina implements in her social programs. Mercedes pulled out her school journal and wrote the mission in it.

I found Mina sitting on our backyard deck watching a deer grazing on our property.

"Hey, you okay" I asked.

"Yeah" she replied without looking at me.

"You sure?"

"I SAID *yes.*"

"Ooooookay," as I turned to walk away.

"Bernie," she called out one of her affectionate role playing names she has for me.

"Yeah."

"Have you forgiven anyone lately?"

"Um, not that I can recall; though I haven't had a need to either. Why?"

"Can you forgive someone?"

"If you mean am I capable of forgiving? I suppose. But my version of forgiveness may not be the same as most."

"Meaning?"

"If someone commits an act egregious enough that it begs my forgiveness, I let go. I let them go and by doing so, I let the act go. Then I'm done. I only hold on to the memory of the matter to serve as a lesson learned so not let it happen again."

"Is that forgiveness though?"

"It is for me."

"I believe you should forgive, but never forget."

"Sounds like we agree" I tell her.

"Thanks *babe*. Would you mind telling Sweet Pea that the deer is back?"

"YOU AIN'T MY DADDY"

When I walked into the bedroom, Mina was packing an overnight bag. My immediate reaction was to think if I had forgotten something, a conversation or plans to travel. Nothing came to mind.

"Hey, what's up? Where are we going?" I asked.

"I'm going to see my father for Father's Day."

"When did you decide this?"

"Today."

"Oh, so you were just going to take off without asking me?"

"Without asking you . . . you ain't my daddy. I don't need to be asking you."

"I didn't mean it like that. I meant, without asking me if I would mind or if I had plans."

"Don't worry; I'm taking Sadie with me."

"I wasn't worried about you taking Sadie. I mean it is Father's Day for me too."

"Well I didn't think you would mind. It's not like you're her *real* father."

I was stunned. The words hit me bluntly.

"WHAT! I'M MORE OF A FATHER TO THAT GIRL than her *real* father. I cannot believe that you just said that to me."

"Why you yellin'?"

"Why do you think?"

"You don't need to holler."

"Don't tell me what I don't need to do. What's going on with you?"

"Nothing."

"Nothing. Out of the blue you decide to leave and without telling me and you're taking Sadie."

"I just feel like I need to go home to see my father." She explained.

"What about Brianna? Is she going with you?"

"I don't know. I can't get in contact with her."

"So she's just going to be here with me?"

"Or wherever."

"What is this Mina? What's going on with you?"

"Nothing. I'm just going home," and that she did. Brianna showed up at the last minute and just in time to leave with them.

As soon as they pulled out of the driveway, I was on the internet buying a round trip airline ticket to Odelot, Ohio. My parents were both glad and surprised to see me. There was the expected onslaught of questions about where was the rest of the family. I told them as much as I knew and cared to share.

It was meant to be a quick weekend getaway visit. I wanted to get away from life's problem. Instead, I created more for myself. My mother was upset that I flew home for Father's Day and not for Mother's Day. I was sitting on my family's porch looking at the neighborhood that I grew up in. My dad came and joined me.

"I sent her two-hundred dollars to buy whatever she wanted. I called her before she went to church to wish her Happy Mother's Day."

"Son, you could have given your mother a two dollar bill for Mother's Day, but if you flew here from Atlanta to give it to her, that would have made it priceless. Now me, I know you didn't come home just to wish me Happy Father's Day. What's going on?"

That's all it took. I broke down and told my father everything real and imagined that was going on in my life. I told him everything from Mina's suspected affair to the possibility of me losing my job. I confessed that I was nearly at a state of despair and the only places where I could turn could possibly lead to more trouble.

Dad sat quietly while I spoke, until he had this to say, "It sounds like you're under attack."

"By what?"

"Whenever you begin to flow in favor, you will come under attack. It sounds like you're under seasons of attacks and summer is just around the corner."

"What does that mean?"

"It's about to get hotter."

My father began talking about the devil coming after people who are blessed and highly favored. I was surprised to hear my father talk about spirituality. This was more my mother's answer to everything. My dad said that he wasn't surprised that Mina and I were under attack because we made a good couple and we had done a godly thing by taking in Mercedes. Then he went on to praise Mina for her kind heart. I didn't know it, but she called my parents once or twice each month for no other reason other than to check on them. Dad didn't believe the implication of Mina's affair. He even got on me for believing it without proof.

"I've seen the way that girl looks at you and it's with love in her eyes."

"Something has changed about her, dad."

"What?"

"I don't know."

"Then you find out. Son, *what you don't deal with in your life, will deal with you.*"

"CO-MISERY LOVES COMPANY"

Sunday morning we went to church. The sermon by Reverend Lowdown was "Man Up." He touched on the stages of manhood – *male* is a matter of birth, *a boy* is a matter of age, *a man* is a matter of maturity, *a husband* is a matter of choice and *a father* is a matter of responsibility. He asked for all the men to become responsible.

After service I took my parents to an early dinner. My mother cheered up when I told her it was to celebrate both Mother's and

Father's Day. Both parents came along to drop me off at Odelot Express Airport.

Before boarding the plane in Odelot, I received a text from Natalie wishing me a Happy Father's Day. During a two hour layover in Cincinnati, I called her. It seemed like a harmful thing to do at the time.

"Hey Sweetie," she cheerfully answered her cell phone.

"Thanks for the text."

"No problem. So what did you get for Father's Day?"

I gave Natalie the honest update that I gave my father, minus the affair part. We spoke for practically the entire layover. It was a call of commissary for the both of us. While I sat in the airport without my immediate family, Natalie was at home with her son. Her Father's Day was spent very similarly to mine. She went to church and dinner with her father and family. After their dinner, her husband went in one direction and she and son went in another.

In the time we were on the phone, Natalie's mood and tone went through stages of fear, anger, blame, and shame over the forgone conclusion of the failure of her marriage. She admitted that they might as well be separated and that they were living a lie for the sake of keeping up appearances. She suspected Vernon was spending more nights and weekends with someone named Adrianne, one of his home inspection appraisers.

We listened and offered one another words of support up until my boarding call. It felt good to have someone to talk to who could relate to what I was feeling and going through with Mina. Also, though I was ashamed to feel it, I felt better knowing that Mina and I had not reached a point of irreconcilable differences. There was still hope for us.

I said goodbye to Natalie, she said "Thank you Matthew. I love you."

"PILLOW TALK"

Around two a.m. Mina climbed in bed smelling of citrus brown sugar lotion. She stirred in the bed and tugged on the covers until she saw evidence that I was awake.

"How are your parents?" She asked.

"They're fine and they said *hello*."

She went on to tell me about her trip. I heard her, but I was half listening. Something about her father's health failing . . . The woman taking care of him was more taking advantage of him . . . Our godchild was getting big . . . Brianna called Mercedes' incarcerated biological father to have her wish him Happy Father's Day . . . Before falling asleep, Mina vowed that her aunt was *trippin'*.

Summer

Brianna had moved in to Mina's townhouse in the Easywick Village.

Mercedes was enrolled in summer camp.

Mina was busily at work, becoming the new face of the ASK ME Foundation.

"HOW TO PLAY THE GAME"

I was getting my desk at work in order to take my leave of absence to work in the Clean Room with the Law Firm of Pennington and Pennington. Mr. Kubiak was calling me in to his office daily; wanting a status on how ready was Satish, the lawyer to who would be performing my work. With a smile I told him, "You'll know soon enough." He didn't seem to appreciate the comment.

Natalie invited me to visit her at the office. The visit would serve as a cursory informal interview. The furnished appearance of the Law Offices of Pennington and Pennington were posh compared to the conservative office in which I worked. They had dark colored deep pile carpet, oak doors, with matching desks and credenzas.

Natalie's office had a little softer touch in decorations and furnishings. On the wall right next to her law degrees and certificate for passing the Georgia Law Board, was a framed clipping from *Jet* magazine featuring she and husband Vernon on the "Love & Happiness" pages.

So Honored: Natalie Annette Pennington became the wife of Vernon Peel at New Birth Baptist Church in Lithonia, Georgia. The bride is a graduate of University of Florida. She is a lawyer for the Law Offices of Pennington and Pennington. The groom is a graduate of Morehouse College. He is a Mortgage Loan Officer for Regal Mortgage, LLC. The newlyweds plan to make their home in North Atlanta, Georgia. They honeymooned in the Netherlands Antilles.

She was a beautiful bride, makeup was impeccable. A funnier thing was the same could be said about Vernon. Seeing him in the photo clipping brought to mind a standup routine by Jamie Foxx, about how a certain kind of man would have to admit that the singer/entertainer Prince could be viewed as pretty.

There were but a few employees in the offices. That evening, there was an after-hours professional mixer being hosted by the prestigious law firm. I met briefly with one of Natalie's uncles about the Clean Room role. He and I got along respectfully when she and I were dating. Our meeting was more of a re-acquaintance with the exception of him telling me that the timeframe of the Clean Room could be up to six months. After our discussion he invited me to the mixer.

"Oh I hope you will come," Natalie pleaded. "Remember the old saying 'It's not what you know, it's who you know?'" she asked. "It no longer applies in Atlanta. Through networking it's not who you know, it's who knows you. You need to establish yourself as the subject matter expert of contract management. You need to be known as the go-to guy."

"I suppose. I'll just need to . . ."

"What, do you need to ask for permission from the wife" was the obvious taunt?

"No. What I was going to say was that I need to let Mina know that I will be late coming home."

"Oh, how sweet," were her words dripping in sarcasm.

"STAY CLOSE TO THE HERD"

My call to Mina went straight to voicemail. I then called Brianna, who said she hadn't heard from her. Calling Mina's cell phone again, I left a message letting her know that I would be late getting in and to remind her that it was her turn to pick up Mercedes from camp.

The networking mixer was at an uptown and chic restaurant, Room at Twelve. This was the world of the Pennington family. I had to admit to myself that it was nice being back there.

As staff from the Pennington firm arrived, they greeted me with open arms, rendering handshakes, hugs and kisses. Many of them I obviously came to know while dating Natalie offered sentiments of how much they missed me. These were people who were the same age as me, come from the same working-class and strata, hold similar political perspectives. It was a comfortable environment. A few the people were candid enough to say that they would have preferred that Natalie had married me instead of Vernon. I respectfully provided no comment.

When Natalie arrived, she quickly found me and latched on to my arm. She escorted me around the private dining room introducing me to clients of theirs. At first, she introduced me as an extended colleague of their firm. As she began drinking more and more free flowing wine, I became her old boyfriend.

"Uncle Charles, you remember Matthew."

"Why yes, Mister King" I was greeted by one of the senior partners.

"Hello Mister Pennington."

"It's been a long time. How's the family? You guys still have property up in the Hamptons?"

"Yes sir."

"Good. We're putting on fireworks on the beach on the fourth. If you're in the neighborhood, by all means drop by."

"Yes sir. Thank you."

"Uncle Charles, Matthew is going to be working in the Clean Room with us."

"Ah yes. Glad to *finally* have you on the Pennington team."

"I appreciate the opportunity sir."

"Your being here tonight confirms that you are an intelligent young man. Natalie has mentioned what's happening over at your firm. These are tough times. We are being reminded that even with all of our technological advances we are animals, resorting to our primal instincts – survival of the fittest. You know what I mean, son?"

"I think so."

"There's an old African saying '*On the plains of the Serengeti, you are either part of the herd, a predator or prey.*' This isn't the time to be a lone creature on the emerging global plains. Stay close to the herd, son. Also remember, *favor has the ability to change your social position.*" The elder statesman offered a firm handshake before parting company with us.

Mr. Pennington's words of support and survival gave me some comfort. They were words that I clearly needed to here. They also gave me a sense of belonging, maybe with the Pennington herd.

Natalie and I strayed from the crowd and found ourselves sitting at the bar. It was bad idea on my part. I was away from the safety of the herd. She had me trapped.

"Matthew, I miss you."

"Well, we'll be working together soon enough. I'm not sure if can pull off the full six months though."

She lowered her head. When she seemed to find the strength within, she lifted her head and placed a hand on mine.

"I mean that I miss this . . . us talking and being together like this." Natalie clarified.

"Natalie, I . . ."

"I know you're married with a family."

"You should learn to stop cutting people off."

"I'm sorry."

"I'm not going to lie to you. There is something that feels good about being here." Her eyes brightened and widened as if with hope and promise in what words were to follow. I was sorry to have to disappoint. "I'm not the only one married sitting here."

"You didn't have to remind me. I know that I'm in a sham of a marriage."

"Then why stay in it?"

"Because it's the right thing to do."

"Right for who?'

"For our child, my family, our people."

"It sounds like you're settling. So you're staying married for everyone but you."

Her hand on mine, tightened. "You've always did care about me didn't you?"

"You bring happiness to others without being happy within yourself."

"What can I do?"

"My father told me 'that what you don't deal with, will eventually deal with you.' You need to deal with Vernon's infidelity. To put it bluntly, ya'll need to either seek counseling or a lawyer."

She sat quiet as if mulling over her options. Suddenly, with the swiftness of a cheetah Natalie's hands moved to the crotch of my pants. With both of my hands I had to grab hold of hers.

"Natalie, what are you doing?"

"I lied. This is what I really miss. This is what I need."

"You don't mean that Natalie."

"The hell I don't. To take away my pain, I need this for sexual healing. We can go up to the Tica Cabins in the Blue Ridge Mountains for the weekend." She made a strong effort to free herself from my restraining grasp.

"It's the wine talking."

"The wine has given me the courage to say I miss making love to you." Leaning in to me to show some discretion, "I told you I've learned a few tricks."

"It doesn't matter, I'm married."

"I noticed you didn't say *happily* married."

"I'm happily married."

"Oh really; I know about your Q'Mina and her friends." I noted that she used Mina's MySpace screen name.

"What about them?"

"Look, I've been open and honest with you about the troubles in my situation. The least you could do is to be honest with me about yours."

"I don't know what you're talking about and I have nothing else to tell you other than I am happily married with my wife."

"Okay then, maybe you do believe you are. Let me ask you this? Is your *wifey* happily married?"

"Yes." I answered without any visual or audible hesitation, but internally I stuttered.

We managed to end the evening with an exchange of amicable apologies, in attempts to maintain a respectable relationship.

"NOT A REAL LAWYER"

We were sitting in Mable's BBQ restaurant, enjoying dinner. Sadie had sauce all around her mouth from the rib bones. Mina was sipping on her Uptown tea. I was talking with one of the restaurant's owners about the possibility of opening a second location, when Mina's cell phone rang.

With a cute and whimsical expression, she looks at the face of the phone before answering and asks "Who is this?" Then answering the call, "Hello. – Come get you. From where? - JAIL! What did you do? – Well what did he do? - What? So what they pick you up for? – DC6?" I assumed Mina looked to me for help in defining what DC6 was. I couldn't. "So what, they let you out on OR, and what about Ty? – No, he can't do anything for him. – Why? Cause Matthew ain't a real lawyer."

Without question, I took exception to the comment.

After Mina ending the call "Oh my God! She was picked up for disorderly conduct in a known drug area and they're holding her in jail." Mina announced.

"Who?" Mercedes asked.

"Your mother." Mina answered.

"What did you mean that I wasn't a real lawyer?"

"Un uh." Mercedes remarked.

"What?" Mina asked.

"You said I wasn't a real lawyer?"

"Un uh." Mercedes remarked.

"No I didn't." Mina stated.

"Yes you did. Mina, you said that."

"You know what I meant."

"Un uh." Mercedes remarked.

"Just because I can't go down there and get your drug dealing boyfriend out of jail, now I'm not a real lawyer."

"What do you mean my boyfriend? You *are trippin'*."

"Un uh." Mercedes remarked for a third time.

"Girl, what are you *'un uhin'* about?" Mina asked.

"You said that my mother is in jail. No she isn't."

"Oh, now both of ya'll *trippin*." Mina exclaimed.

"You're my mother, and you're right here." Mercedes stated outright without looking up from her plate.

"LAW AND DISORDER"

A week later we were at Mina's townhouse. She and her aunt were having a heated discussion about Brianna's lack of owning up to her responsibility. Apparently, Brianna had been placed on suspension three times by LiveOps, which resulted in the temporary cancelation of her account. In other words, she was close to being fired. The reason for the suspensions was because Brianna was arguing with the customers. I sat back in the chair to watch and listen.

"Do you know how this makes me look with you getting suspended?" Mina demanded.

"Why does it have to make you look bad? You didn't do anything." Brianna responded.

"Because I referred you . . . got you on through money from my program."

"Oh, so this is what this is about . . . cause you got me the job you trying to hold it over my head?"

"Why is everyone around me *trippin'*? You *F'd* up, period. So now, what are you going to do?"

"I'm going to get another job. There are plenty of work-out-of-your-home jobs."

"Well, you better find one quick, because I'm tired of this. The utilities are in my name, and if you don't pay me, then I will have them cut off, before I let you mess up my credit."

"So you would do family like that?"

"Damn straight."

"People back home are right. You do think you are better than us?"

"Us who? Don't anybody think they're better than anyone."

"You shouldn't, because I remember when you used to *ho'* for Popeye's chicken."

That caused me to sit up in the chair.

"WHAT!?" Mina shouted.

"Don't act like you don't remember *skeezin'* with the night manager at Popeye's so he would give you the leftover chicken that they was going to throw out."

Mina looked toward me, and then she immediately whipped her head back in the direction of her aunt. Her lustrous head of hair flowed right behind and in place.

"All I did was, flirt a little. And I did that to make sure we had something to eat AND you sure as hell ate your share."

"And . . . and, what about that time at the ATM?

Once again, Mina turned to look at me before addressing the open ended allegation.

"Look, don't be trying to put my business out here to draw the attention off of you."

"That ain't what I'm doing. I'm just showing you that you ain' perfect."

"I never said I was."

"Right, with your big house, big man and with *my* baby, your life is perfect. But you're threatening to put me out on the street."

"Quit being a damn drama queen. Nobody said anything about putting you out on the street."

"Where else do I have to go? I'm living in your house."

There was a long pause.

"Well, I could possibly fix things with LiveOps. But you're going to have to do better."

"I'll try harder, but some of them people *callin' be for real trippin'.*"

Just like that. All was forgiven. All was well. I could hardly believe it.

The last bit of conversation between them was a bonding on how *dirty* the cops were who picked up Tyriq for drug trafficking. It was reported in the newspaper that $15,000 dollars was seized from a drug house raid by the Red Dog Unit of the Atlanta Police force. Brianna said that Tyriq had $25,000 with him. She wanted to know if there was something that could be done about the alleged thievery by the arresting officers.

"*Cuz* that *shit* ain't right. I mean they're going to send him up and all, then they're going to rip him off too. They should go to jail. We need to sue somebody." Brianna lamented and in making the last statement turned toward me.

"Hey don't look at me. Remember, I'm not a real lawyer," I wisecracked.

"YOU DON'T HAVE TO DIE IN THE PLACE WHERE YOU WERE BORN"

We were sitting in the car in front of Mina's townhouse.

"*Babe,* see that girl over there in the pink top?" Mina pointed out.

"Yeah, what about her?" I spotted the attractive young woman, who was very pregnant.

"She's my age. That's her third child. She and her mother have always lived here. That makes the third generation in her family living here. She reminds me of LaDessa."

"Okay. Um, are we god-parents to any of her children?"

"You so silly."

"I'm just checking."

"Am I wrong for wanting more out of my life?"

"No."

"I mean my past isn't perfect, but should I let my past penalize me for the rest of my life?"

"No. You must never allow your past to hold your future hostage."

"Is there anything wrong with me trying to do better and not become a statistic?"

"No Mina. What is this all about?"

"It's what Brianna said; about my family and people back home thinking that I'm 'too good' or that I'm 'better than them.' That's not me Matthew. That's not me at all. I have a lot of people depending on me. So how could I be accused of thinking like that? Even when I'm tired, or it's not the best thing for me personally or financially, if I feel like I can help someone I love, then I'll do things for them."

"I know you will . . . sometimes to a fault."

"I know . . . and I know if I do it too much, people can become codependent. So I'm really working on learning how to say no and not care so much about pleasing everyone. But I couldn't have helped anyone if I didn't do better for myself. Because I got out of the *E'wick* I'm able to help others and my family. That doesn't make me stuck up."

"I know it doesn't. And you shouldn't let what Brianna has to say bother you."

"I know, but it does *Babe*."

"You shouldn't apologize for trying to better your life. What is it that Faulkner is always saying; 'we should live up to our potential not down to others expectations.' That is what you're doing Mina living up to your potential. Just because Brianna and others like her don't want to move beyond the low expectations for themselves or others, doesn't make you a bad person. What they *should* see in you is what you do for others."

"Thanks *Babe* . . . sometimes you have no idea how much you help me. I love you."

"Hey Boo."

"Yes."

"What happened at the ATM?"

She looked at me out of the corner of her eyes, "I'll tell you later" she stated, followed with a chuckle out loud.

"SEPARATE BUT EQUAL"

"For the fourth, let's go up to my family's place at Oak Bluff. We've been sort of invited to a beach party, with fireworks and everything." I called out to Mina who was in the bathroom. She didn't immediately respond. "MINA."

She came out of the bathroom combing her fingers through her hair. The coquettish expression on her face and the actions of her jumping in the bed with and on top of me, said that she had other ideas. She straddled and was looking down at me with a wide grin.

"Bernie . . ."

"Yeeeessss, Wanda."

"I need . . ."

"Yeeeessss."

"I need me some me time."

"What does that mean?"

"Just what I said. I'm tired. I need a vacation and don't take this the wrong way, because I know how sensitive you can be."

"No, go right ahead."

"Synea is home for a little while. She and some of my *HAMS* from college are going to the Essence Music Festival in New Orleans."

"*HAMS?*"

"*Hot Ass Messes* – my girlfriends."

"Okay and how is this 'ME' time if you're going with your *HAMS?*"

"I need a break *babe*. With all that's been going on, I just need to take some time away for me. I know it sounds selfish, but I'm not trying to be."

"So what about me and Sadie?"

"Ya'll can still go to your parent's place without me. I don't mind."

"I don't know. It's going to most likely be more adults than kids."

"That's okay. Then stay here and take her to the *E'wick*. They're throwing a block party before going to see fireworks at South Dekalb Mall."

"Yeah, right . . ., me hanging out at the Easywick. I only go up in there when I have you along for protection."

"What . . . now who's being *shitdiddy*?"

"*Shitdiddy*. No you didn't call me that." I tossed Mina off me and we began wrestling in the bed.

Together we asked Mercedes where she would like go for the 4th. At first she was upset that we weren't spending the holiday together. Mina reminded her of her best friend Uniqua and that she has at the Easywick. Granted there was some reluctance, but our little girl chose being with Brianna and her childhood friends, as opposed to being with me and my family.

"THE VINTAGE – BARBERSHOP"

I was sitting in the barbershop waiting for my barber Diesel to *hook me up* before my trip to Martha's Vineyard for the 4th. Because of the impending holiday and me not calling ahead to make an appointment, I had a bit of a wait. I didn't mind, because the barbershop is the second best place for a man to feel comfortable. The first is in his home – his castle.

The conversation in the barbershop touched on the hot topics of the country – the economy, high gas prices, and the war in IRAQ, whether America was ready for an African-American president and can Barack Obama be successful. *YES WE CAN!*

Mina called me on my mobile phone. "Hey *Babe*, where are you?"

"At the barbershop. *What'sup?*"

"I need some money."

"Oh yeah. Have you heard about those people in hell who need ice water?"

"Funny. I'm for real. I need some money until I get paid."

"Um, don't you work or are you performing community service?"

"You stupid. Paying that five-hundred dollar traffic fine put me behind. So are you going let me borrow some money?"

"Yeah."

"How long are you going to be?"

"Diesel, how long?" I asked the burly barber. He looks at the row of guys seated and counts.

"Two heads after this guy," he answered.

"It's going to be a while."

"Where is this place again?"

"On Forsyth, down and across the street from the Rialto Theatre."

"Right. I'm going to come down to get your check card, okay."

"Um hmm."

"Love you, bye."

She hadn't made it to the shop by the time I made it in the chair. Shame on her, because from the point my butt hits the chair a "do not disturb" sign ought to be draped across my chest on the front of the oversized bib. Aside from a courtesy exchange of greetings and inquiry of one another's significant others, I sat quietly while Diesel performs his grooming artistry.

My usual from Diesel, is a haircut and an *old school*, hot towel straight razor face shave. It's the shave that I mostly look forward to. Once I'm leaned back in the chair, for the fifteen maybe twenty minutes to follow I'm in a personal quiet zone. The water begins running in the sink. That's my cue to close my eyes. Diesel puts on a single latex glove. *Snap.* In my mind, the glove offers little protection against the scalding hot towel that he retrieves from the sink and wrings out excess water. I don't know how he can stand the heat. I can hardly bare the steaming towel that is wrapped around my face from my neck to the top of my head. Only my nose is left exposed to breathe in whatever cool air it can inhale.

From that point I tune out all the voices in the room and those in my head. I'm in a totally quiet zone - my place of peace and I'm at peace with the world. In that state, a five minute power semi-nap can easily be had.

This particular time I don't take advantage of the quiet zone to get in an impromptu snooze. I'm awake when fingers begin carefully prying away the towel from over my mouth. It was because of my wide open nostrils and now heightened sense of smell that I caught a familiar whiff of Hanae Mori, Mina's favorite perfume. Right at the point of recognition, come the pleasure of a pair of soft lips planted on mine.

The kiss lasted but a minute. That was long enough for me to gain an appreciation for the bib draped well past my knees, because it hid the growing erection between my legs. Mina is a sensual kisser. The lips were pulled away and the towel was unwrapped from my face.

"I HOPE HE DON'T THINK THAT WAS YOU D." A patron announced which brought a roar of laughter.

"Oh, I know he knows it wasn't me." Diesel shot back, bringing more laughter.

When my eyes gained focus, there was Mina in a *Next Top Model* kickstand stance. She was looking ravishing in a sleeveless sundress I've always loved the way her full arms look. One hand was on her hip while the other was outstretched.

"Your check card, please." She asked with sass in her voice. That brought on heckles from the barbershop's voyeurs. Playing along, reached in my pocket and retrieved my wallet.

Once I handed her my card, "what's your code?" She asked. All eyes then turned on me. "Never mind, I know what it is." Then she proceeded to leave.

"You're going to leave me something in there right?" I provided to our unrehearsed script.

"WHATEVER." Was her exit line.

The barbershop lit with cheers and jeers, whooping and hollering. When the crescendo of laughter and comments broke, I was given the chance to state that Mina was my wife. That admission quieted some and stirred others. It also brought on a new topic for discussion.

"Man, I wouldn't give my woman my debit card to save *my* life. She would empty my account without hesitation," one freshly clean head shaven guy declared.

"I can't trust my *girl* to bring me back my change from buying a two-piece chicken and biscuit snack," offered a guy getting his shoes shined.

"My *babies' mama* nickels and dimes me to death. Every time she sends me to the store to buy them something, she only gives me the whole dollar amount – knowing damn well that a black man has to pay double in taxes," provides an *old hat* gentleman. Once again, the Vintage Barbershop was filled with laughter. There is always "it's a conspiracy" guy in the bunch.

"GHETTOWAY WEEKEND"

Mina tossed her weekend Coach® bag in the back of Synea's SUV. She was looking quite sexy in her tight fitting Butta Phat Jeans and high heeled shoes. The designer jeans slogan of "It's in the genes" was definitely holding true as Mina was filling her pants with what her mama gave her.

She turned to give us her farewell.

"Goodbye Sweet Pea. I'll call you as soon as I get to where I'm going." She told Sadie.

"Promise" asked the child.

"Promise." The two exchanged pinkie swears to seal the pledge.

"What about me, do I get a pinkie swear too?" I asked.

"I gave you something last night, Mister Stop that Tickles."

"Hey, you said you weren't going to mention that."

"Don't worry. Your secret is safe with me, unless I have a little too much to drink." She teased. We exchanged kisses before she climbed in the SUV with a CAU plate frame on the front and an AKA tag frame on the back.

At the Easywick, I pulled up to Brianna's door front. This is where it all began between Mina and me. One Saturday night, I fell asleep on Mina's couch watching television and holding her in my arms. It was like the movie scene in *Boomerang* between Eddie Murphy and Halley Berry, when they fell asleep watching *Star Trek*.

The next morning Mina made me breakfast. That was before Brianna came home, who had spent the night away. With her, she brought Tyriq, who came in the house demanding that Mina braid his hair. There was a brief verbal altercation between Tyriq and me then him and Mina and then Mina and me. She kicked us both out of her house that morning. He made it back in her house that night. After another week, I made my way into her heart till death do us part.

I turned off the ignition of my CLS500. A young boy in sagging jeans and an oversized white t-shirt came to attention. His face didn't recognize amongst many drug runners.

"You stay close to me when we get out of the car. Okay?" instructed Mercedes.

Just as we reach the teenager, he stepped in our pathway.

"*What'up unc'*? You *a'ight*?" He asked.

"Yeah."

"*Com'on fucwitme. Fucwitme.*"

"What?"

Mercedes pulled at my arm. "He wants you to buy some of hi drugs," offered the apparent streetwise child.

"Look at *chu* young *schawty, teachin' ole school what'sup.*"

"Deke, go on son," commanded a voice approaching us from blind side. It was Tyriq. "Don't mind him Benzo. These young son don't have no respect. They see everybody as a sell. They don't care who it is. That's why I'm getting out of the game. "

"I see."

"Hey Little Mina."

"Hey."

"Why don't you go ahead and ring the doorbell?" I instructed Mercedes, which sends her trotting to the house.

"So you bailed out," I noted to the man.

"Yeah. They can't hold me. They messed me up when they stole some of my stash, though. I was going to make that my last run before I got out." He claimed.

"HEY SWEET PEA." Brianna could be heard behind us. She held open the door for Mercedes to enter. She was wearing a t-shirt which had printed on it "STRETCH MARKS IS GOD SIGNING HIS MASTERPIECE."

"*Aunty* is one of my models for my t-shirts." Tyriq promotes.

"Okay," keeping my responses short. I went inside the house to say goodbye to Mercedes. When I walked in, she's dancing in the middle of the living room to "*Ay Bay Bay.*"

"Look Matthew," Mercedes requested, as she *walked it out.*

I stood there watching proudly as any father would seeing his child perform. I've seen her in a school play and a ballet recital, and the feeling I had then equals the one I had seeing her dancing hip-hop.

"Very nice honey," I encouraged. We hugged and kissed and I left with a heavy heart.

Tyriq was waiting outside, standing near my Benz. A confrontation was inevitable. The image of him kissing Mina flashed before my eyes. My temporary blindness almost caused me to run into him.

"Whoa Benzo."

"Sorry."

"No problem. I wanted to talk to you 'bout something."

"Yeah."

"I know you and I got this beef or whatever. I just want to set the record straight."

"About?"

"Mina."

My curiosity was piqued and I felt my right eyebrow rise. "Go ahead."

"I ain't *goin'* to lie. I still had a thing for your girl. I mean, Mina is like a rose up in this concrete jungle. But she's all about *helpin' a brotha* out. She helped me start my *phat* gear and t-shirt business, by setting up my MySpace page and eBay account. I mean she taught me everything about computers. I was sitting in on her classes in the club house with these welfare *hoes* up in here. Unlike a lot of *dem*, I got *somethin'* out of it."

"And to thank her, that's why you kissed her."

"Oh, you know about that. I *shouda* known she'd tell you. Well . . see, what had happen was . . ." he chuckled. "When she set up the MySpace page I was crazy happy - right, so I grabbed and kissed her I said some bullshit about needing a woman like her having my back. That's where I messed up.

"She snapped on me like a pit bull; told me to keep my hands and lips to myself. You know how she can be when she wants to tear a *brotha* down."

A smile formed across my face.

"Yeah, you know what I'm talkin' about." We shared a brief moment of oneness. "Mina can be a tough one when she wants to be. Well, I just want say, *my bad* Benzo. I didn't mean no real harm."

"Sure you didn't."

"I'm *fo'real*. Besides, it's in the past. Now we're cool."

"And you've moved on to her aunt, just to keep it in the family?"

He didn't get my sarcasm.

"Not really. Brie is just a *jump off girl*." He read the dumbfounded expression on my face and chuckled before explaining, "A chick I use for sex. To make her feel special, I let her model my t-shirts."

"Nice guy."

"Ya know?" He accepted the backhanded compliment. We exchange emotionless glances and a firm handshake. We're not *boys* or friends. Despite his words, he still covets someone I have. As the police would call him, Tyriq remains "a person of interest."

"INDEPENDENCE DAY"

Once I exited the ferry to Martha's Vineyard, I stopped at an eatery called Biscuits, where I had stuffed French toast, fried chicken and of course, coffee and biscuits. On the way to our house on the beach, I remembered the years of coming here since the age of nine, staying with family for two weeks on Beach Road in Oak Bluff. I remember having a sense of freedom on the Vineyard, like now without having Mina or Mercedes along. A quickly passed moment of guilt was washed away with the view of beautiful coastal scenery.

I was the first to reach our house, so I went to my room and took a nap. The next thing I knew was that I'm being pummeled by a pillow in the hands of my cousin Emily. "Get up sleepy head. I didn't come all this way to watch you sleep." She provoked. "And where's the rest of the family?"

Sitting on wooden rocking chairs out on the deck waiting for the rest of the King blood clan to arrive, Emily and I catch up.

"I love it here. It's so relaxing." Emily described.

"Yeah, you sure gain an appreciation for quiet time; away from the hustle and bustle."

"What are you talking about; living out on, what is it three acres of woodland with wild animals running across your property?"

"Three and half," I correct her.

A tone alerted me that I received a phone text. It was from Marcus asking what I and the family were doing for the fourth. I replied "I'm flying solo with family on the Vineyard." No follow-up.

"Who's that, Mina?"

"Nah."

"And why didn't you bring her and Sweet Pea? I wanted to see her."

"Mina's at the Essence Festival in New Orleans and Sadie's with her mother, Brianna."

"Are ya'll okay?"

"Yeah, we're good. Mina said that she needed some 'me time'." I put up my hands to emphasize the quotation marks.

"Well, that was nice of you agreeing to it."

"Let's just say that I didn't object for another reason."

"Such as . . .?"

I told Emily about what was going on with Natalie and me. How it felt comfortable being around her family again. The job opportunity and possibility of more work being thrown my way if I decided to do more independent contracting work. Then I glossed over the sexual advances Natalie had been making.

"WHAT? And you came up here without Mina."

"It's not like anything is going to happen."

"You damn right nothing is going to happen. Because you're not going to leave my sight, you hear me?"

"Emily, it doesn't call for all that. I'm telling you this in the strictness of confidence."

"Hold up. Remember how upset you were when you found out Mina and ole boy had kissed, and now you want to keep secrets from her."

"Why do you always have to *flip the script* on me to prove a point?"

"Because the point needs to be proven. What's good for you mister gander, is good for the goose. I can't believe your ass."

"*Dang*, I can't believe you're getting so worked up about this."

"Damn right I'm worked up. You're about to jeopardize your marriage playing sexual politics with your old girlfriend in hopes of getting a job!"

"I would never let it go that far."

"It's already gone too far. The implication has taken you there. You need to end it. Cut it off the next time you see her."

"And what about doing the work for her family's firm; we're talking five-thousand dollars a week."

Emily stood from her chair and walked to the deck railing. "Answer me this," she turned and asked, "Is it worth the risk of losing your family over?"

It was nice being at the Vineyard with my family. My parents finally arrived; they drove in with my mother's sister and her husband. My mother's sister is Emily's mother. Once they settled in their rooms, the women headed for the kitchen and began preparing the side dishes and the meat for the barbequing. The men sat out on the deck talking. Our work would start tomorrow, with the grilling.

My father complained about the high price of gas and how much the trip would end up costing him. He documented the varying prices he paid comparatively, from state to state. The more he spoke about the poor state of the economy and how we got to this state of the union under the Bush Administration, the more he started sounding like the "it's a conspiracy" guy. Listening to him made me chuckle out loud.

"So why didn't you bring your family along?" My dad asked.

"Mina went to a festival in Louisiana."

"Everything all right?"

"Yes sir."

"This isn't what you all call 'taking a break' from each other is it?"

"No sir. She and some girlfriends went together."

"You sure?"

"Yes sir."

"Okay. Your mother will be glad to hear it. She didn't want to ask, so she had me do it."

"GUESS WHO'S COMING TO DINNER?"

Later the night on the 4th of July Eve, we were all sitting around the living room talking when the doorbell rang. My mother returned from seeing who was at the door. She had a peculiar look on her face when she stepped back in the room. The reason why was following her.

"Look who was at the door. You all know Natalie the lawyer and she brought her baby." My mother announced.

My mother introduced my aunt's husband; "This is William; he's a surgeon at Henry Ford Hospital in Detroit." I wondered if my mother knew that whenever she introduced someone, she does so by giving their name and occupation. I've long time suspected that my mother felt as if she had to impress the Penningtons with whatever she could in order to match their socioeconomic status.

Later, whenever and wherever she could, my mother would compliment how cute the Pennington-Peel child was and how he favored his mother. Then there came the snide remark about wishing she had a grandchild that looked like someone she recognized. Unabashedly, my aunt could be heard asking her husband, "Isn't that the one he was dating before he got married?"

Keeping true to her word, Emily wouldn't let me move far from her. She threw one of her legs across my lap to prevent me from getting up. She then nudged me to take note of the child's shoes. We both laughed at a private joke from way back when we saw the Stride Rites®. When I first saw Natalie on the beach when we were teenagers, Emily joked that my soon to be girlfriend grew up wearing Stride Rites before she stepped in to some all white Pro Keds®. The real joke was that Natalie would not let her natural feet ever touch the sand.

Emily leaned in to whisper, "Your girl is wearing a pair of Birkenstocks."

The brand name reference was lost on me; I didn't know what that meant.

"If Mina was here, she'd know. Those are one-hundred dollar sandals. Most of the affluent, liberal, Buppies own several pairs. I wouldn't be surprised if she has a different pair on tomorrow."

Natalie's visit was to formally invite my family to the Pennington's fireworks show on the beach. She caught the family up on her professional accomplishments, such as passing the Georgia Bar. Her cue that is time to leave came when the two and a half year old got his fill of the attention. With the look of reluctance apparent on her face, she gathered the little one and said her goodbyes. Emily's face was plastered with a wide grin.

"LET THE FIREWORKS BEGIN"

As a family, the Kings walked along the beach to the Pennington's house. We were paired off. Emily and I walked arm in arm. She was taking her bow guard duties seriously.

The hosting Penningtons had a festive spread of food and drinks for their guests. The scent of barbeque being cooked on barrel pits could be smelled for up to a half a mile as we approached. Emily and I headed for the drinks table where bartenders provided whatever alcoholic drink you wanted from Red Stripe Jamaican Lager to wine with actual gold flecks. Emily started with a Mojito; while I had a glass of Gold Chardonnay.

The guests looked like live models right out of a Brooks Brothers, Robert Talbots or Tommy Hilfiger fashion catalogs. Natalie, Vernon and son were dressed alike and color coordinated in powder blue and white, right down to each one having a periwinkle Argyle sweater draped or tied around their shoulders. Emily pointed out that Natalie did indeed have on a different pair of Birkenstocks. We chuckled out loud.

It was nice being there and having a positive connection in a normal day in the life with other African-American families. Granted, most of the people walking the shores of the beach were from upper class families and lived lives far from normal compared to those living in the Easywick community.

Is what we call classism the acknowledgement of the different socio-economic lives of people, or is it the disparagement of the people? The answer to my question came when the thunderous sound of hard rap lyrics coming from a boom box, disturbed the peace. A group of teenagers strolled along, deciding to crash the Pennington's party. As a few of the men went to turn the teens away, I along with Emily overheard an elder woman recite an old racial divisive limerick, "*Niggers* and flies. *Niggers* and flies. The more I see *niggers*, the more I like flies."

"Excuse you," Emily shot at the white haired woman. "This is what's wrong with us as people. We want to tell everyone else to treat us with respect, when we don't respect ourselves." I grabbed Emily by the arm to temper her, which she promptly snatched away "My mother raised me to respect my elders, but I've learned that some respect needs to earned. Just because you're old don't mean you can say whatever the hell you want like some kind of brain fart . ."

The woman gasped along with many of those who were in earshot. Emily would have continued on her rant if her mother hadn't pulled her away. As a herd should and would do, my parent's and I surrounded and walked of went Emily. I trailed behind to protect the rear. That meant I was exposed to the danger of attack.

"*ALL HAIL THE KING,*" hailed Vernon Peel.

"Hello Vernon."

"Is there a problem with your kissing cousin?"

"Kissing cousin . . . oh you mean Emily. No, she's fine."

"Good. So, how does it feel being Matthew *King of the world*? The man giggled.

"I don't know what you mean."

"Oh sure you do. I would imagine the 'king of the world' would be satisfied with having what's his. But you want yours and everybody else's too."

"Is there something that you want to say?"

"A better question is, is there something that you don't want me to say?"

"All right, I'm not getting this. If you've got something on your mind, then come out and say it."

"Let's just say, wouldn't your family be interested in knowing that their precious Matthew King is nothing more than a lowdown cheater . . . on his wife and family."

"What?" I stepped to him out of reflex.

He stumbled backwards. "I . . . I have proof," he stammered.

After a few button clicks, Vernon handed me his red Blackberry showing me text messages from someone to Natalie making arrangements for rendezvous. What caught my attention from some of the texts were the references to when Mina was out of town.

```
-"She's gone again.  Can we meet?  Q'Mina will be
gone for a few days.  When can we do the cabin
thing again?" -
```

I looked at Vernon who had a smug expression of "I gotcha." Instead, what came out of his mouth was, "Oh what now, Your Highness?"

He did have me. I was speechless while trying to mentally put some things together. The texts obviously weren't from me, but from someone else who knew when Mina would be out of town, someone who obviously witnessed her leaving or who was made aware of her whereabouts.

Vernon said he came across the texts when one was sent while Natalie left her cell phone out and she was showering. He then forwarded them to his phone for future leverage. He said that he was "sick and tired of having my name brought up by her and her family as being "the one that got away."

"I also found the receipt for the Movado watch she bought you." He punctuated his claim with a snide, "*Um hmm.*"

Now that I knew what I knew, Vernon's smug accusation seemed comical. It was my turn.

"Does Natalie know that you know?"

"Of course. It's what I use to have her to keep me looking fashion fabulous."

"Along with your appraiser, mistress? What's her name, Adrianne," showing him that I knew a few things too. He laughed in a sissified manner. The more he spoke, the more what Mina suspected about him appeared credible. There was no more truer evidence than his own words.

"Look *atchu*, trying to play tit-for-tat. I didn't think she had the nerve to tell anyone. Wait, you said her?" Again, he let out a high pitched laughed. "My appraisers name is Adrian; but it's A-d-r-i-a-n."

I didn't give him the satisfactory look of surprise.

"That explains, you're not being able to satisfy her in bed."

"*Duh*. I tried to introduce her to some new things."

"I'll bet."

We both laughed. We actually shared a jovial moment. It was strange.

"So now what?" I asked.

"I suppose that depends on what you're willing to give up."

"And why would I be willing to give up anything?"

"Aren't you forgetting about *wifey poo*?"

"Not at all. Vernon, man to man, if you will; I suspect that know with whom Natalie is having an affair. But I can tell you unequivocally that it is not me."

I turned and walked away from the man, leaving him with his neatly trimmed eyebrows arched high in wonderment. I found my family and told them that I had some business to attend to. My next point was to locate Mr. Pennington, the senior partner of their firm. When I found him, I politely and respectfully retracted my bid to work with them in the Clean Room. I had nothing to say to Natalie as I walked passed her to rejoin my family. The last that I saw of her she and Vernon were having what appeared to be a heated discussion.

I told Emily everything as we sat and watched the fireworks. With every bit of information that I told her, she would say in response, "You lying." I would just go on, until she was laughing hysterically.

It wasn't until I was back to our house and getting ready for bed did I notice that I had missed several phone calls from Natalie to my mobile phone. And there were just as many text messages from her pleading for me to call her. In my haste to quickly read and delete them, I almost missed a message from Mina.

-Getting ready to see Frankie Beverly and Maze. *Babe*, I'm so excited. Golden Time of Day...-

There was a voicemail message from her as well.

She didn't speak. Over the phone I could hear the Maze band playing live and the crowd singing the groups signature song "Happy Feelings."

"*I WISH YOU LOVE*"

After the plane landed in Hartsfield-Jackson International Airport and we were able to turn on our electronic devices, I had several more voicemail and text messages from Natalie. On some of the voicemail messages she was sobbing, on others she sounded angry. All of them ended with her pleading with me to return her call to allow her to explain. Her last text message asked me to check my Hotmail account.

Sadie was a little chatter box after I picked her up. She was excitedly telling me of the fun and wonderful time she had staying with Brianna. Seeing and spending extended time with the kids that she's known since she was born, brightened her spirit. She didn't stop talking until she fell asleep on the couch and I had to carry her to bed.

The email from Natalie was three pages long. It began with more apologies for her "improprieties" is what she called it. She blamed her poor behavior as a desperate attempt to find happiness that she had "no chance of having in her own failed relationship." It wasn't so much that she wanted to ruin my marriage, but rather to have part of me, "however that meant and whatever it took."

As with the Bible, it was at the end of the email letter that brought a revelation. Natalie claimed that after reaching out to him, it was Marcus who gladly offered his services to spy on Mina and I, letting her know when it was safe to contact me. Every time Mina would leave town, Marcus would send a text. She said that at first Marcus had such contempt for my wife that he eagerly wanted to be an accomplice to her plan to come between us, for the initially price of luxury gifts.

Then, one night Marcus allegedly called Natalie in a drunken stupor asking for sex. She claimed to have had rejected him, at first. Then he began talking about how hot and sexy Mina was and how he wouldn't mind having a chance at her in the bed. He claimed that Mina would leave me if he had just one time with her. Natalie wrote; --When he said that, I thought to myself, she's taking another man from me and I wasn't going to let her.-- Natalie blamed that and a lapse in judgment as to what caused her to sleep with Marcus. She also said that she had a long time ache and he provided the sexual healing she needed. After being with Vernon, she needed to be in the arms of a real man. In closing, she offered more apologies.

Once I finish reading the email I sent her this reply from an old Nat King Cole title song: "I wish you love. Goodbye." Then I was done with Natalie Pennington-Peel, with no intentions of ever speaking with her again. I erased her contact info from my mobile phone. I lost out on for sure money, but the decision to "let go" of my relationship with Natalie was worth it.

I still had Marcus to deal with.

"LIP SERVICE"

I'm not ashamed to say this; I couldn't wait for my wife to come home so that I could hold her in my arms. It wasn't that I wanted to have sex with her; I just wanted to have her close to me. I resisted the urge to call her to find out what time she was expected home. Instead, I wrote her a note and left it on her pillow.

Dear Mina –
I like you for you.
It may have been your cuteness that attracted me;
but it was your personality that interested me.
Your words touched my mind and my heart.
It was what I saw <u>of</u> you that drew me near.
It was what I saw <u>in</u> you that made me stay.
I love you for you.
- Matthew

At two-something in the morning, a warm body nuzzled close to me. Strong arms pulled on me to turn around. I did. In the dark, I found my baby's lips and kissed them. She winced.

"What?" I asked.

"I had this drink called a *Blue MF* and it burned my lips. You know how sensitive they are." I reached for my jar of Carmex® from the nightstand. "Un uh, you know I can't stand the smell of that stuff."

"What's good for you doesn't always smell good."

"Um hmm."

"Do you trust me to take care of you?"

"Yes."

I put some ointment on my finger and applied it to her mouth."

"Ow. It burns." She protested.

"It's tingling."

"Tingling hell. That burns."

"How about this, then?" I spread a coating of the balm on my lips, and then gave her some light butterfly kisses. After but a few caresses, she began lifting her head to meet me. Naturally, I became aroused.

"*Babe*, I'm tired okay," she stated as she placed her hand on my emerging *jones* to confirm what she suspected.

"Hey, you're the one who started this. I was sound asleep."

"Yeah right, and who tried to be slick with 'how about this, then?"

"I was just trying to help."

"Oh you want to help then put your hot hands on my stomach. I'm cramping." She turned her back to me, pulled my arm around her and placed my open hand just below her navel. We scooted toward one another.

"*Babe*, you're poking me."

"THE CONFRONTATION"

The best man at my wedding accepted my appointment for lunch. I saw Marcus in line getting his food as I was paying for mine. I signaled to him with a head up tic that I'd get a table in the cafeteria seating area. As I watched the man who stood by my side at my wedding approach the table, I still didn't know exactly what I would say to him about his deceit in our friendship.

There was no "Man Law" that applied to this situation, because men simply don't behave this way. At least none of the men thought I knew. This was about behind the back game play. If a man wanted a woman, he simply made his move or play for her. As Marcus approached, the only script that I had to work with was the last email from Natalie.

"*What'up* King? You sounded like you had something on you mind when you called."

"What's up is you and Natalie scheming to breakup my marriage."

His eyes widened, which was the only "tell" that I needed to confirm what Natalie wrote in her email was true. I proceeded to read point-by-point from the highlighted email.

"She said what? No way Matt man, would I do that," He initially denied. "Okay, she called me out of the blue one day and started asking about you, *knowhaimsayin*?" He continued to defend.

"She came on to me with the watch first, and then she asked me to go away to the cabin with her. She said that her husband wasn't man enough for her. I mean all she wanted was for me to let her know when Mina was away, *knowhaimsayin*. I didn't see anything wrong with that. I knew you wouldn't mess around." He deflected.

"So, for a watch and sex you played me?"

"Nah, nah, Matt man. Okay, yeah. But that's because I knew you would do the right thing, *knowhaimsayin*. I mean she told me about how she was going to hook you up with a job and everything; so really, I was looking out for you, *knowhaimsayin*. Come on man, I'm your boy."

"Yeah, that's what's so messed up about this."

"What's that?"

"We aren't boys anymore. You are no longer welcome in my house."

I stood from the table and walked away from a barely touched lunch. I forgave him by letting go of our friendship, just as I did with Natalie. Relationships either build you up or tear you down. Once I recognized the tear down relationships in my life, I cut them out. Anyone you can cut out of your life, were not there for a good purpose.

"LEAVE OF ABSENTMINDEDNESS"

Mr. Kubiak called me into his office. When he started asking me for specific dates of my extended leave of absence without pay, I'm sure I resembled the commonly referred to "deer caught in the headlight." Though I formally told the senior partners of Pennington and Pennington my decision to decline the opportunity to work with them, I failed to mention it to my own firm's operations manager.

"Oh, about that . . . I won't need to take the leave after all."

"Really and why is that?"

"Uh, there's just been a change in plans."

"Change in plans; like you backing out of your agreement to work the Clean Room with Pennington and Pennington?" The headlights were now on high beams.

"How . . ."

"We received an anonymous phone call giving some pretty specific details of dates and times when you were out of the office, which matched when the interviewing was taking place." Immediately I suspected Natalie as the voice of the anonymous caller. "Don't worry. Technically you did nothing to violate firm policy, but there is a bigger issue."

"And that is?"

"As part of my facilities to this firm, I submit a resource planning forecast to the managing partners. I've already submitted the forecast for the next month that the firm would be relieved of your salary. As you can imagine, that is a considerable margin increase to our revenue line."

"So what are you saying?"

"Well, I can't just walk back in their offices and say 'oops, he changed his mind.'"

"Actually you can, because that's what happened."

"Okay, let's say that I could; what would you want me to tell them as to why you changed your mind . . . because you turned down a job with a competing firm?"

"Would that be necessary?"

"Because they sign your check, I believe so."

"Then do it."

Kubiak sat quietly still while he thought over my last words. We maintained eye contact. He blinked first, and then said that he'll see what he can do. I walked out of his office with no confidence that he would actually do anything more than he would have to. Whatever he would decide to do would be in the interest of the firm's bottom line.

Just as I reached Ruby's receptionist desk, she waved me over because she was on the phone. She handed me a message slip.

was for me to call a MEL. I shoved the note in my suit coat pocket and headed out of the office to think of what my options would be if I would be forced to take the unpaid leave.

While I walked around the Bank of America skyscraper, I beat myself up and blamed myself for flirting with an opportunity that put me in the position that I found myself. When it came to jeopardizing the livelihood and security of our household, I should have been more careful. According to Bishop Bronner, *every experience that comes in to your life either has a divine or demonic handle.* I wasn't sure whose hand was on the predicament I was in.

When I came back into the office, Ruby told me Kubiak wanted to see me. What he called a compromise was that I had to take at least one month of time off without pay. Thanks to our savings, there were adequate funds to cover expense, I thanked God.

"A FATHER AND DAUGHTER MOMENT"

My favorite father and daughter moments with Mercedes are when we're together and I'm reading either an *Esquire* or *GQ* magazine. She nudges right by my side leaning against me as I turn the pages. Anxiously she waits for me to come to one of the ad pages with a cologne sample, so that she can tear it open. Next comes a sniff – then it's my turn to wait for either a frown or a smile of approval from her. The next time we're shopping at the mall, we'll go by the men's cologne counter with our torn out pages to check out the real deal and a whiff of love.

"AY BAY BAY"

After tapping our "just in case" emergency account, we paid on our expenses for up to a month. It was Mina's idea to create the "just in case" account to put aside six months worth of income to cover our household bills. When it comes to handling household business, I call Mina "Wanda" in reference to Bernie Mac's television wife who worked for AT&T. In another time, she would be Claire Huxtable and I her Heathcliff. It was our harmless form of role playing.

To take advantage of the time off, I enrolled in an online correspondence course to obtain a global contract management certification from the International Association of Commercial and Contract Management (IACCM).

The day's routine would be that I would drop Mercedes off at summer camp and return home to study. This particular morning, Mina's Sebring was still parked in the driveway. Upon entering the house, I called for her and didn't get an answer. I found her lying in the bed, balled in a fetal position wearing only her bra and panties.

"Hey, are you okay?"

"I'm cramping."

"Do you want some Goody's® powder? You know I've got the Goody's."

"You silly . . . yes."

It was unusual for Mina to accept my offer for Goody's powder. For as long as I've known her she's shown an amazingly high tolerance for period pain. She's never taken as much as an aspirin especially when she's visited by her *Aunty Pearl*. *Aunty Pearl* is our code for on her menstrual cycle, ever since the emergency tampon removal incident.

I returned to Mina's bedside with two packets of red Goody's powder specifically for the body pain and a bottle of Red Rock ginger ale. That combination is my prescription for anything that ails me.

"Thanks *Babe*." She struggled with a cough, choke and gag before she swallowed the fast acting pain reliever.

"That wasn't so bad now was it?"

"I almost choked to death."

"You want me to lay hands on you?"

"Um hmm."

"Just call me Doctor Feel Good."

"Uh, doctor; ever notice how all of women's problems start with MEN? MENtal illness, MENstrual cramps, MENtal breakdown, MENopause, GUY-necologist, and . . ."

"Stop it, I got the same email."

I climbed in bed alongside her and spooned with her. She helped guide my hand to her midriff. I put my other arm beneath her head to be used as a pillow and I wrapped it around to her shoulder. We laid there in an embrace for a quiet five minutes, until –

"Matthew, I'm late."

"I know. That's why I was surprised to see your car in the driveway. Since you're not feeling well, why don't you just call in?"

"You stupid. I'm not talking about that kind of late. *Aunty Pearl* is late."

Palpitations, that's what best describes the sensations I was having in my chest.

"You mean . . . that you're, you're pregnant?"

"GOD GIVETH . . ."

There was no medical science confirmation that Mina was pregnant and she was reluctant to have it confirmed. Instead, she would offer laymen excuses as to what could have caused her period to come late; stress, hormonal imbalance, her eating habit/diet, weight loss or gain. Each time I wanted to talk about the possibility of her having our baby, she would avoid the issue. It almost came to a point of an argument.

"Look Matthew, I'm just late that's all."

"Here, just pee on the stick."

"I can't believe you. You went and bought a pregnancy test?"

"YES! Don't you want to know for sure?"

"No. I will know soon enough."

"Why wait, when you could just go ahead and pee on the stick."

"The only peeing is you pissing me off."

"Funny."

"I'm not trying to be funny. I'm serious Matthew. I knew I shouldn't have told you."

"This involves both of us you know."

"Oh really? You act like it's all about you needing to know. Why, so you can rush and call your mother and finally make her happy?"

"No, it has nothing to do with my mother. And you're the one who's acting like it's all about you."

"Maybe you're not pregnant at all." I tried the reverse psychology approach.

"What?"

"Maybe you aren't pregnant. I mean it's not like you've been pregnant before and would know what it's like."

This is when I realized that I should operate within my own field of profession, meaning leaving psychology to the psychologist. The stern look on Mina's face reminded me at that very delicate moment that I had forgotten her abortion of Tyriq's baby. We stared at each other for about a minute.

"*Babe*, this is one of those times where we need to agree to disagree."

"Mina . . ."

"*Babe* . . ."

"*. . . AND HE TAKETH AWAY*"

Mina came in to the house, slamming the door behind her. heard the footsteps stomping against our hardwood floor getting louder and louder as she neared the den. She was visibly trembling when she shoved a partially crumbled piece of paper in front of me.

"I found this on Brianna's printer. This is some *BULL!*" Min exerted. "AFTER ALL THAT I'VE DONE FOR THAT *SKANK* AND SHE'S GOING TO PULL SOME *SHIT* LIKE THIS!"

Taking the sheet of paper from her shaking hand, I began readin a printout from an Internet page.

Q. If you adopt a family member's child, can the natural parer receive custody again? The adopt parent and natural parent agree t it and everyone agrees that it's in the best interest of the child. How would we go about getting information? – *Anonymous*

A. The answer is that you absolutely can reverse the adoption, but the way to do it is to start all over with a new adoption. It will be expensive, but if everyone consents, it shouldn't be unduly complicated. And then let's please all cooperate to give this poor child some consistency. - *Lee Borden*

"Can you believe that *shit*? If she tries to take Sadie from me, there is going to be some consequences and repercussions. Do you hear me?" Mina threatened with an assuredness.

"Yeh, I'm sitting right here," trying to lighten the mood. I would have teased about her rare use of four syllable words, but then was not the time.

"Matthew, can she do that? Can she take back custody of Mercedes?" She bombarded me with questions I couldn't answer.

"I . . . I honestly don't know. Without being versed in family law, I would say, maybe. But I'm not sure."

"Then you need to find out."

She harassed me to the point of submission to call a colleague attorney to get some advice. I learned just how desperate Mina was when she even suggested that I call Natalie. Instead, I called Kara, the in house attorney on staff of the ASK ME Foundation. What she had to offer was not good news.

"It may come down to a small technicality," Kara sited. She further clarified, "that the father *did not* sign the letter that the mother, Brianna Parker signed away her custodial rights to the child. If she can get him to protest the courts to regain custodial rights, she might be successful."

"BUT HIS ASS IS IN JAIL SOMEWHERE," Mina blurted in to the receiver of the remote phone.

"And thus would be the challenge on your behalf." Kara offered as a slim ray of hope.

Mina was beyond consoling. She threatened everything from putting Brianna out of her house to reporting her to the Dekalb police for aiding and abetting a known drug dealer. Now it was my turn to show the good natured and spirited side.

"Once she has no place to stay, how will she be able to take care of Sadie? They'll see her as an unfit mother, right *Babe*?"

"Yeah, but you don't want to be the one who made her that way."

"And why the hell not?"

"Why provoke her, you don't want to make her hostile in case this does go to court?"

"*COURT*! What the fuck? I can't believe this is happening."

We paid a visit to the ASK ME offices to meet with Kara. What she had to say did not differ much from what she told us over the phone.

"Here's the deal you guys; like I said, she can petition the courts for custody rights on the technicality that the father did not render his consent." Kara provided.

"That's *bullshit*. Like he would even want custody," Mina argued.

"That isn't the point. I'm just pointing out the loophole here. Mercedes' biological father Geoffrey Frazier signed the child's birth certificate, in which the court will view as his document of right. You said that the father might be in jail, meaning that he's not in the picture."

"Brianna called G-Money so Sadie could wish him Happy Father's Day. I wonder if she was planning this then."

"Based on this question she posed online, I'm going to say that she's just begun her fact finding process. We probably know more than she does at the moment. And like whoever responded to her question mentioned, it would be costly for your aunt to regain custody."

"She doesn't have any money. She can barely pay me what she owes to keep a damn roof over her head. How is she going to take care of Sadie too?"

"Then I wouldn't worry about anything until you are served with a petition. If I could offer this word of advice; try to keep the relationship between you and your aunt as amicable as possible. You don't want to create a hostile environment. In Georgia, the family court system tends to lean toward the best interest of the child. Can either of you say how Mercedes would feel about this?"

"VICTORY OVER EVIL"

It was fortunate that Mina and I were on the pew of Word of Faith the morning Bishop Dale C. Bronner preached from the focal scripture of Ephesians 6:11-13; *11 Put on the whole armor of God, that ye may be able to stand against the wiles of the devil. 12 For we wrestle not against flesh and blood, but against principalities, against powers, against the rulers of the darkness of this world, against spiritual wickedness in high places. 13 Wherefore take unto you the whole armor of God, that ye may be able to withstand in the evil day, and having done all, to stand.*

On the ride home, we listened to the Reverend Lowdown's radio ministry program.

"Let go of disappointments, bad memories and anger. All things happen for a reason, even painful experiences. There are no accidents. Replace the pain with forgiveness. When you are driving a car, you can't move forward looking in the rear view mirror. Do you live your life looking in the rear view mirror? Past experiences are behind. They came to pass, not to stay.

"Have an open heart, be willing to forgive. At times, we hold on to old pain because it is safe to hide behind. It gives us reason not to move on. Nothing can hurt me unless I allow it. I release every disappointment.

"In prayer, I ask the Holy Spirit to help me practice forgiveness. The only person I am hurting by not forgiving is me. I release and live harmoniously with a renewed spirit of peace. I replace the seeming hurts with an inner calm. I allow God to be in the middle of every wound, replacing my old thinking with new vision and clarity. God has already healed the situation. I forgive, release and let go. Thanks, God. And so it is

"... and let there be no divisions among you; but be perfectly united in one mind and in one thought. Amen and amen." Concluded the pastor.

"Mina, we've been going through quite a bit here lately. It's like Bishop said, 'Whenever you begin to flow in favor, you will come under attack.'"

"What favor are we flowing in?" Mina challenged as she whipped around in the passenger seat.

"Our marriage and the love that we have for one another and Sadie."

"That ain't no favor."

"In itself it may not be, but the fact that we're still together and have managed to sustain our marriage is in God's favor."

"I love you and Sadie, that's it. God ain't got nothing to do with that."

"IS THIS THE WAY LOVE FEELS?"

I was up late studying in the den. The rest of the family had long gone to bed. By the time I decided to put the books away, I was beyond sleepy but decided to watch television. Flipping through channels I came across the 1999 movie *Love and Action in Chicago* starring Courtney Vance, Regina King and Kathleen Turner.

Mina comes in the family room, sliding her feet across the carpet. She's wearing her frumpy pajamas and squinting through half opened eyes. She pulled back the throw that covered me and climbed beneath it and lay on top of me.

"Your side of the bed was cold." She explained.

"I was studying."

"What *chu* watching?"

I caught her up to the point of the movie. We watched. We laughed.

"*Babe*, rub my back. Lower. It relaxes me."

"Then let daddy take care of his baby girl." I planted a kiss on the top of her silk scarf covered head.

"I need you to go with me somewhere."

"Okay."

"I need to have an outpatient operation." I tried to maneuver our bodies so that I could look at her face, but she fought against me. "No."

"What's the operation for?"

"My doctor says that I have a cyst on my ovary. That's why *Aunty Pearl* was late."

"When did you go to the doctor?"

"Last week."

"When did she tell you about the . . ."

"Yesterday. Are you mad?"

"Yes."

". . . because I'm not pregnant."

"Because you didn't tell me about the doctor's appointment. What do I have to do to prove to you that we're in this love together?"

"I don't know."

"Why don't you?"

"No one has ever cared or encouraged me the way you do."

"I'm not doing anything special here Mina other than loving you the only way I know how."

She clutched a handful of my shirt and exhaled a breath that seemed to deflate her entire body as she sank deeper onto me. I wrapped my arms ever tighter around the 150 pounds of deadweight, showing that I could bear the burden of any problems she wanted me to. The next sound I heard was snoring.

"OUT OF THE BLUE-TOOTH"

Mina was in overdrive trying to make it out of the house and off to work. She had braided Mercedes hair, making sure that she looked every bit of the little princess that she was. We exchanged an impassioned kiss just before she made her way to the front of the house. Grabbing her computer bag, she threw it on her shoulder.

Next, she hung her Bluetooth device on to her ear and she was out the door.

♪*If you walk thru the Easy, you better watch your back. Well I beg your pardon. Walk the straight and narrow track. If you walk with Jesus, he'll save your soul. You gotta keep the devil way down in the hole. Way down in the hole. Way down in the hoooole.* ♪ Mercedes sang as she pranced around the house getting her belongings together for summer camp.

"And where did you hear that song?"

"Over my friend Uniqua's house, when we were watching *The Wire*."

"*The Wire*? What's that about?"

The child went on to explain her version of the HBO series which portrayed the "*drug-infested streets of west Baltimore, where there are good guys and there are bad guys. Sometimes you need more than a badge to tell them apart.*" She continued to run down the plot of this obvious adult drama, its cast of characters and how people in the Easywick were comparing them to Tyriq and his crew.

Leaving the inside of the house, I was listening so intently to Mercedes, that I didn't immediately notice Mina still sitting in her car in the driveway. I instructed Mercedes to get in my car while I went to check on Mina. She was sitting motionless and staring straight ahead.

"Hey, you alright? Is something wrong with the car?"

She gave no response, until I reached for the door handle. That's when she quickly pushed the door-lock and began beating on the door, screaming "NO. NO. NO. YOU STAY AWAY!"

After thirty minutes and with the help of Sheryl, my next-door neighbor we were able to get Mina to open the door and come out of the car. That is when the both of us learned that Mina received a phone call telling her that her father had *passed*.

"YOUR JOY"

Reluctantly, I put Mina on a flight alone to Baton Rouge to take care of her father's affairs. After getting herself appointed the executor of his estate, it made it harder for others that were in William Montague's life to mooch off of him. Marbella even made herself scarce, once Mina took over her father's finances. Yet, it was on one of Marbella's rare visits that she discovered that Mina's father had died in his sleep of natural causes.

I didn't hear from Mina until she had set the date and time of the funeral. Whenever I asked if she was all right, she answered with a matter of fact tone, "I'm fine."

Brianna volunteered to watch Mercedes while I drove to Louisiana. I was packing my clothes for the trip when I came across in my suit coat pocket, the memo message to call MEL. Though several weeks had passed since receiving it, my curiosity got the better of me, so I called.

M.E.L. was the monogram for Mary Elizabeth Levenger from the Straight to the Heart Foundation. She called to offer me a job with their foundation to head their legal department, with a twenty percent increase in salary. Without hesitation, I accepted the position. I let Mary Elizabeth know that I was on a leave of absence and had some personal matters to attend to, before I could start working again. She said for me to give her a call once I was ready.

"FOOL, FOOL HEART"

The funeral home's parlor was filled to capacity. Mina had managed to pull together a family that had been splintered nearly since the time she was a child. Everyone has that moment in their life when they find out their parents are less than perfect. After he left Mina's mother unwed with five children, William Montague personified the singing Temptation's verse ♪*Papa was a rolling stone. Wherever he laid his hat, was his home.*♪ As it turns out, aside from her brothers, Mina had an extended family of stepbrothers and sisters, by other women where Mr. Montague made his temporary home.

Learning this surprising news during this bereavement time, Mina still welcomed her extended family with open arms and heart.

Mina stood at the podium to deliver her father's eulogy. She surveyed the room, just before clearing her throat. With a flinty and steady voice, she began to speak.

"Five days ago today, I lost my daddy, William Albert Montague. No matter how much time passes, I still remember the way I felt when I got that call. I came to know this man better and late in my life. Better late than never, is what they say. For a long time my father was absent from my life. For the short time that he was with me as a child, I loved him deeply. I had no choice. He was my father. Now he's gone.

"I have mastered the art of crying without tears. The uncontrollable sobbing that occurs when your heart has been broken, you stub a toe hard enough to break a toenail, you lose a loved one all can be contained behind my eyes without ever soiling my face.

"It took years to master and I do not think I noticed the first instant I stopped crying so everyone else could see, but the day I did it fascinated me. I looked in the mirror after receiving a blow that would have knocked Laila Ali off her feet and all I saw was sadness even though I felt like I was crying and shaking violently from the inside, no tears emerged to reveal my grief. If only I could elude my heart the same way keeping the pain from penetrating, it would be a great demonstration of control.

"But no, the heart is the one organ I cannot control. It betrays me often. When I do not want it to give, it gives too much, when I want it to give, it tells me it has been hardened and cannot give itself so fiercely or quickly as if my heart learned the art of fear and retreat through consistent defeat. But I tell you one thing, it sure is resilient-picking up its broken pieces and at the slightest glimmer of love, it hopes again for different outcomes trying to forget about the last one." She looked in my direction before continuing.

"It rarely works in conjunction with my eyes who knows that seeing is believing, it says instead, have faith. It doesn't work in union with my mind which fuels on the logic befitting an educated intelligent woman, it goes out on a limb believing in the undeserving, loving the unlovable, and hoping against all odds that 'this time will be different', this one will be different, and everything all the other senses and body parts are experiencing just may not pertain to it because if I love big enough and wide enough maybe I can engulf someone…someone other than myself …this time.

"Maybe someone will see that a love with me is truly worth having, worth fighting for, worth saving, worth never betraying.

"The truth the eyes see and the ears hear; the heart will not process. 'Fool, fool heart', I tell myself.

"I want to leave you all with a few thoughts. When the tears happen; endure, grieve and move on. The only person who is with us our entire life is ourselves. – I ask that everyone here, love people while they're still here. Tell the people that you love, that you love them at every opportunity. *Bookie*, I love you. Family; all of you, I love you too."

Just as she stepped away from the podium, Mina fell faint. Friends and family rushed to her side. Her mother took charge, using her nursing skills to tend to her daughter. Aside from a preliminary diagnosis of low blood pressure, there was no apparent sign of a serious health issue. Rosemary Parker attributed the fainting spell to stress, dealing with her father's death and having to arrange his funeral.

I consigned that she had taken on too much responsibility at work. Also, I inadvertently revealed the pending outpatient operation to remove the cyst from one of Mina's ovaries. That sent her mother in a parental tirade and she began chastising her daughter as if she were a toddler. We were given strict physical health orders to follow as our send off before we hit the road.

"When you get home I want you to tell your boss that you need to slow down and I want you to start getting more rest. Go and see your doctor and have him call me. Do you her me?" Mama bird spoke sternly. Mina nods her reply. Turning to me, "And you make sure she does it."

"Yes ma'am."

"THE DRIVE HOME"

We headed out early for our long ride home. As we merged onto I-59 North, we settled in for the longest stretch of interstate to get us home. On a talk radio show was the discussion on whether there should be a government sponsored program to bolster black families to improve the numbers of their marital unions. *"Last week, we asked callers to go online and vote whether the government should fund programs that promote marriage in the African American community. By the end of the week, fifty-five percent of you said yes,"* stated the talk show host.

"OH HELL NAW. The government should not have to tell black people how to get along as a family." Mina loudly exerted.

"Fifty-five percent of blacks would say otherwise."

"*Babe*, I found that all the drama we have with dealing with people and relationships in our lives are in direct connection to the lives we lived or didn't live with our parents." Mina expounded.

"Really, and what brought you to that conclusion."

"These past few days, I was able to sit and think . . . my most favorite thing to do."

"You could have fooled me. I thought being on your Blackberry was your most favorite thing to do."

"To be honest with you, it's not. I do it because it's necessary. So back to what I was saying; before now, I think I've just been numb when it comes to a lot of things."

"What are you saying?"

"I didn't realize how much my relationship with my father affected me. Even with us, *Babe*; I can't say that I've been in it one hundred percent."

"Oh, really?"

"I'm sorry. I'm not saying that I loved you any less, it's just that may have been holding back."

"Why?"

"Do you know Tyriq has five kids?"

"What, five?"

"So with mine, it would have been six."

"Is that why . . . why you . . ."

"No. About that, I didn't have an abortion."

"Come again?"

"The baby was still-born. God didn't want me to have it."

"Soooooo you wanted to have Tyriq's baby?"

"I wanted somebody who wanted me. I was young, confused and didn't know any better. I didn't know the difference between the lust and love. And I certainly didn't know about *all* of his other baby's mamas until after I lost the baby. One of them actually came to visit me while I was in the hospital and told me."

"Are you serious?"

"Very. That's when I realized that I had made a mistake and that I would never give myself fully like that to a man again."

"So . . . what does that mean about me, us . . . our marriage?"

"I don't know at this point in my life. But I do know that you are showing me what real love is supposed to look like, and act like . . ."

For five miles, I had nothing to say. God moves in mysterious ways. Over the radiocast came a "Relationship Checkup Moment," by personal relationship coach, Dr. William July.

"*Summer is here and people are ready for love; or are they? Are you ready for your next relationship? Note, I didn't ask are you ready for love, everyone deserves to be loved in some way or another. The question is are you ready for a relationship?*

"*. . . I remember this popular piece of jewelry many years ago made of half a heart. You were supposed to wear half and your partner would take the other half. The idea was that you were incomplete without them, only half a person. We also see this pattern in songs we hear on the radio and movies all the time. The message is 'I'm nobody without somebody else.' But that's all romance brainwashing.*

"*The truth is a good relationship only results from two whole people who merge together into one and experience a synthesis of something bigger*

*than themselves. Two half people can't do that because they already come
into a relationship empty. Two half people just create one whole mess. So
remember, it does not take two to make you. This has been Doctor William
July with your Relationship Checkup moment."*

I looked to Mina to view her reaction.

"He's right, *Babe*," she urged.

"About?"

"Two half people make a whole mess. I've been half-in this
relationship. But I didn't want us to be another used to be."

"So is that why you married me?"

"No. I mean I do love you Matthew."

"You're just not in love with me?"

"The truth is most of the time I've been afraid of what I really
thought I felt and couldn't really say 'yes I feel this way or no I don'
feel this way.'"

"It sounds like you're confused again."

"You're right; I may have been. I had unresolved abandonmen
issues. I felt resentment. But I'm passed that now. You aren't Tyriq
or Marcus and you aren't my father."

"Wait, did you say Marcus?"

"Yes. Look, I know he's your boy and all, but he ain't right. You
might not believe me but he sent me some MySpace messages saying
that he wanted to get with me. Once I found out who he was, I had
him blocked."

"I believe you."

"You do?"

"Yeah. It explains why you and he were always going at it. I had
to cut him loose. I found out some things about him that weren'
right."

"Really . . . things like what?"

I told her about the dealings between Marcus and Natalie.

"Are you serious?"

"Yes."

"That no good . . . and I knew *your girl* wanted you?"

"Yes you were right."

"It's funny how God brings some things to light. I guess with me, I needed closure with the issues with my father leaving. While I was focusing on my history with him, I couldn't commit to you and our future. Now I can."

"May I ask what your issue was with your father?"

It took a moment before she responded with, "His leaving our family after I was born had me thinking it was because of me. With that, I thought it was that he either didn't like me or he didn't like having a girl. I couldn't do anything about being a girl. So I focused on being the best in school and whatever else I could get involved in, so that maybe he would then like me. It was like that little girl in that book I bought Sadie. I so badly wanted my father's approval and love.

"And that's how I saw the guys I dated, which wasn't a lot. They either liked me for me or they wanted to get with me for sex. I was happy with trying to please either type of guy because I was looking for that acceptance that I wasn't getting from my father."

"Okay."

"Coming down here on my own to arrange my father's funeral, I thought I had no one to depend on. But wherever I turned, things were there, getting done and falling in to place. That was God showing me that He was with me and that it didn't matter how my father felt about me or any man. My father was now gone and I was still needed to get things done.

"I found that applying my faith that was missing and how I relied on God, everything seemed clear to me. I was never abandoned by who really mattered; He has been with me all along. I never could have made it otherwise. And Matthew . . ."

"Yeah?"

"It takes for someone else to realize who you are before the actual person does. To know that I would be chosen by a King like you speaks beauty and wonders to me! I must say that I am learning to love me. You have taught me so much by allowing me to find my own way and by encouraging and supporting me on that journey. Just by always being here when I needed you and being a good listener has helped me develop. I love you truly, Matthew."

Those words from my wife, my woman; my *babe's* mouth spoke volumes of devotion to my head and to my heart. It was like listening to an Anita Baker love song. Not only did I hear the words but I felt them throughout my body and soul.

"*Babe*, what I'm about to say is going to make me sound *soft*, as you put it. But this is who I am and my mother told me not to change for anyone. Anyway, God brought us together at this time during this season. Why, I don't know, in His time He will reveal the reason.

"But know this; I love you. More importantly, I like you. I like the person you were when I met you and I love the person you've become thus far."

"Thus far!"

"Yeah, thus far. What's wrong with that?"

"Real people don't say thus far."

"Yeah, they do, because I said it."

"I'm sorry *Bookie*, go ahead."

"See, this is what I'm talking about. I like how you keep it real with me; although a better time would be when I'm not confessing my love to you."

"I said that I was sorry."

"What I was saying was that you've matured and improved upon the person who I already felt was the best one to come into my life, to which I've committed to be with for the rest of my life. Neither of us is perfect, but together we make each other better. Together we can work on this not so perfect love story. And I look forward to writing the rest of our story together."

She leaned in to where her lips came to rest on my right cheek, planting a lingering soft kiss. By surprise to me, she gripped my face between her teeth, with a quick release of her playful bite.

"*HEY!* What was that for?" I asked.

"Okay, you're real."

After all that we had been through in the past year and what we had learned had proven to be worth the troubles and losses that we endured. Along the way, we had lost friends and family. But Mina and I had found each other.

There comes a point in your life when you realize who matters, who never did, who won't anymore and who always will. So, don't worry about people from your past, there's a reason why they didn't make it to your future. To everything there is a season, and a time to every purpose.

Happily Continued.

DISCUSSION QUESTIONS

1. Why does the author refer to Later Days & Nights as being a relationship book?

2. Why is the subtitle of LD&N "I want you back?"

3. When it comes to relationships, are old fashion ideas and values a thing of the past?

4. Who should be the head of the household or should there be?

5. If the man is the provider, should he pay all of the bills of the household or should it be based on a percentage of income of both parties as with M&M?

6. What is the difference between Matthew's and Mina's family background? How did it mold them differently as adults?

7. Do Matthew and Mina complement one another as a couple?

8. Did the "birds of a feather" rule apply to Marcus or Synea?

9. Mina is what Mina does, a compassionate caregiver (true or false)?

10. How did Matthew's personal passion for collecting pens help him professionally?

11. Should the government fund a program to promote marriage in the African American community?

SOUNDTRACK FOR LATER DAYS & NIGHTS

♫ *Intro: Loving*, India Arie

♫ *Confessions*, Malcolm Jamal Warner

♫ *Is This the Way Love Feels*, Chrisette Michele

♫ *This Gift of Life*, Teddy Pendergrass

♫ *I'd Rather Be With You*, Bootsy Collins

♫ *I Just Wanna Be Your Girl*, Anita Baker/Chapter 8

♫ *Moments In Love*, Art of Noise

♫ *If This World We Mine*, Cheryl Lynn and Luther Vandross

♫ *Law & Order Theme Song*, Mike Post

♫ *Cherish This Momemt*, Kem

♫ *Alright*, Ledisi

♫ *Happy Feelings (Live)*, Maze

♫ *Can You Believe*, Robin Thicke

♫ *I Believe*, Fantasia

♫ *Window of the Soul*, Chuck Loeb

♫ *A Bit Old Fashion*, Babyface

♫ *Golden*, Chrisette Michele

♫ *Not So Perfect Love Story*, Lorenz Owens

♫ *I Choose*, India Arie

♫ *Another Used to Be*, Joe

♫ *I Wish You Love - Live*, Nat King Cole

♫ *Outro: Learning*, India Arie

FROM THE AUTHOR

People often ask me where I get my story ideas. The answer in a word is "life." Life is truly the greatest muse. We are living our lives and the pen is writing as we go.

Every person, place or thing could potentially contribute to one of my story ideas. It's not that I'm always looking or listening for ideas to tell a story, but life is pretty hard to ignore.

I hope that you truly enjoyed this remarkable love inspired true to life, not so perfect love story.

ABOUT THE AUTHOR

LAWRENCE CHRISTOPHER is the author of the Mick Hart series of mysteries; *Ghettoway Weekend* and the illustrated *The Tickle Finger* children's books and online short stories.

SPECIAL THANK YOU

- 107.5 WJZZ, Smooth Jazz Radio
- Aon'gelle Quinn
- Baraonda *caffé italiano*, Atlanta, Georgia
- Benihana's, Atlanta, Georgia
- Bishop Dale C. Bronner, Word of Faith Church, Austell, GA
- Bobbi Burt, Shoe Studio, Atlanta, Georgia
- Chloe' Clavon
- Clarence Hutcheson, Vintage Barbershop, Atlanta, GA
- Denise Ransom
- Depeaux, Decatur, Georgia
- Dominique Snoddy, Washington Mutual Bank, Atlanta, GA
- Hotel Indigo, Atlanta, Georgia
- Jaiden Craighead-Applewhite
- Lakeshia Stewart-King
- Lakisha Winters
- Mable's Barbeque Restaurant, Lithonia, Georgia
- Nakeisha Brumfield
- Reggie Tolbert, Tolbert Graphics
- Regina Buckmire-Williams
- *Rolling Out* magazine, Atlanta, Georgia
- Saleem Winters
- Starbucks, Barnes & Noble at Georgia Tech, Atlanta, GA
- Starbucks, Downtown Decatur, Georgia
- Stephanie Johnson
- Tanya Jackson
- Tonia Burks
- Vivian Driver

MORE ACKNOWLEDGEMENTS

ThanQ again; to God. I give You praise and glory.

ThanQ to all of my public, Sunday school and life teachers.

ThanQ to my editor, Kimberly; "u no dat I cannot spe wart a lik."

ThanQ fans and readers. A writer is just a write without a reader of his work. I want to thank you for you encouragement, readership, and your "word of mouth' promotion.

ThanQ to the book clubs, who have read my books invited me to your meetings, fed me well and featured m on your websites. Can a *brother* get seconds?

ThanQ, to the Atlanta's Writers Club for you support.

ThanQ, to the owners of independent book stores and t the CRMs of major book stores who have allowed me to si and sign books. ThanQ, to the online booksellers. ThanC to the websites that have featured my writings, poste reviews of my books.

ThanQ, to the editors of print magazines, newsletter and newspapers for giving me exposure.

I have much love and appreciation for all of you!

LAWRENCE CHRISTOPHER'S FAVORITE

Authors, Poets and Writers

- 📖 Aaron McGruder (W)
- 📖 Betty L. Bush (A)
- 📖 Brandon Massey (A)
- 📖 C. A. Lindsey (W)
- 📖 Jeffrey Knuckles (A)
- 📖 Lawrence Christopher (A, P, W) ☺
- 📖 Lester Kern (W)
- 📖 Monique A. Williams – "momowilly" (A, P, W)
- 📖 Sonya Senell Wash (A)
- 📖 The Urban Griot – Omar Tyree (A)
- 📖 Tony Lindsay (A, W)
- 📖 Uyladia Jarmon (P, W)
- 📖 V. Evelyn (W)
- 📖 Valerie Respress (P)
- 📖 Walter Mosley (A)
- 📖 William July, II (A, W)

(A) Author (P) Poet (W) Writer

Printed in the United States
209440BV00001B/303/P

9 780971 227866